"YOU DID US GREAT DAMAGE THEN," SAYS THE ELF.

"It was the last effort we could make and we knew you would take out our last weapons. We had learned to trust your habits even if we didn't understand them. When the shelling came, towers fell; and there were over a thousand of us dead in the cities."

"And you keep coming."

"We will. Until it's over or until we're dead."

DeFranco stares at the elf a moment. The room is a small and sterile place, showing no touches of habitation, but signs of humanity—a quiet bedroom, done in yellow and green. A table. Two chairs. An unused bed. They have faced each other over this table for hours. They have stopped talking theory and begun thinking only of the recent past. And deFranco finds himself lost in elvish thinking again. It never quite makes sense. The assumptions between the lines are not human assumptions.

From "The Scapegoat" by C.J. Cherryh

ALIEN STARS

EDITED BY
**ELIZABETH
MITCHELL**

A BAEN BOOK

ALIEN STARS

This is a work of fiction. All the characters and events portrayed in this book are fictional, and any resemblance to real people or incidents is purely coincidental.

Copyright © 1985 by Baen Enterprises, Inc.

A Baen Book

Baen Enterprises
8-10 W. 36th Street
New York, N.Y. 10018

First printing, January 1985

ISBN: 0-671-55934-6

Cover art by Rick Sternbach

Printed in the United States of America

Distributed by
SIMON & SCHUSTER
MASS MERCHANDISE SALES COMPANY
1230 Avenue of the Americas
New York, N.Y. 10020

CONTENTS

Usually war serves no purpose that would not be better served by negotiation; especially when advanced weapons are involved even the "winner" would have been better off. Still, there are times when we don't have a choice. As long as we partition ourselves into groups—in other words, as long as humans remain human—the means for resolving that which cannot otherwise be resolved will remain the field of battle.

C.J. Cherryh never joined the armed forces, wasn't a Navy brat, hasn't even lived near a military base since a childhood shared with the youngsters of Fort Sill Oklahoma; but she is today one of science fiction's best writers of war. Her Downbelow Station, *which opens amid the panic of refugee influx at a threatened orbital station, gives us a desperate conflict through the eyes of those most closely involved. She does not protect her characters; they fight and die, as soldiers always have and will, and are mourned when time permits.*

As a novel of war, Downbelow Station *might seriously be compared to the classic* All Quiet on the Western Front, *though one conflict was real and the other only imagined. Most of us were born beyond Brest and the Argonne; none will see Downbelow or Pell. But we can feel the fear and the forces which impelled those wars—or any war—in stories like "The Scapegoat."*

THE SCAPEGOAT
By
C.J. Cherryh

I

DeFranco sits across the table from the elf and he dreams for a moment, not a good dream, but recent truth: all part of what surrounds him now, and true as any memory ever is—a bit greater and a bit less than it was when it was happening, because it was gated in through human eyes and ears and a human notices much more and far less than what truly goes on in the world—

—the ground comes up with a bone-penetrating thump and dirt showers down like rain, over and over again; and deFranco wriggles up to his knees with the clods rattling off his armor. He may be moving to a place where a crater will be in a moment, and the place where he is may become one in that same moment. There is no time to think about it. There is only one way off that exposed hillside, which is to go and keep going. DeFranco writhes and wriggles against the weight of the armor, blind for a moment as the breathing system fails to give him as

much as he needs, but his throat is already raw with too much oxygen in three days out. He curses the rig, far more intimate a frustration than the enemy on this last long run to the shelter of the deep tunnels. . . .

He was going home, was John deFranco, if home was still there, and if the shells that had flattened their shield in this zone had not flattened it all along the line and wiped out the base.

The elves had finally learned where to hit them on this weapons system too, that was what; and deFranco cursed them one and all, while the sweat ran in his eyes and the oxy-mix tore his throat and giddied his brain. On this side and that shells shocked the air and the ground and his bones; and not for the first time concussion flung him bodily through the air and slammed him to the churned ground bruised and battered (and but for the armor, dead and shrapnel-riddled). Immediately fragments of wood and metal rang off the hard-suit, and in their gravity-driven sequence clods of earth rained down in a patter mixed with impacts of rocks and larger chunks.

And then, not having been directly in the strike zone and dead, he got his sweating human limbs up again by heaving the armor-weight into its hydraulic joint-locks, and desperately hurled fifty kilos of unsupple ceramics and machinery and ninety of quaking human flesh into a waddling, exhausted run.

Run and fall and run and stagger into a walk when the dizziness got too much and never waste time dodging.

But somewhen the jolts stopped, and the shell-made earthquakes stopped, and deFranco, laboring along the hazard of the shell-cratered ground, became aware of the silence. His staggering steps slowed as he turned with the awkward foot-planting the armor imposed to take a look behind him. The whole smoky valley swung across the narrowed view of his visor, all lit up with ghosty green readout that flickered madly and told him his eyes were jerking in panic, calling up more than he wanted. He feared that he was deaf; it was that profound a silence to his shocked ears. He heard the hum of the fans and the ventilator in the suit, but there would be that sound forever, he heard it in his dreams; so it could be in his head and not coming from his ears. He hit the ceramic-shielded back of his hand against his ceramic-coated helmet and heard the thump, if distantly. So his hearing was all right. There was just the smoke and the desolate cratering of the landscape to show him where the shells had hit.

And suddenly one of those ghosty green readouts in his visor jumped and said **000** and started ticking off, so he lumbered about to get a look up, the viewplate compensating for the sky in a series of flickers and darkenings. The reading kept up, ticking away; and he could see nothing in the sky, but base was still there, it was transmitting, and he knew what was happening. The numbers reached **Critical** and he swung about again and looked toward the plain as the first strikes came in and the smoke went up anew.

He stood there on the hillcrest and watched the airstrike he had called down half an eternity ago pound hell out of the plains. He knew the devastation of the beams and the shells. And his first and immediate thought was that there would be no more penetrations of the screen and human lives were saved. He had outrun the chaos and covered his own mistake in getting damn near on top of the enemy installation trying to find it.

And his second thought, hard on the heels of

triumph, was that there was too noise in the world already, too much death to deal with, vastly too much, and he wanted to cry with the relief and the fear of being alive and moving. Good and proper. The base scout found the damn firepoint, tripped a trap and the whole damn airforce had to come pull him out of the fire with a damn million credits worth of shells laid down out there destroying ten billion credits worth of somebody else's.

Congratulations, deFranco.

A shiver took him. He turned his back to the sight, cued his locator on, and began to walk, slowly, slowly, one foot in front of the other, and if he had not rested now and again, setting the limbs of his armor on lock, he would have fallen down. As it was he walked with his mouth open and his ears full of the harsh sound of his own breathing. He walked, lost and disoriented, till his unit picked up his locator signal and beaconed in the Lost Boy they never hoped to get back.

"You did us great damage then," says the elf. "It was the last effort we could make and we knew you would take out our last weapons. We knew that you would do it quickly and that then you would stop. We had learned to trust your habits even if we didn't understand them. When the shelling came, towers fell; and there were over a thousand of us dead in the city."

"And you keep coming."

"We will. Until it's over or until we're dead."

DeFranco stares at the elf a moment. The room is a small and sterile place, showing no touches of habitation, but all those small signs of humanity—a quiet bedroom, done in yellow and green pastels. A table. Two chairs. An unused bed. They have faced each other over this table for hours. They have stopped talking theory and begun thinking only of the recent past. And deFranco finds himself lost in elvish thinking again. It never quite makes sense. The assumptions between the lines are not human assumptions, though the elf's command of the language is quite thorough.

At last, defeated by logicless logic: "I went back to my base," says deFranco. "I called down the fire; but I just knew the shelling had stopped. We were alive. That was all we knew. Nothing personal."

There was a bath and there was a meal and a little extra ration of whiskey. HQ doled the whiskey out as special privilege and sanity-saver and the scarcity of it made the posts hoard it and ration it with down-to-the-gram precision. And he drank his three days' ration and his bonus drink one after the other when he had scrubbed his rig down and taken a long, long bath beneath the pipe. He took his three days' whiskey all at once because three days out was what he was recovering from, and he sat in his corner in his shorts, the regs going about their business, all of them recognizing a shaken man on a serious drunk and none of them rude or crazy enough to bother him now, not with congratulations for surviving, not with offers of bed, not with a stray glance. The regs were not in his command, he was not strictly anywhere in the chain of command they belonged to, being special ops and assigned there for the reg CO to use when he had to. He was 2nd Lt. John R. deFranco if anyone bothered and no one did hereabouts, in the bunkers. He was special ops and his orders presently came from the senior trooper captain who was the acting CO all along this section of the line, the major having got hisself lately dead, themselves waiting on a replacement, thank you, sir and ma'am; while higher brass kept themselves cool and dry and safe behind the shields on the ground a thousand miles away and up in orbit.

And John deFranco, special ops and walking target, kept his silver world-and-moon pin and his blue beret and his field-browns all tucked up and out of the damp in his mold-proof plastic kit at the end of his bunk. The rig was his working uniform, the damned, cursed rig that found a new spot to rub raw every time he realigned it. And he sat now in his shorts and drank the first glass quickly, the next and the next and the next in slow sips, and blinked sometimes when he remembered to.

The regs, male and female, moved about the underground barracks in their shorts and their T's like khaki ghosts whose gender meant nothing to him or generally to each other. When bunks got double-filled it was friendship or boredom or outright desperation; all their talk was rough and getting rougher, and their eyes when real pinned-down-for-days boredom set in were hell, because they had been out here and down here on this world for thirty-seven months by the tally on bunker 43's main entry wall; while the elves were still holding, still digging in and still dying at unreasonable rates without surrender.

"Get prisoners," HQ said in its blithe simplicity; but prisoners suicided. Elves checked out just by *wanting* to die.

"Establish a contact," HQ said. "Talk *at* them—" meaning by any inventive means they could; but they had failed at that for years in space and they expected no better luck onworld. Talking to an elf meant coming into range with either drones or live bodies. Elves cheerfully shot at any target they could get. Elves had shot at the first human ship they had met twenty years ago and they had killed fifteen hundred men, women, and children at Corby Point for reasons no one ever understood. They kept on shooting at human ships in sporadic incidents that built to a crisis.

Then humanity—all three humanities, Union and Alliance and remote, sullen Earth—had decided there was no restraint possible with a species that persistently attacked modern human ships on sight, with equipage centuries less advanced—*Do we have to wait*, Earth's consensus was, *till they do get their hands on the advanced stuff? Till they hit a world?* Earth worried about such things obsessively, convinced of its paramount worldbound holiness and importance in the universe. The cradle of humankind. Union worried about other things—like breakdown of order, like its colonies slipping loose while it was busy: Union pushed for speed in settling this business. Alliance worried because the elves were on its border right in the direction it wanted to expand to keep ahead of Union's ambitions. So Union wanted speed, Earth wanted to go back to its own convolute affairs, and Alliance wanted the territory, preferring to make haste slowly and not create permanent problems for itself on its flank. There were rumors of other things too, like Alliance picking up signal out this direction, of something other than elves. Real reason to worry. It was at least sure that the war was being pushed and pressed and shoved; and the elves shoved back. Elves died and died, their ships being no match for human-make once humans took after them in earnest and interdicted the jump-points that let them near human space. But elves never surrendered and never quit trying.

"Now what do we do?" the joint command asked

themselves collectively and figuratively—because they were dealing out bloody, unpalatable slaughter against a doggedly determined and under-equipped enemy, and Union and Earth wanted a quick solution. But Union as usual took the Long View: and on this single point there was consensus. "If we take out every ship they put out here and they retreat, how long does it take before they come back at us with more advanced armaments? We're dealing with lunatics."

"Get through to them," the word went out from HQ. "Take them out of our space and carry the war home to them. We've got to make the impression on them now—or take options no one wants later."

Twenty years ago. Underestimating the tenacity of the elves. Removed from the shipping lanes and confined to a single world, the war had sunk away to a local difficulty; Alliance still put money and troops into it; Union still cooperated in a certain measure. Earth sent adventurers and enlistees that often were crazier than the elves: Base culled those in a hurry.

So for seventeen years the matter boiled on and on and elves went on dying and dying in their few and ill-equipped ships, until the joint command decided on a rougher course; quickly took out the elves' pathetic little space station, dropped troops onto the elvish world, and fenced human bases about with antimissile screens to fight a limited and on-world war—while elvish weaponry slowly got more basic and more primitive and the troops drank their little measures of imported whiskey and went slowly crazy.

And humans closely tied to the elvish war adapted, in humanity's own lunatic way. Well behind the lines that had come to exist on the elves' own planet, humans settled in and built permanent structures and scientists came to study the elves and the threatened flora and fauna of a beautiful and earthlike world, while some elvish centers ignored the war, and the bombing went on and on in an inextricable mess, because neither elves nor humans knew how to quit, or knew the enemy enough to know how to disengage. Or figure out what the other wanted. And the war could go on and on—since presumably the computers and the records in those population centers still had the design of starships in them. And no enemy which had taken what the elves had taken by now was ever going to forget.

There were no negotiations. Once, just once, humans had tried to approach one of the few neutral districts to negotiate and it simply and instantly joined the war. So after all the study and all the effort, humans lived on the elves' world and had no idea what to call them or what the world's real name was, because the damn elves had blown their own space station at the last and methodically destroyed every record the way they destroyed every hamlet before its fall and burned every record and every artifact. They died and they died and they died and sometimes (but seldom nowadays) they took humans with them, like the time when they were still in space and hit the base at Ticon with 3/4-cee rocks and left nothing but dust. Thirty thousand dead and not a way in hell to find the pieces.

That was the incident after which the joint command decided to take the elves out of space.

And nowadays humanity invested cities they never planned to take and they tore up roads and

took out all the elves' planes, and they tore up
agriculture with non-nuclear bombs and shells
trying not to ruin the world beyond recovery, hoping eventually to wear the elves down. But the
elves retaliated with gas and chemicals which humans had refrained from using. Humans interdicted supply and still the elves managed to come
up with the wherewithal to strike through their
base defense here as if supply were endless and
they not starving and the world still green and
undamaged.

DeFranco drank and drank with measured slow-
ness, watching regs go to and fro in the slow dance
of their own business. They were good, this Delta
Company of the Eighth. They did faithfully what
regs were supposed to do in this war, which was to
hold a base and keep roads secure that humans
used, and to build landing zones for supply and
sometimes to go out and get killed inching humanity's way toward some goal the joint command
understood and which from here looked only like
some other damn shell-pocked hill. DeFranco's job
was to locate such hills. And to find a prisoner to
take (standing orders) and to figure out the enemy
if he could.

Mostly just to find hills. And sometimes to get
his company into taking one. And right now he
was no more damn good, because they had gotten
as close to this nameless city as there were hills
and vantages to make it profitable, and after that
they went onto the flat and did what?

Take the place inch by inch, street by street and
discover every damn elf they met had suicided?
The elves would do it on them, so in the villages
south of here they had saved the elves the bother,
and got nothing for their trouble but endless, mea-

sured carnage, and smoothskinned corpses that drew the small vermin and the huge winged birds— (they've been careful with their ecology, the Science Bureau reckoned, in their endless reports, in some fool's paper on large winged creatures' chances of survival if a dominant species were not very careful of them—)

(—or the damn birds are bloody-minded mean and tougher than the elves, deFranco mused in his alcoholic fog, knowing that nothing was, in all space and creation, more bloody-minded than the elves.)

He had seen a young elf child holding another, both stone dead, baby locked in baby's arms: they love, dammit, they love— And he had wept while he staggered away from the ruins of a little elvish town, seeing more and more such sights—because the elves had touched off bombs in their own town center, and turned it into a firestorm.

But the two babies had been lying there unburned and no one wanted to touch them or to look at them. Finally the birds came. And the regs shot at the birds until the CO stopped it, because it was a waste: it was killing a non-combatant lifeform, and that (O God!) was against the rules. Most of all the CO stopped it because it was a fraying of human edges, because the birds always were there and the birds were the winners, every time. And the damn birds like the damn elves came again and again, no matter that shots blew them to puffs of feathers. Stubborn, like the elves. Crazy as everything else on the planet, human and elf. It was catching.

DeFranco nursed the last whiskey in the last glass, nursed it with hands going so numb he had to struggle to stay awake. He was a quiet drunk, never untidy. He neatly drank the last and fell over sideways limp as a corpse, and, tender mercy to a hill-finding branch of the service the hill-taking and road-building regs regarded as a sometime natural enemy—one of the women came and got the glass from his numbed fingers and pulled a blanket over him. They were still human here. They tried to be.

"There was nothing more to be done," says the elf. "That was why. We knew that you were coming closer, and that our time was limited." His long white fingers touch the table-surface, the white, plastic table in the ordinary little bedroom. "We died in great numbers, deFranco, and it was cruel that you showed us only slowly what you could do."

"We could have taken you out from the first. You knew that." DeFranco's voice holds an edge of frustration. Of anguish. "Elf, couldn't you ever understand that?"

"You always gave us hope we could win. And so we fought, and so we still fight. Until the peace. My friend."

"Franc, Franc—" —it was a fierce low voice, and deFranco came out of it, in the dark, with his heart doubletiming and the instant realization it was Dibs talking to him in that low tone and wanting him out of that blanket, which meant wire-runners or worse, a night attack. But Dibs grabbed his arm to hold him still before he could flail about. "Franc, we got a move out there, Jake and Cat's headed out down the tunnel, the lieutenant's gone to M1 but M1's on the line, they want you out there, they want a spotter up on hill 24 doublequick."

"Uh." DeFranco rubbed his eyes. "Uh." Sitting upright was brutal. Standing was worse. He staggered two steps and caught the main shell of his armor off the rack, number 12 suit, the lousy stinking armor that always smelled of human or mud or the purge in the ducts and the awful sick-sweet cleaner they wiped it out with when they hung it up. He held the plastron against his body and Dibs started with the clips in the dim light of the single 5-watt they kept going to find the latrine at night— "Damn, damn, I gotta—" He eluded Dibs and got to the toilet, and by now the whole place was astir with shadow-figures like a scene out of a gold-lighted hell. He swigged the stinging mouthwash they had on the shelf by the toilet and did his business while Dibs caught him up from behind and finished the hooks on his left side. "Damn, get him going," the sergeant said, and: "Trying," Dibs said, as others hauled deFranco around and began hooking him up like a baby into its clothes, one piece and the other, the boots, leg and groin-pieces, the sleeves, the gloves, the belly clamp and the backpack and the power-on—his joints ached. He stood there swaying to one and another tug on his body and took the helmet into his hands when Dibs handed it to him.

"Go, go," the sergeant said, who had no more power to give a special op any specific orders than he could fly; but HQ was in a stew, they needed his talents out there, and deFranco let the regs shove him all they liked: it was his accommodation with these regs when there was no peace anywhere else in the world. And once a dozen of these same regs had come out into the heat after him, which he never quite forgot. So he let them hook his weapons-kit on, then ducked his head down and put the damned helmet on and gave it the locking half-twist as he headed away from the safe light of the barracks pit into the long tunnel, splashing along the low spots on the plastic grid that kept heavy armored feet from sinking in the mud.

"Code: *Nightsight*," he told the suit aloud, all wobbly and shivery from too little sleep; and it read his hoarse voice patterns and gave him a filmy image of the tunnel in front of him. "Code: *ID*," he told it, and it started telling the two troopers somewhere up the tunnel that he was there, and on his way. He got readout back as Cat acknowledged. "**la-6yg-p30/30**," the green numbers ghosted up in his visor, telling him Jake and Cat had elves and they had them quasi-solid in the distant-sensors which would have been tripped downland and they themselves were staying where they were and taking no chances on betraying the location of the tunnel. He cut the ID and Cat and Jake cut off too.

They've got to us, deFranco thought. *The damned elves got through our screen and now they've pushed through on foot, and it's going to be hell to pay—*

Back behind him the rest of the troops would be suiting up and making a more leisurely prep for a hard night to come. The elves rarely got as far as human bunkers. They tried. They were, at close range and with hand-weapons, deadly. The dying was not all on the elves' side if they got to you.

A cold sweat had broken out under the suit. His head ached with a vengeance and the suit weighed on his knees and on his back when he bent and it stank with disinfectant that smelled like some damn

tree from some damn forest on the world that had
spawned every human born, he knew that, but it
failed as perfume and failed at masking the stink
of terror and of the tunnels in the cold wet breaths
the suit took in when it was not on self-seal.

He knew nothing about Earth, only dimly remembered Pell, which had trained him and shipped
him here by stages to a world no one bothered to
give a name. Elfland, when High HQ was being
whimsical. Neverneverland, the regs called it after
some old fairy tale, because from it a soldier never
never came home again. They had a song with as
many verses as there were bitches of the things a
soldier in Elfland never found.

Where's my discharge from this war?
Why, it's neverneverwhere, my friend.
Well, when's the next ship off this world?
Why, it's neverneverwhen, my friend.
  And time's what we've got most of,
  And time is what we spend
  And time is what we've got to do
  In Neverneverland.

He hummed this to himself, in a voice jolted and
crazed by the exertion. He wanted to cry like a
baby. He wanted someone to curse for the hour
and his interrupted rest. Most of all he wanted a
few days of quiet on this front, just a few days to
put his nerves back together again and let his head
stop aching. . . .

. . . *Run and run and run, in a suit that keeps you
from the gas and most of the shells the elves can
throw—except for a few. Except for the joints and the
visor, because the elves have been working for twenty
years studying how to kill you. And air runs out and*

*filters fail and every access you have to Elfland is a
way for the elves to get at you.*

*Like the tunnel openings, like the airvents, like the
power plant that keeps the whole base and strung-out
tunnel systems functioning.*

*Troopers scatter to defend these points, and you
run and run, belatedly questioning why troopers want
a special op at a particular point, where the tunnel
most nearly approaches the elves on their plain.*

*Why me, why here—because, fool, HQ wants
close-up reconnaissance, which was what they wanted
the last time they sent you out in the dark beyond the
safe points—twice, now, and they expect you to go out
and do it again because the elves missed you last time.*

*Damn them all. (With the thought that they will
use you till the bone breaks and the flesh refuses.
And then a two-week rest and out to the lines again.)*

*They give you a medical as far as the field hospital;
and there they give you vitamins, two shots of
antibiotic, a bottle of pills and send you out again.
"We got worse," the meds say then.*

There always are worse. Till you're dead.

DeFranco looks at the elf across the table in the
small room and remembers how it was, the smell
of the tunnels, the taste of fear.

II

**So what're the gals like on this world?
Why, you nevernevermind, my friend.
Well, what're the guys like on this world?
Well, you neverneverask, my friend.**

"They sent me out there," deFranco says to the
elf, and the elf—a human might have nodded but

elves have no such habit—stares gravely as they sit opposite each other, hands on the table.

"You alway say 'they,' " says the elf. "We say 'we' decided. But you do things differently."

"Maybe it *is* we," deFranco says. "Maybe it is, at the bottom of things. We. Sometimes it doesn't look that way."

"I think even now you don't understand why we do what we do. I don't really understand why you came here or why you listen to me, or why you stay now— But we won't understand. I don't think we two will. Others maybe. You want what I want. That's what I trust most."

"You believe it'll work?"

"For us, yes. For elves. Absolutely. Even if it's a lie it will work."

"But if it's not a lie—"

"Can you make it true? *You* don't believe. That—I have to find words for this—but I don't understand that either. How you feel. What you do." The elf reaches across the table and slim white hands with overtint like oil on water catch at brown, matte-skinned fingers whose nails (the elf has none) are broken and rough. "It was no choice to you. It never was even a choice to you, to destroy us to the heart and the center. Perhaps it wasn't to stay. I have a deep feeling toward you, deFranco. I had this feeling toward you from when I saw you first; I knew that you were what I had come to find, but whether you were the helping or the damning force I didn't know then, I only knew that what you did when you saw us was what humans had always done to us. And I believed you would show me why."

*　　*　　*

DeFranco moved and sat still a while by turns, in the dark, in the stink and the strictures of his rig; while somewhere two ridges away there were two nervous regs encamped in the entry to the tunnel, sweltering in their own hardsuits and not running their own pumps and fans any more than he was running his—because elvish hearing was legendary, the rigs made noise, and it was hard enough to move in one of the bastards without making a racket: someone in HQ suspected elves could pick up the running noises. Or had other senses.

But without those fans and pumps the below-the-neck part of the suit had no cooling and got warm even in the night. And the gloves and the helmets had to stay on constantly when anyone was outside, it was the rule: no elf ever got a look at a live human, except at places like the Eighth's Gamma Company. Perhaps not there either. Elves were generally thorough.

DeFranco had the kneejoints on lock at the moment, which let him have a solid prop to lean his weary knees and backside against. He leaned there easing the shivers and the quakes out of his lately-wakened and sleep-deprived limbs before he rattled in his armor and alerted a whole hillside full of elves. It was not a well-shielded position he had taken: it had little cover except the hill itself, and these hills had few enough trees that the fires and the shells had spared. But green did struggle up amid the soot and bushes grew on the line down on valley level that had been an elvish road three years ago. His nightsight scanned the brush in shadow-images.

Something touched the sensors as he rested there on watch, a curious whisper of a sound, and an amber readout ghosted up into his visor, dots rippling off in sequence in the direction the pickup came from. It was not the wind: the internal computer zeroed out the white sound of wind and suit-noise. It was anomalies it brought through and amplified; and what it amplified now had the curious regular pulse of engine-sound.

DeFranco ordered the lock off his limbs, slid lower on the hill and moved on toward one with better vantage of the road as it came up from the west—carefully, pausing at irregular intervals as he worked round to get into position to spot that direction. He still had his locator output off. So did everyone else back at the base. HQ had no idea now what sophistication the elves had gained at eavesdropping and homing in on the locators, and how much they could pick up with locators of their own. It was only sure that while some elvish armaments had gotten more primitive and patchwork, their computer tech had nothing at all wrong with it.

DeFranco settled again on a new hillside and listened, wishing he could scratch a dozen maddening itches, and wishing he were safe somewhere else: the whole thing had a disaster-feeling about it from the start, the elves doing something they had never done. He could only think about dead Gamma Company and what might have happened to them before the elves got to them and gassed the bunker and fought their way into it past the few that had almost gotten into their rigs in time—

Had the special op been out there watching too? Had the one at bunker 35 made a wrong choice and had it all started this way the night they died?

The engine-sound was definite. DeFranco edged higher up the new hill and got down flat, belly down on the ridge. He thumbed the magnification plate into the visor and got the handheld camera's snake-head optics over the ridge in the theory it was a smaller target and a preferable target than himself, with far better nightsight.

The filmy nightsight image came back of the road, while the sound persisted. It was distant, his ears and the readout advised him, distant yet, racing the first red edge of a murky dawn that showed far off across the plain and threatened daylight out here.

He still sent no transmission. The orders were stringent. The base either had to remain ignorant that there was a vehicle coming up the road or he had to go back personally to report it; and lose track of whatever-it-was out here just when it was getting near enough to do damage. Damn the lack of specials to team with out here in the hot spots, and damn the lead-footed regs: he had to go it alone, decide things alone, hoping Jake and Cat did the right thing in their spot and hoping the other regs stayed put. And he hated it.

He edged off this hill, keeping it between him and the ruined, shell-pocked road, and began to move to still a third point of vantage, stalking as silently as any man in armor could manage.

And fervently he hoped that the engine sound was not a decoy and that nothing was getting behind him. The elves were deceptive as well and they were canny enemies with extraordinary hearing. He hoped now that the engine-sound had deafened them—but no elf was really fool enough to be coming up the road like this, it was a decoy, it had to be, there was nothing else it could be; and he was going to fall into it nose-down if he was not careful.

He settled belly-down on the next slope and got the camera-snake over the top, froze the suit-joints and lay inert in that overheated ceramic shell, breathing hard through a throat abused by oxygen and whiskey, blinking against a hangover head-ache to end all headaches that the close focus of the visor readout only made worse. His nose itched. A place on his scalp itched behind his ear. He stopped cataloging the places he itched because it was driving him crazy. Instead he blinked and rolled his eyes, calling up readout on the passive systems, and concentrated on that.

Blink. Blink-blink. Numbers jumped. The com-puter had come up with a range as it got passive echo off some hill and checked it against the local topology programmed into its memory. Damn! Close. The computer handed him the velocity. 40 KPH with the 4 and the 0 wobbling back and forth into the 30's. DeFranco held his breath and checked his hand-launcher, loading a set of armor-piercing rounds in, quiet, quiet as a man could move. The clamp went down as softly as long practice could lower it.

And at last a ridiculous open vehicle came jounc-ing and whining its way around potholes and shell craters and generally making a noisy and erratic progress. It was in a considerable hurry despite the potholes, and there were elves in it, four of them, all pale in their robes and one of them with the cold glitter of metal about his/her? person, the one to the right of the driver. The car bounced and wove and zigged and zagged up the hilly road with no slackening of speed, inviting a shot for all it was worth.

Decoy?

Suicide?

They were crazy as elves could be, and that was completely. They were headed straight for the hidden bunker, and it was possible they had gas or a bomb in that car or that they just planned to get themselves shot in a straightforward way, whatever they had in mind, but they were going right where they could do the most damage.

DeFranco unlocked his ceramic limbs, which sagged under his weight until he was down on his belly; and he slowly brought his rifle up, and inched his way up on his belly so it was his vulnerable head over the ridge this time. He shook and he shivered and he reckoned there might be a crater where he was in fair short order if they had a launcher in that car and he gave them time to get it set his way.

But pushing and probing at elves was part of his job. And these were decidedly anomalous. He put a shot in front of the car and half expected elvish suicides on the spot.

The car swerved and jolted into a pothole as the shell hit. It careened to a stop; and he held himself where he was, his heart pounding away and himself not sure why he had put the shot in front and not into the middle of them like a sensible man in spite of HQ's orders.

But the elves recovered from their careening and the car was stopped; and instead of blowing themselves up immediately or going for a launcher of their own, one of the elves bailed out over the side while the helmet-sensor picked up the attempted motor-start. Cough-whine. The car lurched. The elvish driver made a wild turn, but the one who had gotten out just stood there—*stood*, staring up, and lifted his hands together.

DeFranco lay on his hill; and the elves who had

gotten the car started swerved out of the pothole it had stuck itself in and lurched off in escape, not suicide—while the one elf in the robe with the metal border just stood there, the first live prisoner anyone had ever taken, staring up at him, self-offered.

"You damn well stand still," he yelled down at the elf on outside com, and thought of the gas and the chemicals and thought that if elves had come up with a disease that also got to humans here was a way of delivering it that was cussed enough and crazy enough for them.

"Human," a shrill voice called up to him. "Human!"

DeFranco was for the moment paralyzed. An elf knew what to call them; an elf *talked*. An elf stood there staring up at his hill in the beginnings of dawn and all of a sudden nothing was going the way it ever had between elves and humankind.

At least, if it had happened before, no human had ever lived to tell about it.

"Human!" the same voice called—*uu-mann*, as best high elvish voices could manage it. The elf was not suiciding. The elf showed no sign of wanting to do that; and deFranco lay and shivered in his armor and felt a damnable urge to wipe his nose which he could not reach or to get up and run for his life, which was a fool's act. Worse, his bladder suddenly told him it was full. Urgently. Taking his mind down to a ridiculous small matter in the midst of trying to get home alive.

The dawn was coming up the way it did across the plain, light spreading like a flood, so fast in the bizarre angle of the land here that it ran like water on the surface of the plain.

And the elf stood there while the light of dawn

grew more, showing the elf more clearly than
deFranco had ever seen one of the enemy alive,
beautiful the way elves were, not in a human way,
looking, in its robes, like some cross between man
and something spindly and human-skinned and
insectoid. The up-tilted ears never stopped moving,
but the average of their direction was toward him.
Nervous-like.

*What does he want, why does he stand there, why
did they throw him out? A target? A distraction?*

Elvish cussedness. DeFranco waited, and waited,
and the sun came up; while somewhere in the
tunnels there would be troopers wondering and
standing by their weapons, ready to go on self-seal
against gas or whatever these lunatics had brought.

There was light enough now to make out the red
of the robes that fluttered in the breeze. And light
enough to see the elf's hands, which looked—which
looked, crazily enough, to be tied together.

The dawn came on. Water became an obsessive •
thought. DeFranco was thirsty from the whiskey
and agonized between the desire for a drink from
the tube near his mouth or the fear one more drop
of water in his system would make it impossible to ignore his bladder; and he thought about it
and thought about it, because it was a long wait
and a long walk back, and relieving himself outside the suit was a bitch on the one hand and on
the inside was damnable discomfort. But it did get
worse. And while life and death tottered back and
forth and his fingers clutched the launcher and he
faced an elf who was surely up to something, that
small decision was all he could think of clearly—it
was easier to think of than what wanted thinking
out, like what to do and whether to shoot the elf
outright, counter to every instruction and every

order HQ had given, because he wanted to get out of this place.

But he did not—and finally he solved both problems: took his drink, laid the gun down on the ridge like it was still in his hands, performed the necessary maneuver to relieve himself outside the suit as he stayed as flat as he could. Then he put himself back together, collected his gun and lurched up to his feet with small whines of the assisting joint-locks.

The elf never moved in all of this, and deFranco motioned with the gun. "Get up here. . . ."—not expecting the elf to understand either the motion or the shout. But the elf came, slowly, as if the hill was all his (it had been once) and he owned it. The elf stopped still on the slant, at a speaking distance, no more, and stood there with his hands tied (*his*, deFranco decided by the height of him). The elf's white skin all but glowed in the early dawn, the bare skin of the face and arms against the dark, metal-edged red of his robe; and the large eyes were set on him and the ears twitched and quivered with small pulses.

"I am your prisoner," the elf said, plain as any human; and deFranco stood there with his heart hammering away at his ribs.

"Why?" deFranco asked. He was mad, he was quite mad and somewhere he had fallen asleep on the hillside, or elvish gas had gotten to him through the open vents—he was a fool to have gone on open circulation; and he was dying back there somewhere and not talking at all.

The elf lifted his bound hands. "I came here to find you."

It was not a perfect accent. It was what an elvish mouth could come up with. It had music in it.

And deFranco stood and stared and finally motioned with the gun up the hill. "Move," he said, "walk."

Without demur his prisoner began to do that, in the direction he had indicated.

"What did I do that humans always do?" deFranco asks the elf, and the grave sea-colored eyes flicker with changes. Amusement, perhaps. Or distress.

"You fired at us," says the elf in his soft, songlike voice. "And then you stopped and didn't kill me."

"It was a warning."

"To stop. So simple."

"God, what else did you think?"

The elf's eyes flicker again. There is gold in their depths, and gray. And his ears flick nervously. "DeFranco, deFranco, you still don't know why we fight. And I don't truly know what you meant. Are you telling me the truth?"

"We never wanted to fight. It was a warning. Even animals, for God's sake—understand a warning shot."

The elf blinks. (And someone in another room stirs in a chair and curses his own blindness. Aggression and the birds. Different tropisms. All the way through the ecostructure.)

The elf spreads his hands. "I don't know what you mean. I never know. What can we know? That you were there for the same reason I was? Were you?"

"I don't know. I don't even know that. *We never wanted a war.* Do you understand that, at least?"

"You wanted us to stop. So we told you the

same. We sent our ships to hold those places which were ours. And you kept coming to them."

"They were ours."

"Now they are." The elf's face is grave and still. "DeFranco, a mistake was made. A ship of ours fired on yours and this was a mistake. Perhaps it was me who fired. What's in this elf's mind? Fear when a ship will not go away? What's in this human's mind? Fear when we don't go away? It was a stupid thing. It was a mistake. It was our region. Our—"

"Territory. You think you owned the place."

"We were in it. We were there and this ship came. Say that I wasn't there and I heard how it happened. This was a frightened elf who made a stupid mistake. This elf was surprised by this ship and he didn't want to run and give up this jump point. It was ours. You were in it. We wanted you to go. And you stayed."

"So you blew up an unarmed ship."

"Yes. I did it. I destroyed all the others. You destroyed ours. Our space station. You killed thousands of us. I killed thousands of you."

"Not me and not you, elf. That's twenty years, dammit, and you weren't there and I wasn't there—"

"I did it. I say I did. And you killed thousands of us."

"We weren't coming to make a war. We were coming to straighten it out. Do you understand that?"

"We weren't yet willing. Now things are different."

"For God's sake—why did you let so many die?"

"You never gave us defeat enough. You were cruel, deFranco. Not to let us know we couldn't win—that was very cruel. It was very subtle. Even now I'm afraid of your cruelty."

"Don't you understand yet?"

"What do I understand? That you've died in thousands. That you make long war. I thought you would kill me on the hill, on the road, and when you called me I had both hope and fear. Hope that you would take me to higher authority. Fear—well, I am bone and nerve, deFranco. And I never knew whether you would be cruel."

The elf walked and walked. He might have been on holiday, his hands tied in front of him, his red robes a-glitter with their gold borders in the dawn. He never tired. *He* carried no weight of armor; and deFranco went on self-seal and spoke through the mike when he had to give the elf directions.

Germ warfare?

Maybe the elf had a bomb in his gut?

But it began to settle into deFranco that he had done it, he had done it, after years of trying he had himself a live and willing prisoner, and his lower gut was queasy with outright panic and his knees felt like mush. *What's he up to, what's he doing, why's he walk like that— Damn! they'll shoot him on sight, somebody could see him first and shoot him and I can't break silence—maybe that's what I'm supposed to do, maybe that's how they overran Gamma Company—*

But a prisoner, a prisoner speaking human language—

"Where'd you learn," he asked the elf, "where'd you learn to talk human?"

The elf never turned, never stopped walking. "A prisoner."

"Who? Still alive?"

"No."

No. Slender and graceful as a reed and burning as a fire and white as beach sand. *No.* Placidly. Rage rose in deFranco, a blinding urge to put his rifle butt in that straight spine, to muddy and bloody the bastard and make him as dirty and as hurting as himself; but the professional rose up in him too, and the burned hillsides went on and on as they climbed and they walked, the elf just in front of him.

Until they were close to the tunnels and in imminent danger of a human misunderstanding.

He turned his ID and locator on; but they would pick up the elf on his sensors too, and that was no good. "It's deFranco," he said over the com. "I got a prisoner. Get HQ and get me a transport."

Silence from the other end. He cut off the output, figuring they had it by now. "Stop," he said to the elf on outside audio. And he stood and waited until two suited troopers showed up, walking carefully down the hillside from a direction that did not lead to any tunnel opening.

"Damn," came Cat's female voice over his pickup. "Da-amn." In a tone of wonder. And deFranco at first thought it was admiration of him and what he had done, and then he knew with some disgust it was wonder at the elf, it was a human woman looking at the prettiest, cleanest thing she had seen in three long years, icy, fastidious Cat, who was picky what she slept with.

And maybe her partner Jake picked it up, because: "Huh," he said in quite a different tone, but quiet, quiet, the way the elf looked at their faceless faces, as if he still owned the whole world and meant to take it back.

"It's Franc," Jake said then into the com, directed at the base. "And he's right, he's got a live one. Damn, you should *see* this bastard."

III

So where's the generals in this war?
Why, they're neverneverhere, my friend.
Well, what'll we do until they come?
Well, you neverneverask, my friend.

"I was afraid too," deFranco says. "I thought you might have a bomb or something. We were afraid you'd suicide if anyone touched you. That was why we kept you sitting all that time outside."

"Ah," says the elf with a delicate move of his hands. "Ah. I thought it was to make me angry. Like all the rest you did. But you sat with me. And this was hopeful. I was thirsty; I hoped for a drink. That was mostly what I thought about."

"We think too much—elves and humans. We both think too much. *I'd have given you a drink of water, for God's sake.* I guess no one even thought."

"I wouldn't have taken it."

"Dammit, why?"

"Unless you drank with me. Unless you shared what you had. Do you see?"

"Fear of poison?"

"No."

"You mean just my giving it."

"Sharing it. Yes."

"Is pride so much?"

Again the elf touches deFranco's hand as it rests on the table, a nervous, delicate gesture. The elf's ears twitch and collapse and lift again, trembling.

"We always go off course here. I still fail to understand why you fight."

"Dammit, I don't understand why you can't understand why a man'd give you a drink of water. Not to hurt you. Not to prove anything. For the love of God, *mercy*, you ever learn that word? Being decent, so's everything decent doesn't go to hell and we don't act like damn animals!"

The elf stares long and soberly. His small mouth has few expressions. It forms its words carefully. "Is this why you pushed us so long? To show us your control?"

"No, dammit, to hang onto it! So we can find a place to stop this bloody war. It's all we ever wanted."

"Then why did you start?"

"Not to have you push *us*!"

A blink of sea-colored eyes. "Now, now we're understanding. We're like each other."

"But you won't stop, dammit, you wouldn't stop, you haven't stopped yet! People are still dying out there on the front, throwing themselves away without a thing to win. Nothing. *That*'s not like us."

"In starting war we're alike. But not in ending it. You take years. Quickly we show what we can do. Then both sides know. So we make peace. You showed us long cruelty. And we wouldn't give ourselves up to you. What could we expect?"

"Is it that easy?" DeFranco begins to shiver, clenches his hands together on the tabletop and leans there, arms folded. "You're crazy, elf."

"Angan. My personal name is Angan."

"A hundred damn scientists out there trying to figure out how you work and it's that damn simple?"

"I don't think so. I think we maybe went off

course again. But we came close. We at least see there was a mistake. That's the important thing. That's why I came."

DeFranco looks desperately at his watch, at the minutes ticking away. He covers the face of it with his hand and looks up. His brown eyes show anguish. "The colonel said I'd have three hours. It's going. It's going too fast."

"Yes. And we still haven't found out why. I don't think we ever will. Only you share with me now, deFranco. Here. In our little time."

The elf sat, just sat quietly with his hands still tied, on the open hillside, because the acting CO had sent word no elf was setting foot inside the bunker system and no one was laying hands on him to search him.

But the troopers came out one by one in the long afternoon and had their look at him—one after another of them took the trouble to put on the faceless, uncomfortable armor just to come out and stand and stare at what they had been fighting for all these years.

"Damn," was what most of them said, in private, on the com, their suits to his suit; "damn," or variants on that theme.

"We got that transport coming in," the reg lieutenant said when she came out and brought him his kit. Then, unlike herself: "Good job, Franc."

"Thanks," deFranco said, claiming nothing. And he sat calmly, beside his prisoner, on the barren, shell-pocked hill by a dead charcoal tree.

Don't shake him, word had come from the CO. Keep him real happy—don't change the situation and don't threaten him and don't touch him.

For fear of spontaneous suicide.

So no one came to lay official claim to the elf either, not even the captain came. But the word had gone out to base and to HQ and up, deFranco did not doubt, to orbiting ships, because it was the best news a frontline post had had to report since the war started. Maybe it was dreams of leaving Elfland that brought the regs out here, on pilgrimage to see this wonder. And the lieutenant went away when she had stared at him so long.

Hope. DeFranco turned that over and over in his mind and probed at it like a tongue into a sore tooth. Promotion out of the field. No more mud. No more runs like yesterday. No more, no more, no more, the man who broke the Elfland war and cracked the elves and brought in the key—

—to let it all end. For good. *Winning*. Maybe, maybe—

He looked at the elf who sat there with his back straight and his eyes wandering to this and that, to the movement of wind in a forlorn last bit of grass, the drift of a cloud in Elfland's blue sky, the horizons and the dead trees.

"You got a name?" He was careful asking anything. But the elf had talked before.

The elf looked at him. "Saitas," he said.

"Saitas. Mine's deFranco."

The elf blinked. There was no fear in his face. They might have been sitting in the bunker passing the time of day together.

"Why'd they send you?" DeFranco grew bolder.

"I asked to come."

"Why?"

"To stop the war."

Inside his armor deFranco shivered. He blinked and he took a drink from the tube inside the helmet and he tried to think about something else, but the elf sat there staring blandly at him, with his hands tied, resting placidly in his lap. "How?" deFranco asked, "how will you stop the war?"

But the elf said nothing and deFranco knew he had gone further with that question than HQ was going to like, not wanting their subject told anything about human wants and intentions before they had a chance to study the matter and study the elf and hold their conferences.

"They came," says deFranco in that small room, "to know what you looked like."

"You never let us see your faces," says the elf.

"You never let us see yours."

"You knew everything. Far more than we. You knew our world. We had no idea of yours."

"Pride again."

"Don't you know how hard it was to let you lay hands on me? That was the worst thing. You did it again. Like the gunfire. You touch with violence and then expect quiet. But I let this happen. It was what I came to do. And when you spoke to the others for me, that gave me hope."

In time the transport came skimming in low over the hills, and deFranco got to his feet to wave it in. The elf stood up too, graceful and still placid. And waited while the transport sat down and the blades stopped beating.

"Get in," deFranco said then, picking up his scant baggage, putting the gun on safety.

The elf quietly bowed his head and followed instructions, going where he was told. DeFranco never laid a hand on him, until inside, when they had climbed into the dark belly of the transport and guards were waiting there— "Keep your damn

guns down," deFranco said on outside com, because they were light-armed and helmetless. "What
are you going to do if he moves, shoot him? Let me
handle him. He speaks real good." And to the elf:
"Sit down there. I'm going to put a strap across.
Just so you don't fall."

The elf sat without objection, and deFranco got
a cargo strap and hooked it to the rail on one side
and the other, so there was no way the elf was
going to stir or use his hands.

And he sat down himself as the guards took
their places and the transport lifted off and carried them away from the elvish city and the frontline base of the hundreds of such bases in the
world. It began to fly high and fast when it got to
safe airspace, behind the defenses humans had made
about themselves.

There was never fear in the elf. Only placidity.
His eyes traveled over the inside of the transport,
the dark utilitarian hold, the few benches, the cargo
nets, the two guards.

Learning, deFranco thought, still learning everything there was to learn about his enemies.

"Then I was truly afraid," says the elf. "I was
most afraid that they would want to talk to me
and learn from me. And I would have to die then
to no good. For nothing."

"How do you do that?"

"What?"

"Die. Just by wanting to."

"Wanting is the way. I could stop my heart now.
Many things stop the heart. When you stop trying
to live, when you stop going ahead—it's very easy."

"You mean if you quit trying to live you die.
That's crazy."

The elf spreads delicate fingers. "Children can't. Children's hearts can't be stopped that way. You have the hearts of children. Without control. But the older you are the easier and easier it is. Until someday it's easier to stop than to go on. When I learned your language I learned from a man named Tomas. He couldn't die. He and I talked—oh, every day. And one day we brought him a woman we took. She called him a damn traitor. That was what she said. Damn traitor. Then Tomas wanted to die and he couldn't. He told me so. It was the only thing he ever asked of me. Like the water, you see. Because I felt sorry for him I gave him the cup. And to her. Because I had no use for her. But Tomas hated me. He hated me every day. He talked to me because I was all he had to talk to, he would say. Nothing stopped his heart. Until the woman called him traitor. And then his heart stopped, though it went on beating. I only helped. He thanked me. And damned me to hell. And wished me health with his drink."

"Dammit, elf."

"I tried to ask him what hell was. I think it means being still and trapped. So we fight."

("He's very good with words," someone elsewhere says, leaning near the monitor. "He's trying to communicate something but the words aren't equivalent. He's playing on what he does have.")

"For God's sake," says deFranco then, "is that why they fling themselves on the barriers? Is that why they go on dying? Like birds at cage bars?"

The elf flinches. Perhaps it is the image. Perhaps it is a thought. "Fear stops the heart, when fear has nowhere to go. We still have one impulse left. There is still our anger. Everything else has gone. At the last even our children will fight you. So I fight for my children by coming here. I don't want to talk about Tomas any more. The birds have him. *You* are what I was looking for."

"Why?" DeFranco's voice shakes. "Saitas—Angan—I'm scared as hell."

"So am I. Think of all the soldiers. Think of things important to you. I think about my home."

"I think I never had one. —This is crazy. It won't work."

"Don't." The elf reaches and holds a brown wrist. "Don't leave me now, deFranco."

"There's still fifteen minutes. Quarter of an hour."

"That's a very long time ... here. Shall we shorten it?"

"No," deFranco says and draws a deep breath. "Let's use it."

At the base where the on-world authorities and the scientists did their time, there were real buildings, real ground-side buildings, which humans had made. When the transport touched down on a rooftop landing pad, guards took the elf one way and deFranco another. It was debriefing: that he expected. They let him get a shower first with hot water out of real plumbing, in a prefabbed bathroom. And he got into his proper uniform for the first time in half a year, shaved and proper in his blue beret and his brown uniform, fresh and clean and thinking all the while that if a special could get his field promotion it was scented towels every day and soft beds to sleep on and a life expectancy in the decades. He was anxious, because there were ways of snatching credit for a thing and he wanted the credit for this one, wanted it because a body could get killed out there on hillsides where he had been for three years and no desk-sitting officer was going to fail to mention him in the report.

"Sit down," the specials major said, and took him through it all; and that afternoon they let him tell it to a reg colonel and a lieutenant general; and again that afternoon they had him tell it to a tableful of scientists and answer questions and questions and questions until he was hoarse and they forgot to feed him lunch. But he answered on and on until his voice cracked and the science staff took pity on him.

He slept then, in clean sheets in a clean bed and lost touch with the war so that he waked terrified and lost in the middle of the night in the dark and had to get his heart calmed down before he realized he was not crazy and that he really had gotten into a place like this and he really had done what he remembered.

He tucked down babylike into a knot and thought good thoughts all the way back to sleep until a buzzer waked him and told him it was day in this windowless place, and he had an hour to dress again—for more questions, he supposed; and he thought only a little about his elf, *his* elf, who was handed on to the scientists and the generals and the AlSec people, and stopped being his personal business.

"Then," says the elf, "I knew you were the only one I met I could understand. Then I sent for you."

"I still don't know why."

"I said it then. We're both soldiers."

"You're more than that."

"Say that I made one of the great mistakes."

"You mean at the beginning? I don't believe it."

"It could have been. Say that I commanded the

attacking ship. Say that I struck your people on
the world. Say that you destroyed our station and
our cities. We are the makers of mistakes. Say this
of ourselves."

"I," the elf said, his image on the screen much
the same as he had looked on the hillside, straight-
spined, red-robed—only the ropes elves had put on
him had left purpling marks on his wrists, on the
opalescing white of his skin, "I'm clear enough,
aren't I?" The trooper accent was strange coming
from a delicate elvish mouth. The elf's lips were
less mobile. His voice had modulations, like singing,
and occasionally failed to keep its tones flat.

"It's very good," the scientist said, the man in
the white coveralls, who sat at a small desk opposite the elf in a sterile white room and had his
hands laced before him. The camera took both of
them in, elf and swarthy Science Bureau xenologist.
"I understand you learned from prisoners."

The elf seemed to gaze into infinity. "We don't
want to fight anymore."

"Neither do we. Is this why you came?"

A moment the elf studied the scientist, and said
nothing at all.

"What's your people's name?" the scientist asked.

"You call us elves."

"But we want to know what you call yourselves.
What you call this world."

"Why would you want to know that?"

"To respect you. Do you know that word, respect?"

"I don't understand it."

"Because what you call this world and what you
call yourselves *is* the name, the right name, and
we want to call you right. Does that make sense?"

"It makes sense. But what you call us is right too, isn't it?"

"Elves is a made-up word, from our homeworld. A myth. Do you know *myth*? A story. A thing not true."

"Now it's true, isn't it?"

"Do you call your world Earth? Most people do."

"What you call it is its name."

"We call it Elfland."

"That's fine. It doesn't matter."

"Why doesn't it matter?"

"I've said that."

"You learned our language very well. But we don't know anything of yours."

"Yes."

"Well, we'd like to learn. We'd like to be able to talk to you your way. It seems to us this is only polite. Do you know *polite*?"

"No."

A prolonged silence. The scientist's face remained bland as the elf's. "You say you don't want to fight any more. Can you tell us how to stop the war?"

"Yes. But first I want to know what your peace is like. What, for instance, will you do about the damage you've caused us?"

"You mean reparations."

"What's that mean?"

"Payment."

"What do you mean by it?"

The scientist drew a deep breath. "Tell me. Why did your people give you to one of our soldiers? Why didn't they just call on the radio and say they wanted to talk?"

"This is what you'd do."

"It's easier, isn't it? And safer."

The elf blinked. No more than that.

"There was a ship a long time ago," the scientist said after a moment. "It was a human ship minding its own business in a human lane, and elves came and destroyed it and killed everyone in it. Why?"

"What do you want for this ship?"

"So you do understand about payment. Payment's giving something for something."

"I understand." The elvish face was guileless, masklike, the long eyes like the eyes of a pearl-skinned buddha. A saint. "What will you ask? And how will peace with you be? What do you call peace?"

"You mean you don't think our word for it is like your word for it?"

"That's right."

"Well, that's an important thing to understand, isn't it? Before we make agreements. Peace means no fighting."

"That's not enough."

"Well, it means being safe from your enemies."

"That's not enough."

"What is enough?"

The pale face contemplated the floor, something elsewhere.

"What *is* enough, Saitas?"

The elf only stared at the floor, far, far away from the questioner. "I need to talk to deFranco."

"Who?"

"DeFranco." The elf looked up. "DeFranco brought me here. He's a soldier; he'll understand me better than you. Is he still here?"

The colonel reached and cut the tape off. She was SurTac. Agnes Finn was the name on her desk. She could·cut your throat a dozen ways, and do sabotage and mayhem from the refinements of computer theft to the gross tactics of explosives; she would speak a dozen languages, know every culture she had ever dealt with from the inside out, integrating the Science Bureau and the military. And more, she was a SurTac *colonel*, which sent the wind up deFranco's back. It was not a branch of the service that had many high officers; you had to survive more than ten field missions to get your promotion beyond the ubiquitous and courtesy-titled lieutenancy. And this one had. This was Officer with a capital O, and whatever the politics in HQ were, this was a rock around which a lot of other bodies orbited: *this* probably took her orders from the Joint Command, which was months and months away in its closest manifestation. And that meant next to no orders and wide discretion, which was what SurTacs did. Wild card. Joker in the deck. There were the regs; there was special ops, loosely attached; there were the spacers, Union and Alliance, and Union regs were part of that; beyond and above, there was AlSec and Union Intelligence; and then there were the Special Services, and that was this large-boned, red-haired woman who probably had a scant handful of humans and no knowing what else in her direct command, a handful of SurTacs loose in Elfland, and all of them independent operators and as much trouble to the elves as a reg base could be.

DeFranco knew. He had tried that route once. He knew more than most what kind it took to survive that training, let alone the requisite ten missions to get promoted out of the field, and he knew the wit behind that freckled, weathered face and knew it ate special ops lieutenants for appetizers.

"How did you make such an impression on him, Lieutenant?"

"I didn't try to," deFranco said carefully. "Ma'am. I just tried to keep him calm and get in with him alive the way they said. But I was the only one who dealt with him out there, we thought that was safest; maybe he thinks I'm more than I am."

"I compliment you on the job." There was a certain irony in that, he was sure. No SurTac had pulled off what he had, and he felt the slight tension there.

"Yes, ma'am."

"*Yes, ma'am.* There's always the chance, you understand, that you've brought us an absolute lunatic. Or the elves are going an unusual route to lead us into a trap. Or this is an elf who's not too pleased about being tied up and dumped on us, and he wants to get even. Those things occur to me."

"Yes, ma'am." DeFranco thought all those things, face to face with the colonel and trying to be easy as the colonel had told him to be. But the colonel's thin face was sealed and forbidding as the elf's.

"You know what they're doing out there right now? Massive attacks. Hitting that front near 45 with everything they've got. The Eighth's pinned. We're throwing air in. And they've got somewhere over two thousand casualties out there and airstrikes don't stop all of them. Delta took a head-on assault and turned it. There were casualties. Trooper named Herse. Your unit."

Dibs. O God. "Dead?"

"Dead." The colonel's eyes were bleak and expressionless. "Word came in. I know it's more than a stat to you. But that's what's going on. We've got two signals coming from the elves. And

we don't know which one's valid. We have ourselves an alien who claims credentials—*and* comes
with considerable effort from the same site as the
attack."

Dibs. Dead. There seemed a chill in the air, in
this safe, remote place far from the real world, the
mud, the bunkers. Dibs had stopped living yesterday. This morning. Sometime. Dibs had gone and
the world never noticed.

"Other things occur to the science people," the
colonel said. "One of which galls the hell out of
them, deFranco, is what the alien just said.
DeFranco can understand me better. Are you with
me, Lieutenant?"

"Yes, ma'am."

"So the Bureau went to the Secretary, the Secretary went to the Major General on the com; all
this at fifteen hundred yesterday; and *they* hauled
me in on it at two this morning. You know how
many noses you've got out of joint, Lieutenant?
And what the level of concern is about that mess
out there on the front?"

"Yes, ma'am."

"I'm sure you hoped for a commendation and
maybe better, wouldn't that be it? Wouldn't blame
you. Well, I got my hands into this, and I've opted
you under my orders, Lieutenant, because I can do
that and high command's just real worried the
Bureau's going to poke and prod and that elf's
going to leave us on the sudden for elvish heaven.
So let's just keep him moderately happy. He wants
to talk to you. What the Bureau wants to tell you,
but I told them *I'd* make it clear, because they'll
talk tech at you and I want to be sure you've got
it—it's just real simple: you're dealing with an

alien; and you'll have noticed what he says doesn't always make sense."

"Yes, ma'am."

"Don't yes ma'am me, Lieutenant, dammit; just talk to me and look me in the eye. We're talking about communication here."

"Yes—" He stopped short of the ma'am.

"You've got a brain, deFranco, it's all in your record. You almost went Special Services yourself, that was your real ambition, wasn't it? But you had this damn psychotic fear of taking ultimate responsibility. And a wholesome fear of ending up with a commendation, posthumous. Didn't you? It washed you out, so you went special op where you could take orders from someone else and still play bloody hero and prove something to yourself—am I right? I ought to be; I've got your psych record over there. Now I've insulted you and you're sitting there turning red. But I want to know what I'm dealing with. We're in a damn bind. We've got casualties happening out there. Are you and I going to have trouble?"

"No. I understand."

"Good. Very good. Do you think you can go into a room with that elf and talk the truth out of him? More to the point, can you *make* a decision, can you go in there knowing how much is riding on your back?"

"I'm not a—"

"I don't care what you *are*, deFranco. What I want to know is whether *negotiate* is even in that elf's vocabulary. I'm assigning you to guard over there. In the process I want you to sit down with him one to one and just talk away. That's all you've got to do. And because of your background maybe you'll do it with some sense. But maybe if you just

talk for John deFranco and try to get that elf to
deal, that's the best thing. You know when a government sends out a negotiator—or anything like—
that individual's not average. That individual's
probably the smartest, canniest, hardest-nosed bastard they've got, and he probably cheats at dice.
We don't know what this bastard's up to or what
he thinks like, and when you sit down with him
you're talking to a mind that knows a lot more
about humanity than we know about elves. You're
talking to an elvish expert who's here playing games
with us. Who's giving us a real good look-over.
You understand that? What do you say about it?"

"I'm scared of this."

"That's real good. You know we're not sending
in the brightest, most experienced human on two
feet. And that's exactly what that rather canny elf
has arranged for us to do. You understand that?
He's playing us like a keyboard this far. And how
do you cope with that, Lieutenant deFranco?"

"I just ask him questions and answer as little as
I can."

"Wrong. You let him talk. You be real *careful*
what you ask him. What you ask is as dead a
giveaway as what you tell him. Everything you do
and say is cultural. If he's good he'll drain you like
a sponge." The colonel bit her lips. "Damn, you're
not going to be able to handle that, are you?"

"I understand what you're warning me about,
Colonel. I'm not sure I can do it, but I'll try."

"Not sure you can do it. *Peace* may hang on this.
And several billion lives. Your company, out there
on the line. Put it on that level. And you're scared
and you're showing it, Lieutenant; you're too
damned open, no wonder they washed you out.
Got no hard center to you, no place to go to when I

embarrass the hell out of you, and *I'm* on your side. You're probably a damn good special ops, brave as hell, I know, you've got commendations in the field. And that shell-shyness of yours probably makes you drive real hard when you're in trouble. Good man. Honest. If the elf wants a human specimen, we could do worse. You just go in there, son, and you talk to him and you be your nice self, and that's all you've got to do."

"We'll be bugged." DeFranco stared at the colonel deliberately, trying to dredge up some self-defense, give the impression he was no complete fool.

"Damn sure you'll be bugged. Guards right outside if you want them. But you startle that elf I'll fry you."

"That isn't what I meant. I meant—I meant if I could get him to talk there'd be an accurate record."

"Ah. Well. Yes. There will be, absolutely. And yes, I'm a bastard, Lieutenant, same as that elf is, beyond a doubt. And because I'm on your side I want you as prepared as I can get you. But I'm going to give you all the backing you need—you want anything, you just tell that staff and they better jump to do it. I'm giving you carte blanche over there in the Science Wing. Their complaints can come to this desk. You just be yourself with him, watch yourself a little, don't get taken and don't set him off."

"Yes, ma'am."

Another slow, consuming stare and a nod.

He was dismissed.

IV

So where's the hole we're digging end?
Why, it's neverneverdone, my friend.
Well, why's it warm at the other end?
Well, hell's neverneverfar, my friend.

"This colonel," says the elf, "it's her soldiers outside."

"That's the one," says deFranco.

"It's not the highest rank."

"No. It's not. Not even on this world." DeFranco's hands open and close on each other, white-knuckled. His voice stays calm. "But it's a lot of power. She won't be alone. There are others she's acting for. They sent me here. I've figured that now."

"Your dealing confuses me."

"Politics. It's all politics. Higher-ups covering their—" DeFranco rechooses his words. "Some things they have to abide by. They have to do. Like if they don't take a peace offer—that would be trouble back home. Human space is big. But a war—humans want it stopped. I know that. With humans, you can't quiet a mistake down. We've got too many separate interests. . . We got scientists, and a half dozen different commands—"

"Will they all stop fighting?"

"Yes. My side will. I know they will." DeFranco clenches his hands tighter as if the chill has gotten to his bones. "If we can give them something, some solution. You have to understand what they're thinking of. If there's a trouble anywhere, it can grow. There might be others out here, you ever think of that? What if some other species just— wanders through? It's happened. And what if our little war disturbs them? We live in a big house, you know that yet? You're young, you, with your ships, you're a young power out in space. God help us, we've made mistakes, but this time the first one wasn't ours. We've been trying to stop this. All along, we've been trying to stop this."

"You're what I trust," says the elf. "Not your colonel. Not your treaty words. Not your peace. You. Words aren't the belief. What you do—that's the belief. What you do will show us."

"I can't!"

"I can. It's important enough to me and not to you. *Our little war*. I can't understand how you think that way."

"Look at that!" DeFranco waves a desperate hand at the room, the world. Up. "It's so big! Can't you see that? And one planet, one ball of rock. It's a *little* war. Is it worth it all? Is it worth such damn stubbornness? Is it worth dying in?"

"Yes," the elf says simply, and the sea-green eyes and the white face have neither anger nor blame for him.

DeFranco saluted and got out and waited until the colonel's orderly caught him in the hall and gave his escort the necessary authorizations, because *no one* wandered this base without an escort. (But the elves are two hundred klicks out *there*, deFranco thought; and who're we fighting anyway?) In the halls he saw the black of Union elite and the blue of Alliance spacers and the plain drab of the line troop officers, and the white and pale blue of the two Science Bureaus; while everywhere he felt the tenuous peace—damn, maybe we *need* this war, it's keeping humanity talking to each other, they're all fat and sleek and mud never touched them back here— But there was haste in the hallways.

But there were tense looks on faces of people headed purposefully to one place and the other, the look of a place with something on its collective mind, with silent, secret emergencies passing about him— *The attack on the lines*, he thought, and remembered another time that attack had started on one front and spread rapidly to a dozen; and missiles had gone. And towns had died.

And the elvish kids, the babies in each others' arms and the birds fluttering down; and Dibs— Dibs lying in his armor like a broken piece of machinery—when a shot got you, it got the visor and you had no face and never knew it; or it got the joints and you bled to death trapped in the failed shell, you just lay there and bled: he had heard men and women die like that, still in contact on the com, talking to their buddies and going out alone, alone in that damn armor that cut off the sky and the air—

They brought him down tunnels that were poured and cast and hard overnight, *that* kind of construction, which they never got out on the Line. There were bright lights and there were dry floors for the fine officers to walk on; there was, at the end, a new set of doors where guards stood with weapons ready—

—against *us?* DeFranco got that sense of unreality again, blinked as he had to show his tags and IDs to get past even with the colonel's orders directing his escort.

Then they let him through, and further, to another hall with more guards. AlSec MP's. Alliance Security. The intelligence and Special Services. The very air here had a chill about it, with only those uniforms in sight. *They* had the elf. Of course they did. He was diplomatic property and the regs and the generals had nothing to do with it. He was in Finn's territory. Security and the Surface Tactical command, that the reg command only controlled from the top, not inside the structure. Finn had a leash, but she took no orders from sideways in the structure. Not even from AlSec. Check and balance in a joint command structure too many lightyears from home to risk petty dictatorships. He had just crossed a line and might as well have been on another planet.

And evidently a call had come ahead of him, because there were surly Science Bureau types here too, and the one who passed him through hardly glanced at his ID. It was his face the man looked at, long and hard; and it was the Xenbureau interviewer who had been on the tape.

"Good luck," the man said. And a SurTac major arrived dour-faced, a black man in the SurTac's khaki, who did not look like an office-type. *He* took the folder of authorizations and looked at it and at deFranco with a dark-eyed stare and a set of a square, well-muscled jaw. "Colonel's given you three hours, Lieutenant. Use it."

"We're more than one government," says deFranco to the elf, quietly, desperately. "We've fought in the past. We had wars. We made peace and we work together. We may fight again but everyone hopes not and it's less and less likely. War's expensive. It's too damn open out here, that's what I'm trying to tell you. You start a war and you don't know what else might be listening."

The elf leans back in his chair, one arm on the back of it. His face is solemn as ever as he looks at deFranco. "You and I, you-and-I. The world was whole until you found us. How can people do things that don't make sense? The *whole* thing makes sense, the parts of the thing are crazy. You can't put part of one thing into another, leaves won't be feathers, and your mind can't be our mind. I see our mistakes. I want to take them away. Then elves won't have theirs and you won't have yours. But you call it a little war. The lives are only a few. You have so many. You like your mistake. You'll keep it. You'll hold it in your arms. And you'll meet these others with it. But they'll see it, won't they, when they look at you?"

"It's crazy!"

"When we met you in it we assumed *we*. That was our first great mistake. But it's yours too."

DeFranco walked into the room where they kept the elf, a luxurious room, a groundling civ's kind of room, with a bed and a table and two chairs, and some kind of green and yellow pattern on the bedclothes, which were ground-style, free-hanging. And amid this riot of life-colors the elf sat cross-legged on the bed, placid, not caring that the door opened or someone came in—until a flicker of recognition seemed to take hold and grow. It was the first humanlike expression, virtually the only expression, the elf had ever used in deFranco's sight. Of course there were cameras recording it, recording everything. The colonel had said so and probably the elf knew it too.

"Saitas. You wanted to see me."

"DeFranco." The elf's face settled again to inscrutability.

"Shall I sit down?"

There was no answer. DeFranco waited an uncertain moment, then settled into one chair at the table and leaned his elbows on the white plastic surface.

"They treating you all right?" deFranco asked, for the cameras, deliberately, for the colonel— (*Damn you, I'm not a fool, I can play your damn game, colonel, I did what your SurTacs failed at, didn't I? So watch me.*)

"Yes," the elf said. His hands rested loosely in his red-robed lap. He looked down at them and up again.

"I tried to treat you all right. I thought I did."

"Yes."

"Why'd you ask for me?"

"I'm a soldier," the elf said, and put his legs over the side of the bed and stood up. "I know that you are. I think you understand me more."

"I don't know about that. But I'll listen." The thought crossed his mind of being held hostage, of some irrational violent behavior, but he pretended it away and waved a hand at the other chair. "You want to sit down? You want something to drink? They'll get it for you."

"I'll sit with you." The elf came and took the other chair, and leaned his elbows on the table. The bruises on his wrists showed plainly under the light. "I thought you might have gone back to the front by now."

"They give me a little time. I mean, there's—"

(Don't talk to him, the colonel had said. Let him talk.)

"—three hours. A while. You had a reason you wanted to see me. Something you wanted? Or just to talk. I'll do that too."

"Yes," the elf said slowly, in his lilting lisp. And gazed at him with sea-green eyes. "Are you young, deFranco? You make me think of a young man."

It set him off his balance. "I'm not all that young."

"I have a son and a daughter. Have you?"

"No."

"Parents?"

"Why do you want to know?"

"Have you parents?"

"A mother. Long way from here." He resented the questioning. Letters were all Nadya deFranco got, and not enough of them, and thank God she had closer sons. DeFranco sat staring at the elf who had gotten past his guard in two quick questions and managed to hit a sore spot; and he remembered what Finn had warned him. "You, elf?"

"Living parents. Yes. A lot of relatives?"

Damn, what trooper had they stripped getting that part of human language? Whose soul had they gotten into?

"What are you, Saitas? Why'd they hand you over like that?"

"To make peace. So the Saitas always does."

"Tied up like that?"

"I came to be your prisoner. You understood that."

"Well, it worked. I might have shot you; I don't say I would've, but I might, except for that. It was a smart move, I guess it was. But hell, you could have called ahead. You come up on us in the dark— you looked to get your head blown off. Why didn't you use the radio?"

A blink of sea-green eyes. "Others ask me that. Would you have come then?"

"Well, someone would. Listen, you speak at them in human language and they'd listen and they'd arrange something a lot safer."

The elf stared, full of his own obscurities.

"Come on, they throw you out of there? They your enemies?"

"Who?"

"The ones who left you out there on the hill."

"No."

"Friends, huh? *Friends* let you out there?"

"They agreed with me. I agreed to be there. I was most afraid you'd shoot them. But you let them go."

"Hell, look, I just follow orders."

"And orders led you to let them go?"

"No. They say to talk if I ever got the chance. Look, me, personally, I never wanted to kill you guys. I wouldn't, if I had the choice."

"But you do."

"Dammit, you took out our ships. Maybe that wasn't personal on your side either, but we sure as hell can't have you doing it as a habit. All you ever damn well had to do was go away and let us alone. You hit a world, elf. Maybe not much of one, but you killed more than a thousand people on that first ship. Thirty thousand at that base, good God, don't sit there looking at me like that!"

"It was a mistake."

"Mistake." DeFranco found his hands shaking. No. Don't raise the voice. Don't lose it. (Be your own nice self, boy. Patronizingly. The colonel knew he was far out of his depth. And he knew.) "Aren't most wars mistakes?"

"Do you think so?"

"If it is, can't we stop it?" He felt the attention of unseen listeners, diplomats, scientists—himself, special ops, talking to an elvish negotiator and making a mess of it all, losing everything. (Be your own nice self— The colonel was crazy, the elf was, the war and the world were and he lumbered ahead

desperately, attempting subtlety, attempting a cari-
catured simplicity toward a diplomat and knowing the one as transparent as the other.) "You
know all you have to do is say quit and there's
ways to stop the shooting right off, ways to close it
all down and then start talking about how we
settle this. You say that's what you came to do.
You're in the right place. All you have to do is get
your side to stop. They're killing each other out
there, do you know that? You come in here to talk
peace. And they're coming at us all up and down
the front. I just got word I lost a friend of mine out
there. God knows what by now. It's no damn sense.
If you can stop it, then let's stop it."

"I'll tell you what our peace will be." The elf
lifted his face placidly, spread his hands. "There is
a camera, isn't there. At least a microphone. They
do listen."

"Yes. They've got camera and mike. I know they
will."

"But your face is what I see. Your face is all
human faces to me. They can listen, but I talk to
you. Only to you. And this is our peace. The fighting will stop, and we'll build ships again and we'll
go into space, and we won't be enemies. The mistake won't exist. That's the peace I want."

"So how do we do that?" (Be your own nice self,
boy— DeFranco abandoned himself. Don't see the
skin, don't see the face alien-like, just talk, talk
like to a human, don't worry about protocols. *Do*
it, boy.) "How do we get the fighting stopped?"

"I've said it. They've heard."

"Yes. They have."

"They have two days to make this peace."

DeFranco's palms sweated. He clenched his hands
on the chair. "Then what happens?"

"I'll die. The war will go on."

(God, now what do I do, what do I say? How far can I go?) "Listen, you don't understand how long it takes us to make up our minds. We need more than any two days. They're dying out there, your people are killing themselves against our lines, and it's all for nothing. Stop it now. Talk to them. Tell them we're going to talk. Shut it down."

The slitted eyes blinked, remained in their buddha-like abstraction, looking askance into infinity. "DeFranco, there has to be payment."

(Think, deFranco, think. Ask the right things.) "What payment? Just exactly *who* are you talking for? All of you? A city? A district?"

"One peace will be enough for you—won't it? You'll go away. You'll leave and we won't see each other until we've built our ships again. You'll begin to go—as soon as my peace is done."

"Build the ships, for God's sake. And come after us again?"

"No. The war is a mistake. There won't be another war. This is enough."

"But would everyone agree?"

"Everyone does agree. I'll tell you my real name. It's Angan. Angan Anassidi. I'm forty-one years old. I have a son named Agaita; a daughter named Siadi; I was born in a town named Daogisshi, but it's burned now. My wife is Llaothai Sohail, and she was born in the city where we live now. I'm my wife's only husband. My son is aged twelve, my daughter nine. They live in the city with my wife alone now and her parents and mine." The elvish voice acquired a subtle music on the names that lingered to obscure his other speech. "I've written—I told them I would write everything for them. I write in your language."

"Told who?"

"The humans who asked me. I wrote it all."

DeFranco stared at the elf, at a face immaculate and distant as a statue. "I don't think I follow you. I don't understand. We're talking about the front. We're talking about maybe that wife and those kids being in danger, aren't we? About maybe my friends getting killed out there. About shells falling and people getting blown up. Can we do anything about it?"

"I'm here to make the peace. Saitas is what I am. A gift to you. I'm the payment."

DeFranco blinked and shook his head. "Payment? I'm not sure I follow that."

For a long moment there was quiet. "Kill me," the elf said. "That's why I came. To be the last dead. The saitas. To carry the mistake away."

"Hell, no. No. We don't shoot you. Look, elf—all we want is to stop the fighting. We don't want your life. Nobody wants to kill you."

"DeFranco, we haven't any more resources. We want a peace."

"So do we. Look, we just make a treaty—you understand *treaty*?"

"I'm the treaty."

"A treaty, man, a treaty's a piece of paper. We promise peace to each other and not to attack us, we promise not to attack you, we settle our borders, and you just go home to that wife and kids. And I go home and that's it. No more dying. No more killing."

"No." The elf's eyes glistened within the pale mask. "No, deFranco, no paper."

"We make peace with a paper and ink. We *write* peace out and we make agreements and it's good enough; we do what we say we'll do."

"Then write it in your language."

"You have to sign it. Write your name on it. And keep the terms. That's all, you understand that?"

"Two days. I'll sign your paper. I'll make your peace. It's nothing. Our peace is in me. And I'm here to give it."

"Dammit, we don't kill people for treaties."

The sea-colored eyes blinked. "Is one so hard and millions so easy?"

"It's different."

"Why?"

"Because—because—look, war's for killing; peace is for staying alive."

"I don't understand why you fight. Nothing you do makes sense to us. But I think we almost understand. We talk to each other. We use the same words. DeFranco, don't go on killing us."

"Just you. Just you, is that it? Dammit, that's crazy!"

"A cup would do. Or a gun. Whatever you like. DeFranco, have you never shot us before?"

"God, it's not the same!"

"You say paper's enough for you. That paper will take away all your mistakes and make the peace. But paper's not enough for us. I'd never trust it. You have to make my peace too. So both sides will know it's true. But there has to be a saitas for humans. Someone has to come to us."

DeFranco sat there with his hands locked together. "You mean just go to your side and get killed."

"The last dying."

"Dammit, you *are* crazy. You'll wait a long time for that, elf."

"You don't understand."

"You're damn right I don't understand. Damn

bloody-minded lunatics!" DeFranco shoved his hands down, needing to get up, to get away from that infinitely patient and not human face, that face that had somehow acquired subtle expressions, that voice which made him forget where the words had first come from. And then he remembered the listeners, the listeners taking notes, the colonel staring at him across the table. Information. Winning was not the issue. Questions were. Finding out what they could. Peace was no longer the game. They were dealing with the insane, with minds there was no peace with. Elves that died to spite their enemies. That suicided for a whim and thought nothing about wiping out someone else's life.

He stayed in his chair. He drew another breath. He collected his wits and thought of something else worth learning. "What'd you do with the prisoners you learned the language from, huh? Tell me that?"

"Dead. We gave them the cup. One at a time they wanted it."

"Did they."

Again the spread of hands, of graceful fingers. "I'm here for all the mistakes. Whatever will be enough for them."

"Dammit, elf!"

"Don't call me that." The voice acquired a faint music. "Remember my name. Remember my name. DeFranco—"

He had to get up. He had to get up and get clear of the alien, get away from that stare. He thrust himself back from the table and looked back, found the elf had turned. Saitas-Angan smelled of something dry and musky, like spice. The eyes never opened wide, citrine slits. They followed him.

"Talk to me," the elf said. "*Talk* to me, deFranco."

"About what? About handing one of us to you?

It won't happen. It bloody won't happen. We're not crazy."

"Then the war won't stop."

"You'll bloody die, every damn last one of you!"

"If that's your intention," the elf said, "yes. We don't believe you want peace. We haven't any more hope. So I come here. And the rest of us begin to die. Not the quiet dying. Our hearts won't stop. We'll fight."

"Out there on the lines, you mean."

"I'll die as long as you want, here. I won't stop my heart. The saitas can't."

"Dammit, that's not what we're after! That's not what we want."

"Neither can you stop yours. I know that. We're not cruel. I still have hope in you. I still hope."

"It won't work. *We can't do it*, do you understand me? It's against our law. Do you understand law?"

"Law."

"Right and wrong. Morality. For God's sake, killing's wrong."

"Then you've done a lot of wrong. You have your mistake too. DeFranco. You're a soldier like me. You know what your life's value is."

"You're damn right I know. And I'm still alive."

"We go off the course. We lose ourselves. You'll die for war but not for peace. I don't understand."

"*I* don't understand. You think we're just going to pick some poor sod and send him to you."

"You, deFranco. I'm asking you to make the peace."

"Hell." He shook his head, walked away to the door, colonel-be-hanged, listeners-be-hanged. His hand shook on the switch and he was afraid it showed. End the war. "The hell you say."

The door shot open. He expected guards. Expected—

—It was open corridor, clean prefab, tiled floor. On the tiles lay a dark, round object, with the peculiar symmetry and ugliness of things meant to kill. Grenade. Intact.

His heart jolted. He felt the doorframe against his side and the sweat ran cold on his skin, his bowels went to water. He hung there looking at it and it did not go away. He began to shake all over as if it were already armed.

"Colonel Finn." He turned around in the doorway and yelled at the unseen monitors. "Colonel Finn—get me out of here!"

No one answered. No door opened. The elf sat there staring at him in the closest thing to distress he had yet showed.

"Colonel! *Colonel, damn you!*"

More of silence. The elf rose to his feet and stood there staring at him in seeming perplexity, as if he suspected he witnessed some human madness.

"They left us a present," deFranco said. His voice shook and he tried to stop it. "They left us a damn present, elf. And they locked us in."

The elf stared at him; and deFranco went out into the hall, bent and gathered up the deadly black cylinder—held it up. "It's one of yours, elf."

The elf stood there in the doorway. His eyes looking down were the eyes of a carved saint; and looking up they showed color against his white skin. A long nailless hand touched the doorframe as the elf contemplated him and human treachery.

"Is this their way?"

"It's not mine." He closed his hand tightly on the cylinder, in its deadliness like and unlike every weapon he had ever handled. "It's damn well not mine."

"You can't get out."

The shock had robbed him of wits. For a moment he was not thinking. And then he walked down the hall to the main door and tried it. "Locked," he called back to the elf, who had joined him in his possession of the hall. The two of them together. DeFranco walked back again, trying doors as he went. He felt strangely numb. The hall became surreal, his elvish companion belonging like him, elsewhere. "Dammit, what have they got in their minds?"

"They've agreed," the elf said. "They've agreed, deFranco."

"They're out of their minds."

"One door still closes, doesn't it? You can protect your life."

"You still bent on suicide?"

"You'll be safe."

"Damn them!"

The elf gathered his arms about him as if he too felt the chill. "The colonel gave us a time. Is it past?"

"Not bloody yet."

"Come sit with me. Sit and talk. My friend."

"Is it time?" asks the elf, as deFranco looks at his watch again. And deFranco looks up.

"Five minutes. Almost." DeFranco's voice is hoarse.

The elf has a bit of paper in hand. He offers it. A pen lies on the table between them. Along with the grenade. "I've written your peace. I've put my name below it. Put yours."

"I'm nobody. I can't sign a treaty, for God's

sake." DeFranco's face is white. His lips tremble. "What did you write?"

"Peace," says the elf. "I just wrote peace. Does there have to be more?"

DeFranco takes it. Looks at it. And suddenly he picks up the pen and signs it too, a furious scribble. And lays the pen down. "There," he says. "There, they'll have my name on it." And after a moment: "If I could do the other—O God, I'm scared. I'm *scared*."

"You don't have to go to my city," says the elf, softly. His voice wavers like deFranco's. "De-Franco—here, here they record everything. Go with me. Now. The record will last. We have our peace, you and I, we make it together, here, now. The last dying. Don't leave me. And we can end this war."

DeFranco sits a moment. Takes the grenade from the middle of the table, extends his hand with it across the center. He looks nowhere but at the elf. "Pin's yours," he says. "Go on. You pull it, I'll hold it steady."

The elf reaches out his hand, takes the pin and pulls it, quickly.

DeFranco lays the grenade down on the table between them, and his mouth moves in silent counting. But then he looks up at the elf and the elf looks at him. DeFranco manages a smile. "You got the count on this thing?"

The screen breaks up.

The staffer reached out her hand and cut the monitor, and Agnes Finn stared past the occupants of the office for a time. Tears came seldom to her eyes. They were there now, and she chose not to look at the board of inquiry who had gathered there.

"There's a mandatory inquiry," the man from the reg command said. "We'll take testimony from the major this afternoon."

"Responsibility's mine," Finn said.

It was agreed on the staff. It was pre-arranged, the interview, the formalities.

Someone had to take the direct hit. It might have been a SurTac. She would have ordered that too, if things had gone differently. High Command might cover her. Records might be wiped. A tape might be classified. The major general who had handed her the mess and turned his back had done it all through subordinates. And he was clear.

"The paper, Colonel."

She looked at them, slid the simple piece of paper back across the desk. The board member collected it and put it into the folder. Carefully.

"It's more than evidence," she said. "That's a treaty. The indigenes know it is."

They left her office, less than comfortable in their official search for blame and where, officially, to put it.

She was already packed. Going back on the same ship with an elvish corpse, all the way to Pell and Downbelow. There would be a grave there onworld.

It had surprised no one when the broadcast tape got an elvish response. Hopes rose when it got the fighting stopped and brought an elvish delegation to the front; but there was a bit of confusion when the elves viewed both bodies and wanted deFranco's. Only deFranco's.

And they made him a stone grave there on the shell-pocked plain, a stone monument; and they wrote everything they knew about him. *I was John*

Rand deFranco, a graven plaque said. *I was born on a space station twenty lightyears away. I left my mother and my brothers. The friends I had were soldiers and many of them died before me. I came to fight and I died for the peace, even when mine was the winning side. I died at the hand of Angan Anassidi, and he died at mine, for the peace; and we were friends at the end of our lives.*

Elves—*suilti* was one name they called themselves—came to this place and laid gifts of silk ribbons and bunches of flowers—flowers, in all that desolation; and in their thousands they mourned and they wept in their own tearless, expressionless way.

For their enemy.

One of their own was on his way to humankind. For humankind to cry for. *I was Angan Anassidi*, his grave would say; and all the right things. Possibly no human would shed a tear. Except the veterans of Elfland, when they came home, if they got down to the world—they might, like Agnes Finn, in their own way and for their own dead, in front of an alien shrine.

Joe Haldeman, of course, has personal combat experience; he was drafted in 1967 and sent to Vietnam, coming home with a leg injury and the memories which led him to produce several works, fictional and nonfictional, about war and the men who fight it.

High-level strategy may be devised half a world away, but decisions in action are up to the men who lead. Soldiers are drilled to respond unquestioningly to the orders of their superiors—yet this non-negotiable demand for obedience exacts its own price. Combat leaders are the choosers of the slain. Theirs is the knowledge that personal error can mean the death of many—and that even the finest leader cannot protect his men from battle.

"Seasons" involves war on a very small scale, but a war which illustrates nonetheless the demands and the costs of battle. It is the story of one "unit commander" who had never been trained for conflict, and perhaps was not ready for her responsibility.

SEASONS

By

Joe Haldeman

I

Transcripts edited from the last few hundred hours of recordings:

Maria

Forty-one is too young to die. I was never trained to be a soldier. Trained to survive, yes, but not to kill or be killed.

That's the wrong way to start. Let me start this way.

As near as I can reckon, it's mid-Noviembre, AC 238. I am Maria Rubera, chief xenologist for the second Confederación expedition to Sanchrist IV. I am currently standing guard in the mouth of a cave while my five comrades try to sleep. I am armed with a stone axe and flint spear and a pile of rocks for throwing. A cold rain is misting down and I am wearing only a stiff kilt and vest of wet rank fur. I am cold to the very heart but we dare not risk a fire. The Plathys have too acute a sense of smell.

I am sub-vocalizing, recording this into my artificial bicuspid, one of which each of us has; the only post-Stone Age artifacts in this cave. It may survive even if, as is probable, I do not. Or it may not survive. The Plathys have a way of eating animals head first, crunching up skull and brain while the decapitated body writhes at their feet or staggers around, which to them is high humor. Innocent humor but ghastly. I almost came to love them. Which is not to say I understand them.

Let me try to make this document as complete as possible. It gives me something to do. I trust you have a machine that can filter out the sound of my teeth chattering. For a while I could do the zen trick to keep my teeth still. But I'm too cold now. And too certain of death, and afraid.

My specialty is xenology but I do have a doctorate in histori-cultural anthropology, which is essentially the study of dead cultures through the writings of dead anthropologists. In the nineteenth and twentieth centuries, old style, there were dozens of isolated cultures still existing without metals or writing or even, in some cases, agriculture or social organization beyond the family. None of them survived more than a couple of generations beyond their contact with civilization, but civilization by then could afford the luxury of science, and so there are fairly complete records. The records are fascinating not only for the information about the primitives, but also for what they reveal of the investigating cultures' unconscious prejudices. My own specialties were the Maori and Eskimo tribes, and (by necessary association) the European and American cultures that investigated and more or less benignly destroyed them.

I will try not to stray from the point. That training is what led to my appointment as leader of this band of cold, half-naked, probably doomed, pseudo-primitive scientists. We do not repeat the errors of our forebears. We come to the primitives on equal terms, now, so as not to contaminate their habit patterns by superior example. No more than is necessary. Most of us do not bite the heads off living animals or exchange greetings by the tasting of excrement.

Saying that and thinking of it goads me to go down the hill again. We designated a Latrine Rock a few hundred meters away, in sight of the cave entrance but with no obvious path leading here, to throw them off our scent at least temporarily. I will not talk while going there. They also have acute hearing.

Back. Going too often and with too little result. Diet mostly raw meat in small amounts. Only warm place on my body is the hot and itching anus. No proper hygiene in the Stone Age. Just find a smooth rock. I can feel my digestive tract flourishing with worms and bugs. No evidence yet, though, nor blood. Carlos Fleming started passing blood and two days later, something burst and he died in a rush of it. We covered his body with stones. Ground too frozen for grave-digging. He was probably uncovered and eaten.

It can't be the diet. On Earth I paid high prices for raw meat and fish, and never suffered except in the wallet. I'm afraid it may be a virus. We all are, and we indulge discreetly in copromancy, the divining of future events through the inspection of stools. If there is blood your future will be short.

Perhaps it was stress that killed Carlos. We are under unusual stress. But I stray, again.

It was specifically my study of Eskimos that impressed the assigning committee. Eskimos were small bands of hearty folk who lived in the polar regions of North America. Like the Plathys, they were anagricultural carnivores, preying on herds of large animals, sometimes fishing. The Plathys have no need for the Eskimo's fishing skills, since the sea teems with life edible and stupid. But they prefer red meat and the crunch of bone, the chewy liver and long suck of intestinal contents, the warm mush of brains. They are likable but not fastidious. And not predictable, we learned to our grief.

Like the Eskimos, the Plathys relish the cold, and become rather dull and listless during the warm season. Sanchrist IV has no axial tilt, thus no "seasons" in the terran sense, but its orbit is highly elongated, so more than two thirds of its year (three and a half terran years) is spent in cold. We identified six discrete seasons: spring, summer, fall, winter, dead winter, and thaw. The placid sea gets ice skim in mid-fall.

If you are less than totally ignorant of science, you know that Sanchrist IV is one of the very few planets with not only Earthlike conditions but with lifeforms that mimic our own patterns of DNA. There are various theories explaining this coincidence, which can not be coincidence, but you can find them elsewhere. What this meant in terms of our conduct as xenologists was that we could function with minimal ecological impact, living off the fat of the land. And the blood and flesh and marrow, which did require a certain amount of desensitization training. (Less for me than for some of the others, as I've said, since I've always had an atavistic leaning toward dishes like steak tartare and sushi.)

Satellite observation has located 119 bands, or families, of Plathys, and there is no sign of other humanoid life on the planet. All of them live on islands in a southern subtropical sea—at least it would be subtropical on Earth—a shallow sea that freezes solid in dead winter and can be walked over from late fall to early thaw. During the warm months, on those occasions when they actually stir their bones to go someplace, they pole rafts from island to island. During low tide, they can wade most of the way.

We set up our base in the tropics, well beyond their normal range, and hiked south during the late summer. We made contact with a few individuals and small packs during our monthlong trek, but didn't join a family until we reached the southern mountains.

The Plathys aren't too interesting during the warm months, except for the short mating season. Mostly they loll around, conserving energy, living off the meat killed during the thaw, which they smoke and store in covered holes. When the meat gets too old, or starts running out, they bestir themselves to fish, which takes little enough energy. The tides are rather high in summer and fall, and all they have to do is stake down nets in the right spots during high tide. The tide recedes and leaves behind flopping silver bounty. They grumble and joke about the taste of it, though.

They accepted our presence without question, placidly sharing their food and shelter as they would with any wayfaring member of another na-

tive family. They couldn't have mistaken us for
natives, though. The smallest adult Plathy weighed
twice as much as our largest. They stand about
two and a half meters high and span about a
meter and a half across the shoulders. Their heads
are more conical than square, with huge powerful
jaws; a mouth that runs almost ear to ear. Their
eyes are set low, and they have mucous-membrane
slits in place of external ears and noses. They are
covered with sparse silky fur, which coarsens into
thick hair on their heads, shoulders, armpits, and
groins (and on the males' backs). The females have
four teats defining the corners of a rectangular
slab of lactiferous fatty tissue. The openings we
thought were their vaginas are almost dorsal, with
the cloacal openings toward the front. The male
genitals are completely ventral, normally hidden
under a mat of hair. (This took a bit of snooping.
In all but the hottest times and mating season,
both genders wear a "modest" kilt of skin.)

We had been observing them about three weeks
when the females went into estrous—every mature
female, all on the same day. Their sexuality was
prodigious.

Everybody shed their kilts and went into a
weeklong unrelenting spasm of sexual activity.
There is nothing like it among any of the sentient
cultures—or animal species!—that I have studied.
To call it an orgy would be misleading, and I think
demeaning to the Plathys. The phenomenon was
more like a tropism, in plants, than any animal or
human instinct. They quite simply did not do anything else for six days.

The adults in our family numbered 82 males
and 19 females (the terrible reason for the dispar-
ity would become clear in a later season), so the

females were engaged all the time. Even while they slept. While one male copulated, two or three others would be waiting their turn, prancing impatiently, masturbating; sometimes indulging in homosexual coupling. ("Indulging" is the wrong word. There was no sense that they took pleasure in any sexual activity; it was more like the temporary relief of a terrible pressure that quickly built up again.) They attempted coupling with children and with the humans of my expedition. Fortunately, for all their huge strength they are rather slow, and for all the pressure of their "desire," easily deflected. A kick in the knee was enough to send them stumping off toward someone else.

No adult Plathys ate during the six days. They slept more and more toward the end of the period, the males sometimes falling asleep in the middle of copulation. (Conversely, we saw several instances of involuntary erection and ejaculation while sleeping.) When it was finally over, everyone sat around dazed for a while, and then the females retired to the storage holes and came back with armloads of dried and smoked meat and fish. Each one ate a mountain of food and fell into a coma.

There are interesting synchronies involved. At other times of the year, this long period of vulnerability would mean extinction of the family or of the whole species, since they evidently all copulate at the same time. But the large predators from the north do not swim down at that time of year. And when the litters were dropped, about 500 days later, it would be not long after the time of easiest food gathering, as herds of small animals migrated north for warmth.

Of course we never had a chance to dissect a Plathy. It would have been fascinating to investigate the internal makeup that impels the bizarre sexual behavior. External observation gives some hint as to the strangeness. The vulva is a small opening, a little over a centimeter in extent, that stays sealed except when the female is in estrous. The penis, normally an almost invisible nub, becomes a prehensile purple worm about twenty centimeters long. No external testicles; there must be an internal reservoir (quite large) for seminal fluid.

The anatomical particulars of pregnancy and birth are even more strange. The females become almost immobilized, gaining perhaps fifty percent in weight. When it comes time to give birth, the female makes an actual skeletal accommodation, evidently similar to the way a snake unhinges its jaw when ingesting large prey. It is obviously quite painful. The vulva (or whatever new name applies to that opening) is not involved; instead, a slit opens along the entire perineal area, nearly half a meter long, exposing a milky white membrane. The female claws the membrane open and expels the litter in a series of shuddering contractions. Then she pushes her pelvic bones back into shape with a painful grinding sound. She remains immobile and insensate for several days, nursing. The males bring females food and clean them during this period.

None of the data from the first expedition had prepared us for this. They had come during dead winter, and stayed one (terran) year, so they missed the entire birth cycle. They had noted that there were evidently strong taboos against discussing sexual matters and birth. I think "taboo" is the wrong word. It's not as if there were guilt or shame associated with the processes. Rather, they appear to enter a different state of consciousness when the females are in heat and giving birth, a state that seems to blank out their verbal intelligence. They can no more discuss their sexuality than you or I could sit and chat about how our pancreas was doing.

There was an amusing, and revealing, episode after we had been with the family for several months. I had been getting along well with Tybru, a female elder with unusual linguistic ability. She was perplexed at what one of the children had told her.

The Plathys have no concept of privacy; they wander in and out of each other's *maffas* (the yurt-like tents of hide they use as shelter) at any time of day or night, on random whim. It was inevitable that sooner or later they would observe humans having sex. The child had described what she'd seen fairly accurately. I had tried to explain human sexuality to Tybru earlier, as a way to get her to talk about that aspect of her own life. She would smile and nod diagonally through the whole thing, a rather infuriating gesture they normally use only with children prattling nonsense.

This time I was going to be blunt. I opened the *maffa* flap so there was plenty of light, then shed my kilt and got up on a table. I lay down on my back and tried to explain with simple words and gestures what went where and who did what to whom, and what might or might not happen nine months later.

She was more inclined to take me seriously this time. (The child who had witnessed copulation was four, pubescent, and thus too old to have fantasies.) After I explained she explored me herself, which was not pleasant, since her four-fingered hand was larger than a human foot, quite filthy, and equipped with deadly nails.

She admitted that all she really understood was the breasts. She could remember some weeks of nursing after the blackout period the female language calls "(big) pain-in-hips." (Their phrase for the other blackout period is literally "pain-in-the-ass.") She asked, logically enough, whether I could find a male and demonstrate.

Actually, I'm an objective enough person to have gone along with it, if I could have found a man able and willing to rise to the occasion. If it had been near the end of our stay, I probably would have done it. But leadership is a ticklish thing, even when you're leading a dozen highly educated, professionally detached people, and we still had three years to go.

I explained that the most-elder doesn't do this with the men she's in charge of, and Tybru accepted that. They don't have much of a handle on discipline, but they do understand politeness and social form. She said she would ask the other human females.

Perhaps it should have been me who did the asking, but I didn't suggest it. I was glad to get off the hook, and also curious as to my people's reactions.

The couple who volunteered were the last ones I would have predicted. Both of them were shy, almost diffident, with the rest of us. Good field workers but not the sort of people you would let your hair down with. I suppose they had better "anthropological perspective" on their own behavior than the rest of us.

At any rate, they retired to the *maffa* that was nominally Tybru's, and she let out the ululation that means "All free females come here." I wondered whether our couple could actually perform in a cramped little yurt filled with sweaty giants asking questions in a weird language.

All of the females did crowd into the tent, and after a couple of minutes a strange sound began to emanate from them. At first it puzzled me, but then I recognized it as laughter! I had heard individual Plathys laugh, a sort of inhaled croak—but nineteen of them at once was an unearthly din.

They were in there a long time, but I never did find out whether the demonstration was actually consummated. They came out of the *maffa* beet-red and staring at the ground, the laughter behind them not abating. I never talked to either of them about it, and whenever I asked Tybru or the others, all I got was choked laughter. I think we invented the dirty joke. (In exchange, I'm sure that Plathy sexuality will eventually see service in the ribald metaphor of every human culture.)

But let me go back to the beginning.

We came to Sanchrist IV armed with a small vocabulary and a great deal of misinformation. I don't mean to denigrate my colleagues' skill or application. The Garcia expedition just came at the wrong time and didn't stay long enough.

Most of their experience with the Plathys was during deep winter, which is their most lively and civilized season. They spend their indoor time creating the complex sculptures that so impressed the art world ten years ago, and performing improvisational music and dance that is delightful in its alien grace. Outdoors, they indulge in complicated games and athletic exhibitions. The larders are full, the time of birthing and nursing is well over, and the family exudes happiness, well into the thaw. We experienced this euphoria ourselves. I can't blame Garcia's people for their enthusiastic report.

We still don't know what happened. Or why it happened. Perhaps if these data survive, the next researchers . . .

Trouble.

Gabriel

I was having a strange dream of food—real food, cooked—when suddenly there was Maria, tugging on my arm, keeping me away from the table. She was whispering "Gab, wake up!" and so I did, cold and aching and hungry.

"What's—" She put her hand on my mouth, lightly.

"There's one outside. Mylab, I think." He had just turned three this winter, and been given his name. We crept together back to the mouth of the cave, and both jumped when my ankle gave a loud pop.

It was Mylab, all right; the fur around one earlobe was almost white against the blond. I was glad it wasn't an adult. He was only about a head taller than me. Stronger, though, and well fed.

We watched from the cave's darkness as he investigated the latrine rock, sniffing and licking, circling.

"Maybe he's a scout for a hunting party," I whispered. "Hunting us."

"Too young, I think." She passed me a stone axe. "Hope we don't have to kill him."

As if on cue, the Plathy walked directly away from the rock and stood, hands on hips, sniffing the air. His head wagged back and forth slowly, as if he were triangulating. He shuffled in a half circle and stood looking in our direction.

"Stay still."

"He can't see us in the shadow."

"Maybe not." Their eyesight was more acute than ours, but they didn't have good night vision.

Behind us, someone woke up and sneezed. Mylab gave a little start, and then began loping toward the cave.

"Damn it," Maria whispered. She stood up and huddled into the side of the cave entrance. "You get over there." I stationed myself opposite her, somewhat better hidden because of a projecting lip of rock.

Mylab slowed down a few meters from the cave entrance and walked warily forward, sniffing and blinking. Maria crouched, gripping her spear with both hands, for thrusting.

It was over in a couple of seconds, but my memory of it goes in slow motion: He saw Maria, or sensed her, and lumbered straight for her, claws out, growling. She thrust twice into his chest while I stepped forward and delivered a two-handed blow to the top of his head.

That axe would have cracked a human head from crown to jaw. Instead, it glanced off his thick skull and hit his shoulder, then spun out of my grip.

Shaking his head, he stepped around and swung a long arm at me. I was just out of range, staggering back; one claw opened up my cheek and the tip of my nose. Blood was spouting from two wounds in his chest. He stepped forward to finish me off and Maria plunged the spear into the back of his neck. The flint blade burst out under his chin in a spray of blood.

He stood staggering between us for a moment, trying to reach the spear shaft behind him. Two stones flew up from the rear of the cave; one missed, but the other hit his cheek with a loud crack. He turned and stumbled away down the slope, the spear bouncing grotesquely behind him.

The other six joined us at the cave entrance. Brenda, our doctor, looked at my wound and regretted her lack of equipment. So did I.

"Have to go after him," Derek said. "Kill him."

Maria shook her head. "He's still dangerous. Wait a few minutes, then we can follow the blood trail."

"He's dead," Brenda said. "His body just doesn't know it yet."

"Maybe so," Maria said, her shoulders slumping sadly. "Anyhow, we can't stay here. Hate to move during daylight, but we don't have any choice."

"We're not the only ones who can follow a blood trail," Herb said. He had a talent for stating the obvious.

We gathered up our few weapons, water bladders, and food sack, to which we had just added five small bat-like creatures, mostly fur and bone. None of us looked forward to being hungry enough to eat them.

The trail was easy to follow, several bright red spatters per meter. He had gone about three hundred meters before collapsing.

We found him lying behind a rock in a widening pool of blood, the spear sticking straight up. When I pulled it out he made a terrible gurgling sound. Brenda made sure he was dead.

Maria looked very upset, biting her lip, I think to keep tears away. She is a strange woman. Hard and soft. She treats the Plathys by the book but obviously has a sentimental streak toward them. I sort of like them too, but don't think I'd want to take one home with me.

Brenda's upset too, retching now. My fault; I should have offered to do the knife. But she didn't ask.

I'd better take point position. Stop recording now. Concentrate on not getting surprised.

Maria

Back to the beginning. Quite hot when we were set down on the tropical mainland. It was the middle of the night, and we worked quickly, with no lights (what I'd give for nightglasses now) to set up our domed base.

In a way it's a misnomer to call it a "base," since we left it the next night, not to return for three and a half years. We thought. It was really just a staging area and a place where we would wait for pickup after our mission was ended. We really didn't foresee having to run back to it to hide from the Plathys.

It was halfheartedly camouflaged, looking like a dome of rock in the middle of a jungle terrain that featured no other domes of rock. To our knowledge at the time, no Plathy ever ventured that far north, so that gesture toward noninterference was a matter of form rather than of actual caution. Now we know that some Plathys do go that far, on their rite-of-passage wanderings. So it's a good thing we didn't simply set up a force field.

I think the closest terrestrial match to the biome there would be the jungles of the Amazon basin.

Plus volcanos, for a little extra heat and interest. Sort of a steam bath with a whiff of sulfur dioxide added to the rich smell of decaying vegetable matter. In the clearings, riots of extravagant flowers, most of which gave off the aroma of rotting meat.

For the first leg of our journey we had modern energy weapons hidden inside conventional-looking spears and axes. It would have been more sporting to face the Mesozoic fauna with primitive weapons, but of course we had no interest in that sort of adventure. We often did run into creatures resembling the Deinonychus (Lower Cretaceous period)—about the size of a human, but fast, and all claws and teeth. They travel in packs, evidently preying on the large placid herbivores. We never saw fewer than six in a group, and once were cornered by a pack of twenty. We had to kill all of them, our beams silently slashing them into steaming chunks of meat. None paid any attention to what was happening to his comrades, but just kept advancing, bent low to the ground, claws out, teeth bared, roaring. Their meat tasted like chicken, but very tough.

It took us nine days to reach the coast, following a river. (Did I mention that days here are 28 hours long? Our circadic rhythms had been adjusted accordingly, but there are other physiological factors. Mostly having to do with fatigue.) We found a conspicuous rock formation and buried our modern weapons a hundred meters to the north of it. Then we buried their power sources another hundred paces north. We kept one crazer for group defense, to be discarded before we reached the first island, but otherwise all we had was flint and stone and bicuspids with amazing memories.

We had built several boats with these tools dur-

ing our training on Selva, but of course it was
rather different here. The long day, and no comfortable cot to retire to at night. No tent to keep out
the flying insects, no clean soft clothes in the
morning, no this no that. Terrible heat and a per-
vasive moldy smell that kept us all sniffling in
spite of the anti-allergenic drugs that our modified
endocrine systems fed us. We did manage to get a
fire going, which gave us security and roast fish
and greatly simplified the boat-building. We felled
two large trees and used fire to hollow them out,
making outrigger canoes similar to the ones the
Maori used to populate the sparse South Pacific.
We weren't able to raise sails, though, since the
Plathys did not have that technology. They wouldn't
have helped much, anyway; summer was usually
dead calm. We didn't look forward to rowing 250
kilometers in the subtropical heat. But we would
do it systematically.

Herb was good at pottery, so I exempted him
from boat-building in exchange for crafting and
firing dozens of water jugs. That was going to be
our main survival problem, since it was not likely
to rain during the couple of weeks we'd be at sea.
Food was no problem; we could spear fish and
probably birds (though eating a raw bird was not
an experiment even I could look forward to), and
also had a supply of smoked dinosaur.

I designed the boats so that either one would be
big enough to carry all twelve of us, in case of
trouble. As a further safeguard, we took a shake-
down cruise, a night and a day of paddling and
staying anchored near shore. We took our last fresh-
water bath, topped off the jugs, loaded our gear
and cast off at sundown.

The idea had been to row all night, with ten

minutes' rest each hour, and keep going for a couple of hours after sunup, for as long as we could reliably gauge our direction from the angle of the sun. Then anchor (the sea was nowhere more than ten or twelve meters deep) and hide from the sun all day under woven shades, fishing and sleeping and engaging in elevated discourse. Start paddling again when the sun was low enough to tell us where north was. It did go that way for several days, until the weather changed.

It was just a thin haze, but it was enough to stop us dead. We had no navigational instruments, relying on the dim triangle of stars that marked the south celestial pole. No stars, no progress.

This was when I found out that I had chosen my party well. When the sky cleared two nights later, there was no talk of turning back, though everyone was capable of counting the water jugs and doing long division. A few more days becalmed and we would be in real danger of dying from dehydration, unable to make landfall in either direction.

I figured we had been making about 25 kilometers per night. We rowed harder and cut the break time down to five minutes, and kept rowing an extra hour or so after dawn, taking a chance on dead reckoning.

Daytime became a period of grim silence. People who were not sleeping spent the time fishing the way I had taught them. Eskimo-style, though those folks did it through a hole in the ice: arm cocked, spear raised, staring at one point slightly under the surface; when a fish approaches a handspan above that point, let fly the spear. No Eskimo ever applied greater concentration to the task; none of them was ever fishing for water as well as food. Over the course of days we learned which kinds of fish had flesh that could be sucked for moisture, and which had to be avoided, for the salty blood that suffused their tissues.

We rationed water fairly severely, doling it out in measures that would allow us to lose one night out of three to haze. As it turned out, that never happened again, and when we sighted land finally, there was water enough for another four days of short rations. We stifled the impulse to drink it all in celebration; we still had to find a stream.

I'd memorized maps and satellite photos, but terrain looks much different seen horizontally. It took several hours of hugging the shore before I could figure out where we were; fortunately, the landmark was a broad shallow river.

Before we threw away the crazer and its power source, we used it to light a torch. When the Plathys traveled, they carried hot coals from the previous night's fire, insulated in ash inside a basket of tough fiber. We would do the same, rather than spend an hour each day resolutely sawing two pieces of dry wood together. We beached the canoes and hauled them a couple of hundred meters inland, to a stand of bushes where they could be reasonably well camouflaged. Perhaps not much chance they would still be there after a full year, but it was better than simply abandoning them.

We walked inland far enough for there to be no trace of salt in the muddy water, and cavorted in it like schoolchildren. Then Brenda and I built a fire while the others stalked out in search of food.

Game was fairly plentiful near the river, but we were not yet skilled hunters. There was no way to move quietly through the grass, which was shoulder-high and stiff. So the hunters who had the best luck were the ones who tip-toed up the bank of the stream. They came back with five good-sized snakes, which we skinned and cleaned and roasted on sticks. After two weeks of raw fish, the sizzling fatty meat was delicious, though for most of us it went through the gut like a dropped rock.

We made pallets of soft grass, and most of us slept well, though I didn't. Combination of worry and indigestion. I was awake enough to notice that various couples took advantage of the relative privacy of the riverbank, which made me feel vaguely jealous and deprived. I toyed with the idea of asking somebody, but instead waited for somebody to ask me, and wound up listening to contented snores half the night.

A personal note, to be edited out if this tooth survives for publication. Gabriel. All of us women had been studying his naked body for the past two weeks, quite remarkable in proportion and endowment, and I suppose the younger women had been even more imaginative than me in theorizing about it. So I was a little dismayed when he went off to the riverbank with a male, his Selvan crony Marcus. I didn't know at the time that their generation on Selva is very casual about such things, and at any rate I should have been anthropologist enough to be objective about it. But I have my own cultural biases, too, and (perhaps more to the point) so do the terran males in the party. As a scientist, I can appreciate the fact that homosexuality is common and natural and only attitudes about it change. That attitude is not currently very enlightened on Earth; I resolved to warn them the next day to be discreet. (Neither of them is exclusively homosexual, as it turned out; they both left their pallets with women later in the night, Gabriel at least twice.)

We had rolled two large and fairly dry logs over

the fire before bedding down, orienting them so as to take advantage of the slight breeze, and the fire burned brightly all night without attention. That probably saved our lives. When we broke camp in the morning and headed south, we found hundreds of tracks just downwind, the footpads of large cat-like creatures. What an idiot I had been, not to post guards! Everyone else was sheepish at not having thought of it themselves. The numb routine and hard labor of the past two weeks had dulled us; now we were properly galvanized by fear. We realized that for all our survival training, we still had the instincts of city folk, and those instincts could kill us all.

This island was roughly circular, about a hundred kilometers in diameter, with a central crater lake. We would follow this river to the lake, and then go counterclockwise to the third stream, and follow it to the southern shore. Then we would hop down an archipelago of small islands, another eighty kilometers, to the large island that was our final destination.

The scrub of the coastal lowland soon gave way to tangled forest, dominated by trees like Earth's banyan—a large central trunk with dozens or hundreds of subsidiary trunks holding up an extensive canopy of branches. It was impossible to tell where one tree's territory ended and another's began, but some of the largest must have commanded one or two ares of ground. Their bark was ashen white, relieved by splotches of rainbow lichen. No direct sunlight reached the ground through their dense foliage; only a few spindly bushes with pale yellow leaves pushed out of the rotting humus. Hard for anything to sneak up on us at ground level, but we could hear creatures moving overhead. I wondered whether the branches were strong enough to support the animals that had watched us the night before, and felt unseen cats' eyes everywhere.

We stopped to eat in a weird clearing. Something had killed one of the huge trees: its rotting stump dominated the clearing, and the remnants of its smaller trunks stood around like ghostly guardians, most of them dead but some of them starting to sprout green. I supposed one would eventually take over the space. After feasting on cold snake, we practiced spear-throwing, using the punky old stump as a target. I was the least competent, both in range and accuracy, which had also been the case on Selva. As a girl I'd shown no talent for athletics beyond jacks and playing doctor.

Suddenly all hell broke loose. Three cat-beasts leaped down from the forest canopy behind us and bounded in for the kill. I thrust out my spear and got one in the shoulder, the force of the impact knocking me over. Brenda killed it with a well-aimed throw. The other two cats checked their advance and circled warily. They dodged thrown spears; I shouted for everyone to hold their fire.

Brenda and I retrieved our weapons and, along with Gabriel and Martin, closed in on the beasts, moving them away from where the thrown spears lay. In a few seconds the twelve of us had them encircled, and I suddenly remembered the old English expression "having a tiger by the tail." The beasts were only about half the size of a human, but all muscle and teeth. They growled and snapped at us, heads wagging, saliva drooling.

I shouted "Now, Gab!"—he was the best shot—and he flung his spear at the closest one. It sank deep in the animal's side and it fell over, mewling and pawing the air. The other beast saw its chance

and leaped straight at Gab, who instinctively
ducked under it. It bounded off his back and sprang
for the safety of the trees. Six or seven spears
showered after it, but missed.

Gabriel had four puncture wounds under each
shoulderblade from the cat's front paws. Brenda
washed them out thoroughly but decided against
improvising a dressing out of leaf and vine. Just
stay clean, always good advice.

We skinned and gutted the two cats and labori-
ously sliced their flesh into long thin strips for
jerky. The old stump made a good smoky fire for
the purpose. As darkness fell, we built another
bright fire next to it.

I set up a guard schedule, with teams of three
each standing three-hour shifts while the rest slept,
but none of us slept too soundly. Over the crackle of
the fires I was sure I could hear things moving
restlessly in the woods. If they were there, though,
they weren't bold enough to attack. During my
watch a couple of dog-sized animals with large
eyes came to the periphery of the clearing, to feast
on the cat-beasts' entrails. We threw sticks at them
but they just looked at us, and left after they had
eaten their fill.

If my estimate of our progress was correct, we
had about thirty kilometers of deep woods to go,
until the topography opened up into rolling hills
of grassland. Everyone agreed that we should try
to make it in one push. There was no guarantee we
could find another clearing, and nobody wanted to
spend a night under the canopy. So at first light,
we bundled the jerky up inside a stiff cat skin and
headed south.

As we moved along the river the nature of the

trees changed, the banyans eventually being replaced by a variety of smaller trees—damn! Two
of them!

Brenda

I wasn't paying close attention, still grieving
over Mylab—actually, grieving for myself, for having committed murder. I've had patients die under
my care, but the feeling isn't even remotely similar.
His eyes, when I drew the flint across his throat—
they went bright with pain and then immediately
dull.

We'd been walking for about an hour after leaving the cave, picking our way down the north
slope of the mountain, when Maria, in the lead,
suddenly squatted down and made a silent patting
gesture. We all crouched and moved forward.

Ahead of us on the trail, two adult Plathys sat
together with their backs to us, talking quietly
while they ate. They were armed with spear and
broadaxe and knives. I doubted that the six of us
could have taken even one of them in a face-to-face
combat.

Maria stared, probably considering ambush, and
then motioned for us to go back up the trail. I kept
looking over my shoulder, every small scuff and
scrape terribly amplified in my mind, expecting at
any moment to see the two huge brutes charging
after us. But their eating noise must have masked
the sound of our retreat.

We crept back a couple of hundred meters to a
fork in the trail, and cautiously made our way
down a roughly parallel track, going as fast as
silence would allow. The light breeze was coming

from behind us; we wanted to be past the Plathys—
downwind of them—before they finished eating.
We passed close enough to hear their talking, but
didn't see them.

After about a kilometer the trail disappeared,
and we had to pick our way down a steep defile
and couldn't help making noise, dislodging peb-
bles that often cascaded into small rattling ava-
lanches. We were only a few meters from the bottom of the cliff when the two Plathys appeared
above us. They discussed the situation loudly for a
few moments—using the hunting language, which
none of us had been allowed to learn—and then
set aside their weapons in favor of rocks.

When I saw what they were doing I slid right to
the bottom, willing to take a few abrasions rather
than present too tempting a target. Most of the
others did the same. Herb took a glancing blow to
the head and fell backwards, landing roughly. I
ran over to him, afraid he was unconscious. Gab
beat me to him and hauled him roughly to his
feet; he was dazed but awake. We each took an
arm and staggered away as fast as we could, zig-
zagging as Gab muttered a "go left" and "right,"
so as to present a more difficult target. I sustained
one hard blow to the left buttock, which knocked
me down. It was going to make sitting uncomfortable, but we wouldn't have to worry about
that for a while.

We were lucky the Plathys hadn't brought rope,
as a larger hunting party in the mountains would
have done. They are rather clumsy rock climbers
(though with their long arms they can run up a
steep slope very fast). One of them started down
after us, but after a nearly fatal slip he scrambled
back up.

We pressed our advantage, such as it was. To pursue us they would have to make a detour of a couple of kilometers, and at any rate we could go downhill faster then they could. It seemed likely that they would instead go back to their main group to report our whereabouts, and then all of them try to catch us in the veldt. On level ground they could easily run us down, once they caught our scent.

Maria, xenologist to the end, remarked how lucky we were that they had never developed the idea of signal drums. It is strange, since they use such a variety of percussion instruments in their music and dancing.

Such music and dancing. They seemed so human.

Our only chance for survival was to try to confuse them by splitting up. Maria breathlessly outlined a plan as we hurried down the slope. When we reached the valley we would get a bearing on the stream we'd followed here, then go six different ways, rendezvousing at the stream's outlet to the sea three days later; at nightfall, whoever was there would cross to the next island. Even at high tide it should be possible to wade most of the way.

I suggested we make it three pairs rather than six loners, but Maria pointed out that two of us really didn't stand a much better chance against an armed Plathy than one—in either case, the only way we could kill them would be by stealth. Murder. I told her I didn't think I would be able to do it, and she nodded. Probably thinking that she would have said the same thing a few days ago.

We stopped for a few minutes to rest on a plateau overlooking the veldt, where Maria pointed out the paths she wanted each of us to take. Herb and Derek would go the most direct route, more or less north, but twining in and out of each other's path so as to throw off the scent. Gab, being the fastest, would run halfway around the mountain, then make a broad arc north. She would go straight northeast for about half the distance, and then cut back; Martin would do the opposite. I was to head due west, straight for the stream, and follow it down, in and out of the water. All of us were to "leave scent" at the places where our paths diverged the most from straight north.

A compass would have been nice. At night we'd be okay if it didn't cloud up again, but during the day we'd just have to follow our direction bump through the tall grass. I was glad I had an easy path.

Not all that easy. The three water bladders went to the ones who would be farthest from the stream, of course. So I had to go a good half-day without water. Assuming I didn't get lost. We divided the food and scrambled down in six different directions.

Maria

Where was I? Coming here, we got around the crater lake without incident, but the descent to the shore was more difficult than I had anticipated. It was not terribly steep, but the dense undergrowth of vines and bushes impeded our progress. After two days we emerged on the shore, covered with scratches and bruises. At least we'd encountered no large fauna.

By this time I had a great deal of sympathy for the lazybones minority on the Planning Committee who'd contended that we were being overly cautious in putting the base so far from the Plathy island. They'd recommended we put it on this island, with only 80 kilometers of shallow sea separating us from our destination. I'd voted, along with the majority, for the northern mainland, partly out of a boneheaded desire for adventure.

What we faced was a chain of six small islands and countless sandbars, in a puddle of a sea hardly anywhere more than a meter deep. We knew from Garcia's experience that a boat would be useless. With vine and driftwood we lashed together a raft to carry our weapons and provisions, filled the water jugs and splashed south.

It was tiring. The sand underfoot was firm, but sloshing through the shallow water was like walking with heavy weights attached to your ankles. We had to make good progress, though; the only island we were sure had fresh water was 40 kilometers south, halfway.

We made a good 25 kilometers the first day, dragging our weary bones up onto an island that actually had trees. Marcus and Gab went off in search of water, finding none, while the rest of us gathered driftwood for a fire or tried lackadaisically to fish. Nanci speared a gruesome thing that no one would touch, including her, and nobody else caught anything. Susan and Brenda dug up a couple of dozen shellfish, though, which obediently popped open when roasted. They tasted like abalone with sulfur sauce.

As we were settling in for the night, we met our first Plathy. She walked silently up to the fire, as if it were the most normal thing in the world to happen upon a dozen creatures from another planet. She was young, only a little larger than me (now, of course, we know she was on her Walk North). When I stood up and tried to say "Welcome, sister" in the female language, she screamed and ran. We heard her splashing away for some time, headed for the next county.

The next day was harder, though we didn't have as far to go. Some geological gremlin had raked channels across our path, new features since Garcia's mission, and several times we had to swim as much as two hundred meters before slogging again. (Thank the gods for Gab, who would gamely paddle out toward the horizon in search of solid ground, and for Marcus, who could swim strongly enough one-handed to tow the raft.)

It was dark by the time we got to the water hole island, and we had lost our coals to an inopportune wave. We were cold and terminally wrinkled, but so parched from sucking salt water that we staggered around like maniacs, even laughing like maniacs, searching blindly for the artesian well that Garcia's records said was there. Finally Joanna found it, stumbling in head-first and coming up choking and laughing. We all gorged ourselves, wallowing. In my case the relief was more than mouth and throat and stomach. At sundown I'd squatted in the shallows and squeezed out piss dark with stringy blood. That scared me. But the fresh water evidently cleared it up.

There were no more surprises the next two days of island-hopping, except the pleasant one of finding another water source. We couldn't find any wood dry enough to start a fire with, but it didn't get all that cold at night.

Late afternoon of the second day we slogged into the swamp that was the northern edge of the Plathy island. The dominant form of life was a kind of bilious spotted serpent that would swim heavily away as we approached. We were out of food but didn't go after them. Before nightfall the swamp had given way to rather damp forest; but we found dry dead wood suspended in branches and spun up a bright fire. We dug up a kind of tuber that Garcia's group had identified as edible and roasted them. Then tried to sleep in spite of the noises in the darkness. At first light we moved out fast, knowing that in thirty or so kilometers the forest would give way to open grassland.

The change from forest to veldt was abrupt. We were so happy to be out of the shadow of it—funny that in my present situation I feel exactly the opposite; I feel exposed, and hurry toward the concealment of the thick underbrush and close-spaced heavy trunks. I feel so visible, so vulnerable. And I probably won't find water until I get there. I'm going to turn off this tooth for a few minutes and try not to scream.

* * *

All right. Let me see. On our way to the Plathys, we walked across the veldt for two days. Food was plentiful; the *zamri* are like rabbits, but slow. For some reason they liked to cluster around the *ecivrel* bush, a thorny malodorous plant, and all we would have to do to bag several of them was form a loose circle around the bush and move in, clubbing them as they tried to escape. I would like to find one now. Their blood is sweet.

There's a Plathy song:

Sim garlish a sim garlish farla tob—!ka.
Soo pan du mairly garlish ezda tob—!ka.
Oe vairly tem se garlish mizga mer—!ka.
Garlish. !ka. Tem se garlish. !ka.

Translating it into my own language doesn't work well:

Sacar sangre y sacar sangre para vivir—sí
En sangre damos muerte y sacamos vida—sí
Alabamos la sangre de vida que Usted nos da—sí
Sangre—sí—sangre de vida—sí

Herb, who's a linguist, did a more accurate rendering in English: "Take blood and take blood for living—yes/in blood we give death and take living—yes/we worship the blood of life you give us—yes/blood—yes—blood of life—yes!" But there is really no translation. Except in the love of sweet blood.

I've become too much like them. My human instinct is to keep running, and when I can't run, to hide. But a strong Plathy feeling is to stand in a clearing and shout for them—let them come for me, let me die in a terrible ecstasy of tearing flesh and cracking bone. Let them suck my soft guts so I can live in them—

God. I have to stop. You'll think I'm crazy. Maybe I'm getting there. Why won't it rain?

Gabriel

Turned on the tooth while I sit by the water and rest. Maria wants us to record as much as we can, in case. Just in case.

Why the hell did I sign up for this? I was going to switch out of xenology and work for an advanced degree in business. But she came on campus recruiting, with all those exotic Earth women. They're just like women anywhere, big surprise. Except her. She is truly weird. Listen to this, tooth: I want her. She is such a mystery. Maybe if we live through this I'll get up the courage to ask. Plumb her, so to speak; make her open up to me, so to speak; get to the bottom of her, so to speak. A nice bottom for a woman of her advanced years.

How can I think of sex at a time like this? With a woman twice my age. If somebody on a follow-up expedition finds this tooth in a fossilized pile of Plathy shit, please excuse my digression. If I live to have the tooth extracted and played back, I don't think it will make much difference to my professional reputation. I'll be writing poetry and clerking for my father's export firm.

I ran around the mountain. Collapsed once and slept for I don't know how long. Got up and ran to the river. Drank too much. Here I sit, too bloated to move. If a Plathy finds me I won't be a fun meal.

I was really getting to like them, before they turned on us. They seemed like such vegetables until it started to get cold. Then it was as if they had turned into a different species. With hindsight, it's no big surprise that they should change again. Or that they should be capable of such terrible violence. We were lulled by their tenderness toward each other and their friendliness toward us, and the subtle alien grace of their dancing and music and sculpture. We should have been cautious, having witnessed the two other changes: the overnight transformation into completely sexual creatures and the slower evolution from lumpish primitives to charming creators, when the snow started to fall.

The change was obvious after the first heavy snowfall, which left about a half-meter of the stuff on the ground. The Plathys started singing and laughing spontaneously. They rolled up their *maffas* and stored them in a cave, and began playing in the snow—or at least it seemed like play, they were so carefree and childlike about it. Actually, they were building a city of snow.

The individual buildings, *lacules*, were uniform domes built up from blocks of snow. Maria called them igloos, after a similar primitive structure on Earth, and the name stuck. Even some of the Plathys used it.

There were 29 domes arranged in a circle, eventually connected by tunnels as the snow deepened. The inside of the circle was kept clear, the snow being constantly shoveled into the spaces between the domes. The result was a high circular wall that kept the wind out. Later we learned it would also keep humans *in*.

They had a fire going most of the time in the middle of the circle, which served as a center for their daytime activities: music, dance, tumbling, athletic competition, and storytelling (which seemed to be a kind of fanciful history lesson combined with moral instruction). Even with the sun up the temperature rarely got above freezing, but the Plathys thrived in the cold. They would sit for hours on the ice, watching the performances, wearing only their kilts. We wore leggings and boots, jackets, and hats. The Plathys would only dress up if they had to go out at night (which they often did, for reasons they couldn't or wouldn't explain to us), when the temperature dropped to forty or fifty below.

I went out at night a couple of times, but I didn't go far. Too easy to get lost. If it was clear you could see the ring of igloos ghostly in the starlight, but if there was any weather you couldn't see your own hand in front of your face.

The igloos were surprisingly warm, though the

only source of heat was one or two small oil lamps, plus metabolism. That metabolism also permeated everything with the weird smell of Plathy sweat, which resembled rotten citrus fruit. Our own dome got pretty high with the aroma of unwashed humans; Plathys would rarely visit for more than a minute or two.

Seems odd to me that the Plathys didn't continue some of their activities, like music and storytelling, during the long nights. Some of them did routine housekeeping chores, mending and straightening, while others concentrated on sculpture. The sculptors seemed to go into a kind of a trance, scraping patiently away at their rock or wood with teeth and claws. I never saw one use a tool, though they did carve and whittle when making everyday objects. I once watched an elder through the whole process. He sorted through a pile of rocks and logs until he found a rock he liked. Then he sat back and studied it from every angle, staring for more than an hour before beginning. Then he closed his eyes and started gnawing and scratching. I don't think he opened his eyes until he was done. When I asked him, he said, "Of course not."

Over the course of six nights he must have spent about sixty hours on the stone. When he finished, it was a delicate lacy abstraction. The other Plathys came by, one at a time, to compliment him on it—the older ones offering gentle criticism—and after everyone had seen it, he threw it outside for the children to play with. I retrieved it and kept it, which he thought was funny. It had served its purpose, as he had served his purpose, for it: finding its soul (its "face inside") and releasing it.

I shouldn't talk about sculpture; that's Herb's

area of expertise. The assignment Maria gave me was to memorize the patterns of the athletic competitions. (I was an athlete in school, twice winning the Hombre de Hierro award for my district.) There's not much to say about it, though. How high can you jump, how fast can you run, how far can you spit. That was an interesting one. They can spit with great force. Another interesting one was wood-eating. Two contestants are given similar pieces of wood—kindling, a few centimeters wide by half a meter long—and they crunch away until one has consumed the whole thing. Since the other doesn't have to continue eating afterwards, it's hard to say which one is the actual winner. When I first saw the contest, I thought they must derive some pleasure from eating wood. When I asked one about it, though, he said it tastes terrible and hurts at both ends. I can imagine.

Another painful sport is hitting. It's unlike boxing in that there's no aggression, no real sense of a fight. One contestant hits the other on the head or body with a club. Then he (or she) hands the club to the opponent who returns the blow precisely. The contest goes on until one of them drops, which can take several hours.

You ask them why they do this and most of them will not understand—"why" is a really difficult concept in the Plathy language; they have no word for it—but when you do get a response it's on the order of "This is part of life." Which is uninformative but not so alien. Why do humans lift heavy weights or run till they drop or beat each other senseless in a ring?

Oh my god. Here comes one.

*   *   *

Maria

Finally water. I wish there were some way to play back this tooth and edit it. I must have raved for some time, before I fell unconscious a few kilometers from here. I woke up with a curious *zamri* licking my face. I broke its neck and tore open its throat and drank deeply. That gave me the strength to get here. I drank my fill and then moved one thousand steps downstream, through the cold water, where I now sit concealed behind a bush, picking morsels from the *zamri*'s carcass. When I get back to Earth I think I'll become a vegetarian.

This is very close to the place were we met our first cooperative Plathy. There were three of them, young; two ran away when they spotted us, but the third clapped a greeting, and when we clapped back he cautiously joined us. We talked for an hour or so, the other two watching from behind trees.

They were from the Tumlil family, providentially; the family that had hosted Garcia's expedition. This male was too young to actually remember the humans, but he had heard stories about them.

He explained about the Walk North. In their third or fourth year, every Plathy goes off on his own, going far enough north to get to where "things are different." He brings back something odd. The elders then rule on how powerful the oddness of the thing is, and according to that power, the youngster is assigned his preliminary rank in the tribe.

(They know that this can eventually make the difference between life and death. The higher up you start, the more likely you are to wind up an elder. Those who aren't elders are allowed to die when they can no longer provide for themselves; elders are fed and protected indefinitely.)

Most of them travel as far as the crater lake island, but a few go all the way to the northern mainland. That was the ambition of the one we were talking to. I interrogated him as to his preparations for a boat, food, and water, and he said a boat would be nice but not necessary, and the sea was full of food and water. He figured he could swim it in three hands of days—twelve. Unless he was chaffing me, they evidently sleep floating, and drink salt water. That will complicate our escape, if they keep pursuing.

I take it that the three of them were cheating a bit by banding together. He stressed repeatedly that they would be going their separate ways as soon as they got to the archipelago. I hope they stayed together the whole way. I'd hate to face that forest alone. Maybe I'll have to, though.

Before he left he gave us directions to his family, but we'd decided to start out, at least, with a different one from Garcia's, in the interests of objectivity and to see how much information travelled from family to family. Little or none, it turned out. Our Camchai family knew about the Tumlils, since they shared the same area of veldt during the late summer, but none of the Tumlils had mentioned that ten hairless dwarves had spent the winter with them.

After two days of relatively easy travel, we found the Camchais in their late-summer habitat, the almost treeless grassland at the foot of the southern mountains. Duplicating the experience of Garcia's group, we found ourselves unexcitedly welcomed into the tribe: we were shown where the food was and various Plathys scrounged up the

framework and hides to cobble together a *maffa*
for us. Then we joined the family in their typical
summertime activity, sitting around. After a few
weeks of trying to cajole information out of them,
we witnessed the sudden explosion of sexual activity described earlier. Then they rested some more,
five or six days, and began to pull up stakes.

Their supply of stored food was getting low and
there was no easy hunting left in that part of the
veldt, so they had to move around the mountains
to the seashore and a wretched diet of fish.

The trek was organized and led by Kalyym, who
by virtue of being the youngest elder was considered chief for such practical matters. She was one
of the few Plathy we met who wore ornaments;
hers was a necklace of dinosaur teeth she'd brought
back from her Walk North, the teeth of a large
carnivore. She claimed to have killed it, but everyone knew that was a lie, and respected her for
being capable of lying past puberty.

It was significantly cooler on the other side of
the mountains, with a chilly south wind in the
evening warning that fall had begun and frost was
near. The Plathys still lazed through midday, but
in the mornings and evenings they fished with
some energy and prepared for the stampede. They
stockpiled driftwood and salt and sat around the
fire chipping extra flints, complaining about eating fish and looking forward to bounty.

We spent several months in this transitional state,
until one morning a lookout shouted a happy cry
and the whole family went down to the shore with
clubs. Each adult took about three meters of
shoreline, the children standing behind them with
knives.

We could hear them before we could see them—

the *tolliws*, rabbit-sized mammals that chirped like birds. They sounded like what I imagine a distant cloud of locusts sounded like, in old times. The Plathys laughed excitedly.

Then they were visible, one whirring mass from horizon to horizon, like an island-sized mat of wriggling wet fur. Mammals schooling like fish. They spilled on to dry land and staggered into the line of waiting Plathys.

At first there was more enthusiasm than result. Everybody had to pick up his first *tolliw* and bite off its head and extol its gustatory virtues to the others, in as gruesome a display of bad table manners as you could find anywhere in the Confederación. Then, after a few too-energetic smashings, they settled into a productive routine: with the little animals milling around their ankles in an almost continuous stream, the adult would choose a large and healthy-looking one and club it with a backhand swipe that lofted the stunned animal in an arc, back to where the child waited with the knife. The child would slit the animal's throat and set it on a large hide to bleed, and then wait happily for the next one. When the carcass had bled itself nearly dry, the child would give it a squeeze and transfer it to a stack on the sand, eventually working in a smooth assembly-line fashion. The purpose of the systematic bleeding was to build up on the hide layers of coagulated blood that, when dry, would be cut up into squares and eaten for snacks.

Large predators were scattered here and there through the swimming herd, fawn-colored animals resembling terrestrial kangaroos, but with finger-long fangs overhanging the lower jaw. Most of them successfully evaded the Plathys, but occasion-

ally one would be surrounded and clubbed to death
amidst jubilant screeching and singing.

This went on for what seemed to be a little less
than two hours, during which time the oldest elders busied themselves filling a long trench with
wood and collecting wet seaweed. When the last
stragglers of the school crawled out of the water
and followed the others down the beach, there
were sixty pyramidal stacks of bunny bodies, each
stack nearly tall as a Plathy, ranged down the
beach. We could hear the family west of us laughing and clubbing away.

The statistics of the process bothered me. They
seemed to have killed about one out of a hundred
of the beasts, and then sent the remainder on down
the beach, where the next family would presumably do the same, and so on. There were more than
a hundred families, we knew. Why didn't they run
out of *tolliws*? For once, Tybru gave me a straightforward answer: they take turns. Only sixteen families "gather" the creatures during each migration,
alternating in a rotating order that had been fixed
since the dawn of time. The other families took
advantage of other migrations; she was looking
forward to two years hence, when it would be
their turn for the *jukha* slaughter. They were the
tastiest, and kept well.

By this time it was getting dark. I had been
helping the elders set up the long trench of bonfires;
now we lit them, and with the evening chill coming in over the sea I was grateful for the snapping
flames.

Tybru demonstrated the butchering process so
we could lend a hand. Selected internal organs
went into hides of brine for pickling; then the skin
was torn off and the yellow layer of fat that clung

to it was scraped into clay jars for reducing to oil. More fat was flensed from the body, and then the meat was cut off in thin strips, which were draped over green sticks for smoking. Alas, they had no way to preserve the brain meat, so most of the Plathys crunched and sucked all night while they worked.

We weren't strong enough or experienced enough to keep up with even the children, but we gamely butchered through the night, trying not to cut ourselves on the slippery flint razors, working in the light of guttering torches. The seaweed produced an acrid halogen-smelling smoke that Tybru claimed was good for the lungs. Maybe because of its preservative effect.

The sun came up on a scene out of Heironymous Bosch. Smoke swirling over bloody sands littered with bones and heaps of entrails. Plathys and people blood-smeared and haggard with fatigue. We splashed into the icy water and scrubbed off dried blood with handfuls of sand, then stood in the stinging smoke trying to thaw out.

It was time to pack up and go. Already the rich smell of fresh blood was underlaid with a whiff of rot; insects were buzzing and hardshell scavengers were scuttling up onto the beach. When the sun got high the place would become unlivable, even by Plathy standards.

We rolled up the smoked meat and blood squares into the raw scraped hides, which would later be pegged out and dried in the sun, and followed a trail up into the mountains. We set up our *maffas* on a plateau about a thousand meters up, and waited placidly for the snow.

Someone coming.

* * *

Derek

I can no longer view them as other than dangerous animals. They mimic humanity—no, what I mean is that *we* interpret in human terms the things they do. The animal things they do. Maria, I'm sorry. I can't be a scientist about this, not any more. Not after what I just saw.

Herb and I were supposed to criss-cross, going northeast a thousand steps, then northwest a thousand, and so forth. That was supposed to confuse them. They caught Herb.

I heard the scream. Maybe half a kilometer away. I should have run, knowing that there was nothing I could do, but Herb and I've been close since school. Undergraduate. And there he—

Two of them had run him down in a small clearing, killed him and taken off his head. They were, one of them was . . . I can't.

I hid in the underbrush. All I had was a club there was nothing I could do. One of them was eating his, his private parts. The other was scooping him out, curious, dissecting him. I ran away. It's a wonder they didn't—

Oh shit. Here they come.

Gabriel

I think my wrist is broken. Maybe just sprained. But I killed the son of a bitch. He came around a bend in the river and I was on him with the spear. Element of surprise. I got him two good ones in the thorax before he grabbed me—where are their god-damned vital organs? A human would've dropped dead. He grabbed me by the wrist and slammed me to the ground. I rolled away, retrieved the spear, and impaled him as he jumped on me. He made a lot of noise and finally decided to die, after scraping my arm pretty well. For some reason he wasn't armed. Thank God. He was Embrek, the one who taught me how to fish Plathy-style. We got along so well. What the hell happened?

It was the first time it rained instead of snowing. All the music and everything stopped. They moped around all day and wouldn't talk. When it got dark they went wild.

They burst into our igloo, four of them, and started ripping off our clothes. Nanci, Susan, and Marcus resisted, and were killed right there. One bite each. The rest of us were stripped and led or carried out into the cold, into the center of the compound. The cheerful fire was black mud now, starting to glaze with ice.

All of the family except the oldest elders were there, standing around like zombies. No one spoke; no one took notice of anybody else. We all stood naked in the darkness. Kalyym eventually brought out a single oil candle, so we could be mocked by its flickering warm light.

The nature of the rite became clear after a couple of hours. It was a winnowing process. If you lost consciousness the others would gather around you and try to poke and kick you awake. If you stood up they would go back to ignoring you. If you stayed down, you would die. After a certain number of pokes and kicks, Kalyym or some other elder would tear open the thorax in a single rip. Even worse than the blood was the sudden rush of steam into the cold air. Like life escaping the body.

The ones most susceptible to the cold were the very old non-elders and the youngest females. The first three butchered were girls in their first year. So that was why the family had so few females.

We knew we wouldn't last the night. But the slippery walls were impossible to scale, and the largest Plathys stood guard at every entrance to the ring of igloos.

After some whispered discussion, we agreed we had to do the obvious: rush the guard who stood in front of our own igloo. The ones who survived would rush in, quickly gather weapons and clothing, and try to make it out the back entrance before the Plathys could react. Then run for the caves.

We were lucky. We rushed the guard from six directions. Crouching to slash at Derek, he turned his back to me, and I leaped, striking him between the shoulders with both feet. He sprawled face-down in the mud, and didn't get up. We scrambled into the igloo and I stood guard with a spear while the others gathered up things. A couple of Plathys stuck their heads in the entrance and snarled, but they evidently didn't want to risk the spear.

We weren't immediately followed, and for the first hour or so we made good time. Then it started to rain again, which slowed us down to a crawl. With no stars, we had to rely on Maria's sense of direction, which is pretty good. We found the caves just at dawn, and got a few hours' sleep before Mylab found us and we had to kill him.

How long is this phase going to last? If it goes as long as the summer or winter phases, they're sure to track us down. We may be safe inside the dome, if we can get that far—

Noise . . . Maria!

Maria

I might as well say it. It might be of some interest. None of us is going to live anyhow. I'm beyond embarrassment, beyond dignity. Nothing to be embarrassed about anyhow, not really.

The thing that was splashing up the stream turned out to be Gabriel. I ran out of hiding and grabbed him, hugged him, and we were both a little hysterical about it. Anyhow he got hard and we took care of it, and then we went back to my hiding place and took care of it again. It was the first happy thing that's happened to me in a long time. Now I'm watching him sleep and fighting the impulse to wake him up to try for thirds. One more time before we die.

It's a strange state, feeling like a girl again, all tickled and excited inside, and at the same time feeling doomed. Like a patient with a terminal disease, high on medicine and mortality. There's no way we can outrun them. They'll sniff us down and tear us apart, maybe today, maybe tomorrow. They'll get us. Oh wake up, Gab.

Be rational. This ferocity is just another change of state. They don't know what they're doing. Like the sex and birth phases. Tomorrow they may go back to being bovine sweet things. Or artisans again. Or maybe they'll discover the wheel for a week. What a weird, fucked-up bunch of . . .

There must be some survival value in it. Certainly it serves to cull the weakest members out. And killing most of the females before puberty compensates for the size of the litters—or could the size of the litters be a response to the scarcity of females? Lamarckism either way. Can't think straight.

At any rate it certainly can't be instinctive behavior in regard to us, since we aren't part of their normal environment. Maybe we've unknowingly triggered aberrant behavior. Stress response. Olfactory catalyst. Violent displacement activity. Who knows? Maybe whoever reads this tooth will be able to make some sense of it. You will excuse me for the time being. I have to wake him up.

Brenda

Maria and Gab were waiting for me when I got to the mouth of the river. Gab has a badly sprained wrist; I splinted and bound it. His grip is still good, and fortunately he's left-handed. Maria's okay physically, just a little weak, but I wonder about her psychological state. Almost euphoric, which hardly seems appropriate.

We waited an extra half day, but the others are either dead or lost. They can catch up with us at the dome. We have axe, spear, and two knives. Gab turned one of the knives into a spear for me. Two water bladders. We filled the bladders, drank to saturation, and waded out into the sea.

The water seems icy cold, probably more than ten degrees colder than when we walked through it before. Numb from the waist down after a few minutes. When the water is shallow or you get to walk along a sandbar, sensation returns, deep stinging pain. It was a good thing we'd found that second water island; only ten kilometers of wading and limping along the wet sand.

We'd rolled up our furs and shouldered them, so they were fairly dry. Couldn't risk a fire (and probably couldn't have found enough dry stuff to make one) so we just huddled together for warmth. We whispered, mapping out our strategy, such as it was, and kept an eye out to the south. Though if we'd been followed by even one Plathy we'd be pretty helpless.

Thirty kilometers to the next water hole. We decided to stay here for a couple of days, eating the sulfurous oysters and regaining strength. It would have to be a fast push, going all the way on less than five liters of water.

In fact we stayed four days. Gab came down with bad diarrhea, and we couldn't push on until his body could hold fluid. It was just as well. We were all bone-tired and stressed to the limit.

The first night we just collapsed in a hamster pile and slept like the dead. The next day we gathered enough soft dry grass to make a kind of mattress, and spread our furs into a piecemeal blanket. We still huddled for warmth and reassurance, and after a certain amount of nonverbal discussion, Gab unleashed his singular talent on both of us impartially.

That was interesting. Something Maria said indicated that Gab was new to her. I'd thought that nothing—male, female, or Plathy—was safe around him. Maybe Maria's strength had intimidated him before now, or her age. Or being the authority figure. That must be why she was in such a strange mood when I caught up with them. Anyhow, I'm glad for her.

Gab entertained us with poetry and songs in three languages. It's odd that all three of us know English. Maria had to learn it for her study of the Esquimaux, and I did a residency in Massachusetts. Gab picked it up just for the hell of it, along with a couple of other Earth languages, besides Spanish and Pan-Swahili, and all three Selvan dialects. He's quite a boy. Maria was the only one who could speak Plathy better than he. They tried duets on the blood songs and shit songs, but it doesn't sound too convincing. The consonants *!ka* and *!ko* you just can't do unless you have teeth like beartraps.

The stress triggered my period a week early. When we fled the igloo I hadn't had time to gather up my moss pads and leather strap contraption, so I just sort of dripped all over the island. It obviously upset Gab, but I'm not going to waddle around with a handful of grass for his precious male sensibilities. (His rather gruesome sickness didn't do much for *my* sensibilities, either, doctor or no.)

We spent the last day in futile basket weaving, trying to craft something that would hold water for more than a few minutes. We all knew that it could be done, but it couldn't be done by us, not with the grass on the island. Maria did manage to cobble together a bucket out of her kilt by working a framework of sticks around it. That will double our amount of water, but she'll have to cradle it with both arms. We'll drink from it first, of course.

Thirty kilometers. I hope we make it.

Maria

We were almost dead from thirst and exposure by the time we got to the water hole island. We had long since lost track of our progress, since the vegetation on the islands was radically different from summer's, and some of the shorelines had changed. We just hoped each large island would be the one, and finally one was.

Alongside the water hole we found the fresh remains of a fire. At first that gave us a little hope, since it was possible that the rest of our team had leapfrogged us while Gab was convalescing. But then we found the dropping place, and the excrement was Plathy. Three or four of them, by the looks of it. A day or so ahead of us.

We didn't know what to do. Were they hunters searching us out, or a group on their Walk North? If the latter, it would probably be smartest to stay here for a couple of days; let them get way ahead. If they were hunters, though, they might still be on the island, and it would be smarter for us to move on.

Gab didn't think they were hunters, since they would've overtaken us earlier and made lunchmeat out of us. I wasn't sure. There were at least three logical paths through the archipelago; they might have taken one of the others. Since they could drink salt water, they didn't have to go out of their way to get to the island we first stopped at.

None of us felt up to pushing on. The going would be easier, but it would still be at least ten hours of sloshing through cold water on small rations. So we compromised.

In case there were hunters on the island, we made camp on the southern tip (the wind was from the north) in a small clearing almost completely surrounded by thick brambles. If we had to stand and fight, there was really only one direction they could approach us from. We didn't risk a fire, and sent out only one person at a time for water or shellfish. One stayed awake while the other two slept.

Our precautions wouldn't amount to much if there actually were three or four of them and they all came after us. But they might be split up, and both Gab and I had proved they could be killed, at least one at a time.

We spent two uneventful days regaining our strength. About midday on the third, Gab went out for water and came back with Derek.

He was half-dead from exposure and hunger. We fed him tiny bits of shellfish in water, and after a day of intermittent sleeping and raving, he came around enough to talk.

He'd seen two Plathys in the process of eating Herb. They ran after him, but he plunged blindly into brambles (his arms and lower legs were covered with festering scratches) and they evidently didn't follow him very far. He'd found the river and run out to sea in a blind panic. Got to the first water island and lay there for days. He couldn't remember whether he'd eaten.

Then he heard Plathys, or thought he did, and took off north as fast as he could manage. He didn't remember getting here. Gab found him unconscious at the water's edge.

So now the plan is to wait here two or three more days, until Derek feels strong enough for the next push.

Hardest part still ahead. Even if we don't run into Plathys. What if the boats are gone?

Gabriel

We didn't see any further sign of the Plathys. After four days Derek was ready to go. For a full day we drank all the water we could hold, and then at sundown set out.

There was only one place so deep we had to

swim. I tried to carry Maria's water basket, side-stroking, but it didn't work. So the last twenty or twenty-five kilometers we were racing against the dwindling supply of water in the two bladders.

At first light there was still no sight of land, and we had to proceed by dead reckoning. (The Plathys evidently don't have this problem; they're some-how sensitive to the planet's magnetic field, like some Selvan migrating birds.) We saved a few spoonfuls of water to drink when we finally sighted land.

We went along in silence for an hour or so, and then Derek had a brainstorm. We were scanning the horizon from only a meter or so above sea level; if someone stood on my shoulders, he could see twice as far. Derek was the tallest. I ducked under and hoisted him up. He could only stay balanced for a second, but it did work—he saw a green smudge off to the left. We adjusted our course and slogged on with new energy. When all of us could see the smudge, we celebrated with a last sip of water.

Of course the stream that would be our guide uphill was nowhere to be seen. We stumbled ashore and did manage to lick enough moisture from fo-liage to partly allay our terrible thirst, though the bitter flavor soured my stomach.

We marked the spot with a large X in the sand, and split into pairs, Brenda and I going one direc-tion and Maria and Derek going the other, each with a water bladder to fill when one pair found the river. We agreed to turn back after no more than ten thousand steps. If neither pair found the river within ten kilometers of our starting place, we'd just work our way uphill toward the crater lake. It would be slower going than following the stream's course, but we could probably manage it, licking leaves and splitting some kinds of stalks for water. And we'd be less likely to run into an ambush, if there were hunters waiting ahead.

We were lucky. In a sense. Brenda and I stumbled on the stream less than two kilometers from where we started. I drank deeply and then jogged back to catch up with Maria and Derek.

We made an overnight camp some distance from the stream, and foraged for food. There were no fish in the shallows, and none of the sulfurous oysters. There were small crabs, but they were hard to catch and had only a pinch of meat. We wound up digging tubers, which were not very palatable raw but would sustain us until we got to the lake, where fish were plentiful.

It might have been a little safer to travel by night, but we remembered how the brambles had flayed us before, and decided to take the chance. It was a mistake.

As we had hoped, progress was a lot faster and easier going up than it had been coming down. Less slipping. It was obvious that Plathys had preceded us, though, from footprints and freshly broken vegetation, so we climbed as quietly as possible.

Not quietly enough, perhaps, or maybe our luck just ran out. Damn it, we lost Derek. He had to be the one in front.

Maria

We couldn't see the sun because of the forest canopy, but it was obvious from the reddening of the light that we would soon have to decide whether to make camp or push on through the darkness.

Gab and I were discussing this, whispering, when the Plathy attacked.

Derek was in front. The spear hit him in the center of the chest and passed almost completely through his body. I think it killed him instantly. The Plathy, a lone young female, came charging down the stream bed toward us, roaring. She tripped and fell almost at our feet. Gab and I killed her with spear and axe. After she was dead, Gab hacked off her head and threw it into the bush.

We waited for the rest of them, but evidently she had been alone. Gab had a hard time controlling his grief.

When it got dark we pushed on. The stream was slightly phosphorescent, but we relied mainly on feeling our way. A kind of fungus on the forest floor always grew in pairs, and it glowed dull red, like pairs of sullen eyes watching us.

We made more noise than we had during the daytime, but there was probably little risk. Plathys sleep like dead things, and in this kind of terrain they don't post guard at night, since none of the predators here is big enough to bother them. Big enough to give us trouble, though. Three times we moved to the middle of the stream, when we thought we heard something stalking us.

The slope began to level off before it got light, and by dawn we were moving through the marshy grassland that bordered the crater lake.

We had unbelievable luck with the lake fish. Hundreds of large females lay almost immobile in the shallows. They were full of delicious roe. We gorged ourselves and then cut strips of flesh to dry in the sun. Not as effective as smoking, but we couldn't risk a fire.

We decided it would be safest to sleep separately, in case someone had picked up our trail. Like Gab, I found a tree to drape myself in. Brenda just found a patch of sunlight, arranged her furs on the wet ground, and collapsed. I thought I was too jangled to sleep, after Derek, but in fact I barely had time to find a reasonably secure set of branches before my body turned itself off.

Our survival reflexes have improved. A few hours later—it was not quite noon—I woke up suddenly in response to a slight vibration. One of the cat creatures was creeping toward me along another branch.

I didn't want to throw the spear, of course. So I took the offensive, crawling closer to the beast. He snarled and backed up warily. When I was a couple of spear lengths from him I started poking toward his face. Eventually I forced him onto too small a limb, and he crashed to the ground. He lay there a moment, then heaved himself up, growled at the world, and limped away. I went back to my branch and slept a few more hours unmolested.

Gab woke me up with the bad news that Brenda was gone. There was no sign of violence at the spot where she'd settled down, though, and we eventually found her hiding in a tree as we had. She'd heard a noise.

We gathered up our dried fish—that it hadn't been disturbed was encouraging—and killed a few fresh ones to carry along for dinner. Then we moved with some haste down along the river we had followed up so long ago. If all goes well we will be able to duplicate in reverse the earlier sequence: rest tonight on this side of the banyan forest, then push through to the large clearing; spend the night there, and at first light press on to the sea.

Gabriel

The sea. I was never so glad to see water.

The first boat we found was beyond use, burned in two, but the water jugs nearby were unharmed, curiously enough. It's possible some immature Plathys had come upon it and not recognized that it was a boat; just a hollow log that had burned partway through. So they may have innocently used it for fuel.

The other boat, farther away from the river, was untouched. If anything, it might be in better shape now than when we left it, since it had been propped up on two logs, hollow side down. It was dryer and harder, and apparently had no insect damage.

Unfortunately, it was too heavy for three people to lift; it had been something of a struggle for all twelve of us. We went back upstream a couple of kilometers to where Maria remembered having seen a stand of saplings. Stripped of branches, they looked like they would make good rollers. We each took an armload. It was dark by the time we got back to the boat.

It might have been prudent to try to launch it in the darkness, and paddle out to comparative safety. But there hadn't been any sign of Plathys on this side of the island, and we were exhausted. I stood first watch, and had to trudge around in circles to stay awake. A couple of times I heard something out in the grass, but it never came close. Maria and Brenda heard it on their shifts, but it left before dawn.

At first light we started rolling the boat. A good three hours of hard labor, since when the saplings got into sand they forgot how to be wheels. We dragged it the last hundred meters, one bonecracking centimeter after another. Once it was floating free, we anchored it and sat in the shallow water for a long time, poleaxed by fatigue. It was amazing how much warmer the water was here, just a hundred or so kilometers north of the Plathy island. Volcanic activity coupled with distance from the continental shelf dropoff.

We dragged ourselves back to the place we'd slept and found that all of our food was gone. Animals; the weapons were still there. Rather than start off with no reserve food, we spent the rest of the morning hunting. A dozen large snakes and seven small animals like *zamri*, but with six legs. We risked a fire to smoke them, which perhaps was not wise. One of us guarded the fire while the other two loaded all the jars and then arranged a makeshift vessel in the stern, pegging the largest fur out in a cup shape.

Finally we loaded all the food and weapons aboard and swung up over the side (the outriggers kept us from losing too much water from the stern). We paddled almost hysterically for an hour or so, and then, with the island just a whisper of dark on the horizon, anchored to sleep until the guide stars came out.

Brenda

It was smart of Maria to pick a beefy young athlete as one of her graduate assistants. I don't think that she and I would have stood a chance alone, pushing this heavy old log 250 kilometers. We're all pretty tough and stringy after months of playing caveman, but the forced march has drained us. Last night I paddled more and more feebly until, just before dawn, I simply passed out. It's a good thing Gab was in the rear position. He heard me slump over and grabbed the paddle as it floated by. When the sun got too high to continue, he massaged the knots out of my arms and shoulders, and when I fell asleep again he was doing the same for Maria.

Perhaps we should have delayed our launch long enough to weave a sunshield. It isn't all that hot but it must have some dehydrating effect. And it would be easier to sleep. But Martin was the only one who could weave very well, and he—

Oh my God. My God, we left him for dead and I haven't even thought about him since, since we met up at the river mouth. Now we've left him behind with no boat. He could have been just a day or an hour behind us and if he was we've murdered him.

Maria

Brenda suddenly burst into tears and started going on about Martin. I gave him up before we left the Plathy island. His route was a mirror image of mine and he was a much faster runner. They must have caught him.

I pointed out to Brenda that if Martin did make it to the coast of the crater lake island, he could probably survive indefinitely with his primitive skills, since it would be fairly easy for one man alone to stay away from the Plathys who occasionally passed through there. Surely he would be intelligent enough to stamp out a regular marking in the sand, easily visible from the satellite. Then the next expedition could rescue him. That fantasy calmed her down a bit. Now she's sleeping.

I'm starting to think we might make it. We have water enough for twenty days and food for half that time, even if we don't catch any fish. Admittedly it's harder to keep a straight course when the guiding stars are behind you, but it shouldn't take us twice as long as the trip south, especially if there are no clouds.

Once we get to the mainland and retrieve the modern weapons, the trek back to the base will be simple. And the year waiting inside the dome will be sybaritic luxury. Real food. Chairs. No bugs. Books. Wonder if I can still read?

Gabriel

Seven days of uneventful routine. On the eighth day I woke up in the afternoon and took a spear up to the bow to stare at the water. I stood up to piss overboard, which sometimes attracts fish, and saw a Plathy swimming straight toward us.

He stopped and treaded water about eight meters away, staring at me and the spear. I called out to him but he didn't answer. Just stared for several minutes in what seemed to be a calculating way. Then he turned his back and swam on, powerful strokes that gave him more speed than we could ever muster.

Could he tip us over? Probably not, with nothing to stand on. Once in the water, though, we'd be no match for one of them. My brain started to run away with fear, after a week of the luxury and novelty of not being afraid. He could approach underwater and pull us overboard one by one. He could grab an outrigger while we were sleeping and rock us out. He could for God's sake bite a *hole* in the boat!

When the women woke up I told them, and we made the obvious decision to maintain a rotating watch. I wondered privately how much good it would do. I suspected that a Plathy could hold his breath for a long time; if he approached underwater we might not be able to see him until he was right by the boat. Or one might overtake us in darkness. I didn't give voice to any of these specific fears. Neither of them lacks imagination, and they didn't need my scenarios to add to their own private apprehensions.

How much farther? I suspect we'll be making better time from now on.

Maria

I began to have a recurrent dream that we'd somehow got turned around, and were paddling furiously back to the waiting Plathys. This daymare even began invading my waking hours, especially toward dawn, when I was in that vulnerable, suggestible mental state that extreme fatigue and undirected anxiety can bring on.

So when in the first light I saw land, the emotion I felt was speechless apprehension. We'd been paddling eleven days. We *must* have gotten turned around; we couldn't have covered the distance in that time. I stared at it for half a minute before Brenda mumbled something about it being too early to take a break.

Then Gab also saw the faint green line on the horizon, and we chattered on about it for a while, drifting. As it got lighter we could see the purple cones of distant volcanoes, which put my subconscious to rest.

The volcanos simplified navigation, since I could remember what their relative positions had been on the way out. It looked as if we were going to land ten or fifteen kilometers west of the mouth of the river that led to the base. The question was whether to alter our course off to the right, so as to land closer to the river, or go straight in and walk along the beach. We were safer on the water but terminally tired of paddling, so we opted for the short approach.

It was little more than an hour before the canoe landed with a solid crunch. We jumped out and immediately fell down. No land legs. I could stand up, but the ground seemed to teeter. For some reason it was a lot worse than it had been on the outward trip. There had been a little more wave action this time, which could account for that. It might also account for the good time we made; some sort of seasonal current.

Using the spears as canes, we practiced walking for a while. When we could stagger pretty well unsupported, we gathered our stuff and started down the beach as quickly as possible. It would be a good idea to find the weapons and dig them up before dark.

Eventually we were making pretty good progress, though when we stopped the ground would still rock back and forth. The musty jungle actually smelled good, reassuring. We ate the last of the smoked snake while hungrily discussing the culinary miracles waiting for us at the base. There was enough food there to last twelve people for more than a year, a precaution against disaster.

We reached the mouth of the river before midday. But when we paced off from the rock to where the weapons were supposed to be buried, we got a nasty surprise: someone had already dug them up. Humus had filled the hole, but there was a definite depression there, and the ground was soft.

Dejected and frightened, we paced on to the next site, and it had also been dug up—but we found three of the exhumed fuel cells lying in the brush. The Plathy wouldn't know how to install them, of course. Even if, as was likely, they had been watching us when we first buried them, they wouldn't have been able to find the hidden studs that had to be pushed simultaneously to open the camouflaged weapons. Even if they somehow got one open, they wouldn't know how to screw in the fuel cell and unsafe it.

We went back to the first site on the off-chance that they might have discarded the weapons, too, since ours weren't superior, in conventional capabilities, to what they would normally carry. That turned out to be a smart move: we found a club and a spear snarled in the undergrowth, waiting for their power cells. (They'd been crafted of Bruuchian ironwood, and so were impervious to moisture and mold.)

We armed the two and confirmed that they worked. There were probably others hidden more deeply in the brush, but we were too tired to continue the search. We'd been pushing for most of a day, burning adrenaline. The two weapons would be enough to protect us while we slept.

*   *   *

Gabriel

Brenda woke me up delightfully. I was having an interesting dream, and then it wasn't a dream.

I had the last guard shift before dawn. Scouting the perimeter of our site for firewood, I almost stumbled over a slow lizard about a meter long, and fat. Skinned and cleaned him and had him roasting on a spit by the time the women woke up.

After breakfast, we spent a good two hours searching the area around the weapons pit, spiraling out systematically, but didn't find anything further. Well, it was good luck we even had the two weapons. We were considerably better with spear, knife, and club than we had been when we landed, but probably not good enough for an extended trek through the mainland. Packs of hungry carnivores, even if no Plathys waiting in ambush.

Combing the other side did find us two more fuel cells, which should be plenty. Each one is good for more than an hour of continuous firing when new, and none of them was even half used up. We could even afford to use the weapons to light fires.

So we started off in pretty high spirits. By noon we weren't quite so springy. One long sleep isn't enough to turn night creatures into day creatures, and though walking is easier than paddling, our leg muscles were weak from disuse. There was a bare rock island in the middle of the broad river; we waded out to it and made camp. That consisted of laying down our furs and collapsing.

Brenda usually takes the first watch, but she couldn't keep her eyes open, so I did odds-and-evens with Maria, and lost. And so I was the one to see the first Plathy.

I was gathering driftwood for the night's fire. I'd been concentrating my watch on the nearer bank, the one we'd come from. No telling how long the Plathy had been looking at me, standing quietly on the other side.

Our side was relatively open; compact stands of bamboo-like grass every 20 or 30 meters, with only low bushes in between. The other bank was dense jungle, which was why we avoided it. The Plathy was making no special effort to conceal himself but was hard to see in the dappled shade. I continued picking up wood, studying him out of the corner of my eye.

He was an adult male, carrying a spear. That was bad. If he had been a child he might have been on his Walk North, accidentally stumbling on us. An adult had no reason to be here except us, and he wouldn't be here alone.

I didn't recognize him. If he wasn't from the Camchai family, that probably meant they had enlisted the aid of other families, so we might be up against any number. But I couldn't be sure; even in social situations I often got individuals mixed up. Maria was good at telling them apart. I took an armload of wood back to the camp and quietly woke her up and explained what was happening. She walked over to the other side of the island, casually picking up sticks, and took a look. But he was gone.

We had a whispered conference and decided to stay on the island. They would have a hard time rushing us; the river bottom was too muddy for running. And their spears couldn't reach us from either bank.

She's taken over the watch now. Enough talking. Try to sleep.

Brenda

What a terrible night. Nobody woke me for my afternoon watch turn, so I slept almost until dark. Maria said she hadn't awakened me because she was too nervous to sleep anyhow, and explained about Gab seeing the Plathy.

When the sun went down we lit the fire, and Gab joined us. We decided to double the watch—two on, one off—one person with a crazer watching each bank. Maria curled up by the fire and tried to sleep.

They hit us about an hour before midnight, coming from Gab's side, the near bank. He called out and I ran over.

Spears falling out of the darkness. We had the fire behind us, and so were pretty good targets. Crazers don't make much light; we had to fan them and hope we hit someone. All the time running back and forth sideways, trying to spoil their aim. Maria woke up and I gave her the club-crazer, then retired to the other side of the island, under Gab's orders: watch for an "envelopment." But they weren't that sophisticated.

No way to tell how many we killed. The spears came less and less frequently, and then there were rocks, and then nothing. When dawn came, pieces of four or five sliced-up Pathy bodies lay on the shore, any number having been washed downstream.

I wish I could feel guilty about it. Two weeks ago, I would have. Instead, I have to admit to a kind of manic glee. We beat them. They snuck up on us and we beat them.

Maria

We burned both crazers down to quarter-charge. A little more than half-charge on the two backup cells. But I don't expect any more attacks like last night. They aren't dumb.

So much for the First Commandment. We've demonstrated high technology. Some of them must have survived, to go back and tell others about the magic. But we had no choice.

From now on we'll have to assume we're being followed, of course, and be triply careful about ambush setups. That won't be a real problem until the last day or two, traveling with thick jungle on both sides of the river. Why did we have to be so cautious in siting the dome?

Well, it may turn out that we'll be glad it's where it is. What if they follow us all the way there? If they try to encircle the clearing and wait us out, the jungle will get them; we won't have to do a thing. Plathy skills work fine down on their friendly island, but up where the dome is situated a hunting party armed with clubs and spears wouldn't last a week. Free lunch for the fauna.

We have to push on fast. Islands like this one will be common while the river is wide and slow. We'll be fairly safe. When the jungle closes in on both sides, though, the river will become a narrow twisting cataract. No island protection but its noise might confound Plathy hearing; make it harder for them to ambush us.

At any rate, this is the plan: each day on the plain, cover as much ground as possible, consistent with getting a few hours of sleep each night. Rest up just south of the jungle and then make a forced march, two days to the dome.

Maybe this haste is unnecessary. If the Plathys were their normal, rather sensible selves, they'd cut their losses and go home. But now we have no idea of what's normal. They may harry us until we kill them all. That would be good for the race, leaving it relatively uncontaminated culturally. Bad for us. A few more engagements like last night and we won't have enough power in the crazers to make it through the jungle. Might as well stand by the river and sing blood song to the hungry lizards.

Gabriel

Five days of no contact but I can't shake the feeling we're being watched. Have been watched all the way. Now an afternoon and night of rest on this last island, and Maria wants us to push all the way to the dome.

Physically, I suppose we can do it. The terrain isn't difficult, since a game trail parallels the water all the way up. But the game that made the trail are formidable. They gave us plenty of trouble when there were twelve of us. And theoretically no Plathys.

I wonder about that now, though. Surely someone was watching us back when we buried the weapons. How long had they been following us? They claimed that they never go to the mainland, except for a few brave Walkers, and of course they always tell the truth. About what they remember, anyhow.

I haven't recorded anything for a long time. Waiting for my state of mind to improve. After the night of the attack I ran out of hope. Things haven't improved but I'm talking to myself to stay awake for the rest of this watch. I think Brenda's doing the same thing. Sitting on the other side of the island staring at the water, mumbling. I should go remind her to pay attention. But I can cover both banks from this side.

Besides, if they're going to hit us, I wish they'd hit us here. Clear fields of fire all around. Of course they won't; they learn from their mistakes. Maria says.

I'm being paranoaic. They're gone. The being-watched feeling, I don't know. Ever since Derek got it I've been a, I've been . . . loose in the head. Trying to control this, this panic. They look to me for strength, even Maria does, but all I have is muscle, jaw muscle to keep the screams in. When that one swam by us headed for the mainland I knew we were deep in shit.

Derek had religion. We argued long nights about that. What would he be doing now, praying? *"Nuestro Señor que vives en el cielo, alabado sea tu nombre . . ."* Good spear repellent. I miss him so.

Nobody will ever find this tooth with its feeble beep transmitter. When they come back and find the dome empty, that will be the end of it. Not enough budget for a search through obviously hostile territory. Not enough resources on this planet for anybody to want to exploit it, so no new money to find our teeth. We'll pass into Plathy legend and be forgotten, or distorted beyond recognition.

A good thing for them. If there was anything of use here, we'd be like the Eskimo anthropologists Maria talks about, recording the ways of a race doomed by the fact of recording. So maybe the Plathys will have another million years of untroubled evolution. Maybe they'll learn table manners.

I'm afraid of them but can't be mad at them.
Even after Derek. They are what they are and we
should have been more careful. Maybe I'm becoming a real xenologist, at this late date. Derek would
say I'm trying to compose myself into a state of
grace. Before dying.

It infuriated me that he always had answers. All
I ever had was questions.

So two days' push and we're safe inside the
dome. Food and cube and books and spears bounce
off. Maybe I've read too much, written too much;
the pattern seems inescapable. We're at death's
door. Capital Death's Door. If we make it to the
dome we'll break the rules.

Cálmate. Calm. Maybe I'm projecting, making
patterns. Here there's only real things; cause, effect,
randomness, entropy—your death is like the falling of a leaf, Derek said; like the leaf falling, it's a
small tragedy, but necessary. If everything lived
forever the universe would fill up in short order.

Mustn't blather. Reality, not philosophy. We rest
so we can be alert. If we're alert enough we'll beat
the jungle. Beat the Plathys that aren't there. It's
all in my head. For the next two days take the
head out of the circuit. Only reflex. Smell, listen,
watch: react. React fast enough, you live.

Only I keep thinking about Derek. He never knew
what hit him.

Brenda

Gab asked me to watch both banks for a while
so he could give love to Maria before it got dark.
Hard to watch both banks when I want to watch
him. Men look so vulnerable from this angle,

bouncing; a new perspective for me. I've never been an audience except for watching on the cube. It's different.

Admit I'm jealous of her. She's fifteen years older than me and shows it. But he wants her for his last one. That was obvious in his tone of voice. At some level I think he's as scared as I am.

If he thinks this is his last one he doesn't know much about women. Maria will let me wake him up when our shift is over. If I can wait that long. I've watched him sleeping; he has the refraction period of a twelve-year-old. To be exact, I know from observation that he can do it twice and still get an erection in his sleep. No privacy under our circumstances.

Funny friendly sound, don't hear it like that while you're doing it—what was that? Something move?

Just a lizard, I guess. Nothing now. We've been seeing them the last two days on the jungle side, around dusk and in the firelight. They don't come in the water. What's going to happen tomorrow night, no island, no fire. Don't want to die that way, jumped by a pack of dinosaurs. Nor have my head bitten off by a sentient primitive. I was going to be a grandmother and sit on the porch and tell doctor stories and die with no fuss.

Why won't they attack? I know they're out there, waiting. If they would only come now, I could die that way. I remember the feeling, fifty or a hundred of them against the three of us and our two crazers. Not a fair fight, perhaps, but God it did feel good, holding our own, epinephrine from head to toe. This waiting and worrying. Light the fire.

Stack the wet wood around to dry. Gives me something to do while they're finishing up. Being quiet for the sake of my sensibilities, or theirs. Just heavier breathing and a faster rhythm of liquid sounds. I've followed that unspoken code, too; we haven't been all three together since the water hole. She's had him seven times since, to my four. To my knowledge. Why am I keeping score? They were made for each other. Iron man, iron woman.

I was in love once or twice and know this is something else. Not just sex; I've been that way before, too. Hysteria is part of it, but not in the old-fashioned womanish sense. The womb taking over. This is a certainty-of-death hysteria, to coin a category. It's different from just fear. It's like, it's like—I don't know. As if you had never tasted water before, or seen colors, and suddenly here is a cold spring or a rainbow. Minus the joy. Just something primal and unlike anything before. Does that make sense? We've been in danger God knows constantly for how long? Not the same. There was always hope. Now we're two days away from total sanctuary and for some reason I know we won't make it.

I remember from psych class a lesson about people who seemed to know they were going to die. Not sick people; soldiers, adventurers, whose sudden violent death seemed to resonate backwards in time—they told their friends that somehow they felt that this was it, and by God it was. You can call it coincidence or invoke pragmatic casuality— they were nervous and therefore careless and therefore died—but here and now I think there's more to it. Once I'm safe inside the dome I'll publish a retraction. Right now I feel my death as strongly as I feel the need for that man inside of me.

Maria

Somehow we lived through that one.

We'd been in the jungle for perhaps twelve hours, dusk approaching, when a lizard pack hit us, or two packs, from in front and behind. The trail is scarcely two meters wide, which saved us. The carcasses piled up and impeded their charge. We must have killed forty of them, man-sized or slightly smaller. Not a type we'd seen on the way down.

Were they intelligent enough to coordinate their charge, or is it some kind of instinctive attack pattern? Scary either way. Used up a lot of energy. If it happens a few more times . . . it happens. No use thinking about it.

At least the action seems to have been good for morale. Both of them have been radiating depression and fear since we started out this morning. Reinforcing each other's premonitions of doom. I shouldn't have let her go to him at watch change, or I should have admonished her to fuck, don't talk. It was too much like saying goodbye. I got that feeling from Gab too, last night, but I tried to reassure him. Words.

By my reckoning we have fourteen to eighteen hours to go, depending on how much ground we can cover without light. Decided against torches, of course. The Plathys don't normally hunt at night, but they sure as hell attacked us in the dark.

Natural impulse is to climb a tree and wait for dawn. That would be suicidal. The jungle canopy is thick and supports its own very active ecology. We can't take to the water because the current's too swift, even if we wanted to chance the snakes.

We'll stay within touching distance, Gab in front because he has the best hearing. Brenda hears better than me, so she should bring up the rear, but I think she'll be better off in the middle, feeling protected. Besides, I want to have one of the weapons.

Gabriel

Never another night like that. I wound up firing at every sound, jumpy. But a few times there actually was something waiting in front of us, once something that wasn't a lizard. Big shaggy animal that stood up on its hind legs and reared over us, all teeth and claws and a dick the size of my arm. He was too dumb to know he was dead, and actually kept scrabbling toward us after I cut him off at the knees. If we'd gone a few steps farther before I fired he would have gotten at least me, maybe all of us. The crazer light was almost bright in the pitch blackness, a lurid strobe. I used up the last of one fuel cell and had to reload by touch.

At least we don't have to worry about the Plathys. Nothing remotely edible could make it through a night like that without energy weapons.

When I mentioned that to Maria, she said not to be too sure. They were tracking us on the jungle side before. Not the same, though. This jungle makes that one look like a park.

Dead tired but moving fast. We're looking for a pink granite outcropping. Fifty paces upstream from it there's a minor trail to the right; the dome clearing is about half a kilometer in. Can't be more than a few hours away.

Brenda

There it is! The rock! Hard to ... talk ... running ...

Maria

Slow down! Careful! That's better. Not a sound now.

Gabriel

Oh, no. Shit, no.

Brenda

They ... burned it?

Gabriel

Spears—

Maria

Take his weapon! Get to cover! Here!

Brenda

I—oh!

Maria

So . . . so this is how it ends. Gab died about ten minutes ago, in the first moment of the attack. A spear in the back of his head. Brenda was hit then too, a spear that went in her shoulder and came out her back. She lived for several minutes, though, and acquitted herself well when the Plathys charged. I think we killed them all, 37 by my count. If there are any left in the jungle they are staying there for the time being.

They must have piled wood up around the dome and kept a bonfire going until the force field overloaded and collapsed. It wasn't engineered for that kind of punishment, I suppose. Obviously.

Little of use left in the ruins. Rations destroyed, fuel cells popped by the heat. There's a tool box not badly harmed. Nothing around to repair with it, though. Maybe if I dug I could find some rations merely overcooked. But I don't want to stay around to search. Doubt that I'll live long enough to have another meal, anyhow.

My fault. Eleven good people dead, and how many innocent savages, because I wasn't prudent. With that first abrupt life change, the frenzied breeding, I should have ordered us to tiptoe away. Another decade of satellite surveillance and we would have learned which times were safe to come in for close-up study. Now everything is a shambles.

Racial vanity is part of it, I guess, or my vanity. Thinking we could come naked into a heavily armed Stone Age culture and survive by our superior intelligence and advanced perspective. It worked before. But this place is not Obelobel.

I guess all I can do now is be sure a record survives. These teeth might not make it through a

Plathy or lizard digestive system. I'll ... I'll use
the pliers from the tool kit. Leave the teeth here in
the ruins. Buried enough so the Plathys can't find
them easily. One hell of a prize to bring back from
your Walk North.

I have only about a tenth-charge left. Brenda used
up all of the other before she died. Not enough to get
out of the jungle, not even if it were all daylight.
One woman alone doesn't have a bloody fucking
chance on this world. I'll try the river. Maybe I can
find a log that will float me down to the savannah.
Then hike to the coast. If I can make it to the beach
maybe I can stay alive there for awhile. Sleep with
one eye open. I don't know. Look for me there. But
don't bother to look for too long. The pliers.

Sorry, Brenda ...

Sorry ... Gab. Sweet Gab. Still warm.

Now mine. One jerk. Some blood, some pain.
Tem se garlish. !ka.

*   *   *

To: Ahmadou Masire, Coordinator
Selva Sector Recreational Facilities
Confederación Office Building, Suite 100
Bolivar, 243 488 739
Selva

From: Federico Santesteban, Publicity Director
Office of Resources Allocation
Chimbarazo Interplanetario
Ecuador 3874658
Terra

Dr. Masire:

I hope you will find the enclosed transcript of
some use. Your assistant, Sra. Videla, mentioned

the possibility of a documentary cube show to generate interest in the hunting trips to Sanchrist IV. Seems to me that if you inject some romance into this you have a natural story—sacrifice, tragedy, brave kids battling against impossible odds.

We could save you some production costs by getting a few Plathys shipped to your studio via our xenological division on Perrin's World. We have a hundred or so there and keep their stock stable by cloning. You'll have to have somebody put together a grant proposal demonstrating that they'll be put to legitimate scholarly use. Garcia Belaunde at your Instituto Xenológico is a tame one, as you probably know. Have him talk to Leon Jawara at the PW Xenological Exchange Commission. He'll make sure you get the beasts at the right part of their life cycle. Otherwise they'd eat all of your actors.

I tried to pull some strings but I'm afraid there's no way we can get you permission to take a crew onto the Plathy island itself. That's a xenological preserve now, isolated by a force field, the few remaining Plathys constantly monitored by flying bugs. You can shoot on the mainland, if your actors are as crazy as your hunters, or use the crater lake island. There are a few feral Plathys roaming there, though, so take precautions, no matter what the season. Use a restraining field if that's within your budget; otherwise, regrettably, the smartest thing would be to kill them on sight. Their behavior patterns become erratic if they're separated from family for more than a year.

The search party that followed up on Dr. Rubera's expedition could find only four of the tooth transmitters. There was no other trace of Maria Rubera, or any human remains.

A sad story but I think a useful one for your purposes. Gives your expeditions a dramatic historical context.

Let me know if I can be of further service. And by all means send us a copy of the cube, if you decide to go into production.

Your servant,
Federico Santesteban

Most human conflicts offer the possibility, at least, of a negotiated peace. Any such resolution not forced upon one side by its failure on the battlefield demands much of the combatants. It is rarely successful; war incites too much emotional fervor. The need for revenge, the inability to compromise, pure and simple anger—these are the human feelings that stand in the way of peace. We can recognize them, if we cannot condone their effect.

But how frightening to face an enemy which cannot possibly negotiate—even to accept a surrender. In this example of the scientific "puzzle" story Timothy Zahn has produced so often for Analog Science Fiction/Science Fact, *a band of humans encounters alien soldiers utterly incapable of intelligent communication—much less of talking peace.*

CORDON SANITAIRE

By

Timothy Zahn

For Mitch Drzewicki, the day began like most of the previous hundred or so: he was ripped slap-dash from a sound sleep by the screech of a tarsapien at the edge of the forest. For a few moments he just lay there, letting his heartbeat catch up with him and wondering why the hell his brain couldn't edit out the caterwauling and let him sleep through it. Certainly his subconscious had learned that trick with the dozens of alarm clocks he'd gone through in his thirty-six years. . . . With a sigh he looked at his watch, decided against trying for the last hour of sleep he'd allotted himself, and climbed stiffly out of bed.

The not-quite-warm-enough shower finished the waking-up process, and by the time he'd wolfed down a quick breakfast he was almost over his grouch. Coffee cup in hand, he stepped outside for a breath of fresh air and a final settling of nerves.

A ritual that nearly always worked . . . because

whatever Pallas lacked regarding the courtesy of its indigenous animals, it more than made up in beauty. The forest surrounding their little settlement had an unusual feeling of vitality about it, both in the way it pressed right to the edge of their protective herbicide ring and in its unashamed delight with bursts of color. In the six months since the four men and two women of their study team had arrived here Mitch had solved some of the botanical puzzles behind the ripples of red and pale orange that swept through the ginkgap and manzani trees' leaves every couple of weeks, but he was a long way from a complete explanation of the whys and hows of the phenomenon.

Only three months remained until the university-hired ship would come to pick them up; and despite the normal strains their group was starting to feel, Mitch almost wished it was possible to call across the light-years and ask for an extension. It was always like this, he knew from experience: study expeditions were never long enough for anything but a tantalizing taste of a new world's phytobiology. Still, it was possible that after he published the papers from this trip some other university would decide it worth its while to fund another Pallas study, and if so perhaps he could talk his way aboard. Unless a more eminent botanist decided to bid for such a slot . . . but perhaps by then Mitch would have enough prestige himself to get every field trip he wanted. *Dreamer*, he told himself; and draining his coffee cup he headed back inside to the biology lab and the day's activities.

The first and most pleasurable of which was going to be saying good-morning to Kata Belen. The petite biologist was already up, hunched in familiar posture over her work table as she fiddled with her recorder and computer terminal.

" 'Morning, Kata," Mitch said, coming up to her and looking over her shoulder. The computer displayed a wiggly graph; some kind of spectrum, he guessed.

Kata looked up and smiled. "Well, hi, Mitch. I thought you were going to sleep in today."

"So did I. I really think you should cancel Swizzle's wake-up service."

She chuckled, the action accentuating the tiny crinkles around her eyes. She'd once commented that the lines made her look distinguished, but Mitch thought she was much too cheerful to approach any kind of academic stodginess. "You're the only one that tarsapien wakes up," she said. "Swizzle's always up ahead of time, sitting quietly and munching his manzani fruit, for all the world like he's waiting for the morning news to start."

Mitch glanced over to the cage that dominated the far wall of the lab. Kata's pet-*cum*-test subject was anything but quiet now, his long arms swinging him through and around the makeshift jungle gym with unlikely speed and grace. "I hope you don't intend to put leading similes like that into your report," he warned Kata. "Lyell's firmly convinced the tarsaps rate a four at the most on the Bateson-DuPre. Not high enough for anything but the most rudimentary information exchange."

"Well, Lyell's just wrong," she said firmly. "His sole criterion for that is the Bateson neural dexterity index, and all that really says is that tarsapiens aren't anywhere near the tool-building stage of development."

"I thought you'd taught Swizzle to use simple tools," Mitch said, looking back at the cage. Resembling nothing so much as a chimp-sized Terran tarsier with twin-thumbed gorilla arms, Swizzle always seemed to him more akin emotionally to a canine puppy. Certainly his face—all eyes, mouth, and nostrils—never seemed to show the seriousness Mitch had often sensed in borderline-intelligent animals. Possibly one reason the forest was so pleasant, he thought suddenly: nothing existed on Pallas capable of exploiting its resources. At least not any more. The scattered ruins . . . but those were the archeologists' worry.

"Tool use *per se* is only part of the Bateson index," Kata said, breaking into his drifting thoughts. "Most of it's concerned with cerebral and fingertip neuron density and firing speed, and in those I concede the tarsapiens rate relatively low. Besides which, whether Swizzle's really *using* those tools is still pretty debatable. *But.* Communication skill is also part of the Bateson-DuPre, and I think I've finally figured out what the tarsapiens are doing."

She tapped the pattern on her computer display. "The screeches all sound the same to *us*, but the ultrasonic pattern fluctuates like crazy as the sound hits peak volume and then trails off. I'm guessing the first, more static segment of the howl is something like personal or maybe territorial identification, and the second is then whatever message is being delivered." Tapping a key, she replaced the graph by a series of others, all showing the basic pattern she had described.

"You may be right," Mitch agreed cautiously, "but Lyell's going to want proof."

"He'll get it." Blanking the screen, she typed a short message into her private log and stood up. "I've got a new routine in mind for Swizzle, one that ought to bounce Lyell's guesstimate up at least a couple of points. Want to watch?"

"Sure." Sliding into one of the other chairs, Mitch watched as Kata crossed to Swizzle's cage and extended a hand through the mesh. The tarsapien leaned forward, his floppy nostrils molding themselves briefly around her wrist before he rocked back on his haunches. At one end of the cage was a sliding door leading to a transparent, three-dimensional maze with a small control box mounted on one wall. Kata stepped to the latter and began pressing buttons, and Mitch found himself wondering—again—what in starnation she was doing on Pallas with what could only be described as a second-class university survey team. As a botanist, Mitch's professional interests overlapped hers only slightly, but even he knew something of her reputation and wide range of accomplishments. Why wasn't she with some major planetary development corporation, or at the very least one of the top megaversities?

The answer, of course, was Lyell Moffit; but there were several different flavors to that answer, not all of them especially palatable. Certainly Lyell was one of the more gifted persuaders he had ever run into, as well as one of the most persistent; Mitch had turned down the genial biologist/physician's two previous recruitment pitches, but that hadn't kept the other from coming back a third time. Certainly too the name Lyell Moffit, though relatively fresh on the scene, was becoming more and more recognizable, and not only among the scientific community. Mitch had a sneaking suspicion that at least one of the expedition's six members had joined in hopes of slingshotting a sagging career with the aid of Lyell's growing reputation.

But Mitch rather thought Kata's reasons were more of a personal nature . . . though it was none of his business, of course. Nor likely ever would be.

Kata finished her programming and moved to the sliding panel separating the cage and maze. As if that were the signal he'd been waiting for, Swizzle scampered over to the panel and sat there expectantly. "All right, now," Kata said to Mitch over her shoulder, "I've set up a path with drops of jasmine through holes in that pipe network in the plastic. Watch."

Pulling on a rope, she raised the barrier. Swizzle was through the hole like a furry shot, his nostrils flaring like twin vacuum cleaners as he grabbed tiny handholds to pull himself up a long vertical shaft. Mitch watched him negotiate a right-angle turn, drop down a short segment—and come to an abrupt halt. "Lost?"

Kata shook her head. "He's blocked by a sliding panel. Let's see if he can figure out how to get it open."

But after a couple of minutes it was clear the tarsapien wasn't going to do so. "Oh, well," Kata sighed. "It wasn't a major part of the test, anyway." Touching a switch on the control box, she sent the barrier sliding upward out of the way. As it moved, the overhead lights reflected briefly from it, giving Mitch a glimpse of two hand-sized slots in the bottom which Swizzle could have used to raise the panel himself. With the obstruction gone, the tarsapien rapidly completed the maze, ending up at the far end and three stalks of *pora* grass.

Kata closed off the maze and opened the tunnel that would enable Swizzle to return to his cage, then walked back to Mitch. "He'll get it eventually," she said. "And when he does, Lyell and I will have to spend another couple of days setting up nets out in the forest."

"Ah," Mitch nodded. "You'll trap another tarsap and see if Swizzle can talk *him* through the maze."

"And what exactly will that prove?" a deep voice asked from the door, and Mitch turned as Lyell Moffit sauntered into the lab.

There was no question whatsoever that Lyell was leaving in shreds the popular image of scientists as a sub-species of hominid—superhuman in intelligence and language, subhuman in personality, taste, and social skill. Even on a field expedition a dozen light-years from the nearest newscaster, Lyell was impeccably dressed, his wardrobe complemented by his easy smile and natural charm. Mitch had been somewhat surprised when he found the other maintained his image off-camera as well as on; only gradually was he beginning to admit that Lyell's charisma was simply a part of the man himself.

All that, Mitch thought glumly, *and a top-class scientist, too. Some people have it all.*

Kata had turned toward Lyell, but at the moment seemed entirely unconscious of his charm. "What do you mean, what'll it prove?" she snorted. "It'll prove the existence of detailed communication between them, that's what."

"Like communication between bees?" he countered dryly.

"Not at all. This kind of maze and trick door are completely out of their normal experience. They'll need to exchange abstract information—and they will."

"Only if Swizzle can be persuaded to cooperate." Oddly enough, Lyell didn't seem to be worried about the threatened attack on his theory. "You'd better make it worth his while to give any newcomer the right information. A reward of his own, I'd say, for getting the other through the maze."

Kata's eyes had taken on a knowing look. "Uh-*huh*. So you *do* think they're intelligent. Your famous devil's advocate role, I suppose?"

Lyell winked at her and turned to Mitch. "Kata's worked with me before. She knows that half the results my people get are inspired by the monomaniacal urge to prove something I've said is pure Frensky moss."

"We've yet to make him admit out loud that he does it on purpose," Kata added, sending a mock glower in Lyell's direction. "Usually he tries to claim he's simply dumber than the popular media make him out to be."

"Well, I am," Lyell said, managing to look innocent, hurt, and amused all at once. "All that aside . . . when do you want to start setting the nets?"

"Any time," Kata said. "We've got room for a temporary cage in the Endurssons' lab, and if we can get a female I'll want to do some studies before letting her into the maze. A few days' worth, anyway—plenty of time for Swizzle to master the barrier trick."

Lyell pursed his lips. "Rom won't be happy if he and Shannon come back early and find a tarsap sitting on his isotope counter."

Kata shrugged. "The only other choices are Adler's lab, the common room, or one of our bedrooms. *You* want to tell Adler he's going to have to move all those neat piles of rocks he's been making in order to accommodate a guest?"

"Besides which," Mitch put in, "the Endurssons

aren't likely to come back ahead of schedule. Even if the ruins they found peter out faster than they expect, Rom'll find some reason to stay out there the full fifteen days."

"Um," Lyell said noncommittally . . . but Mitch saw the corner of his lip twitch. Rom Endursson was the thorn in Lyell's organizational flesh, the exception to the rule that Lyell's teams bubbled with harmony and professional camaraderie. Rom was a quiet, moody man who spent little of his time and even less of his attention on the others. Adler Zimmerman, the geologist, had once suggested that after twenty-five years of digging around the leavings of dead civilizations Rom may simply have forgotten how to deal with living human beings. Mitch privately thought that theory simplistic; but whatever the reasons behind his personality, Rom was very definitely the type who improved social gatherings mainly by his absence from them. Fortunately, he seemed to recognize this effect and spent as much time as possible at the handful of suspected ruins the original discovery team had spotted from space.

Mitch sometimes wondered how Shannon stood him; but then, she must have had some idea what she was getting into when she married him. The fact they'd been together for ten years now implied she saw something in him the others were missing.

"All right," Lyell said, breaking into Mitch's thoughts. "I need to wait a couple of hours for some culture plates to come out of the autoclave, but any time after that I could give you a hand with the traps. You'll need the morning to get the nets deodorized, anyway."

"Not to mention assembling the other cage,"

Kata agreed. "We should be able to head out right after lunch, though."

"Fine. Well, if you'll both excuse me, I have some tissue samples to analyze." With a nod at Mitch, he headed off toward his own lab table.

"Anything I can do to help?" Mitch asked Kata as she signed off her terminal.

"No, thanks," she told him. "The nets and caging material's all together out in the number three shed; I can bring all of it in on a single dolly. See you later."

"Sure." Mitch watched her leave the room. Then, with a glance at the back of Lyell's head, he crossed over to his own work bench, piled high with lichen samples he'd spent the last week collecting. *Should I tell her how I feel?* he wondered for the umpteenth time—and for the umpteenth time the same answer came back. *No. I'd just be making a fool of myself. Anyone who's got Lyell doesn't need me.*

And putting Kata out of his mind as best he could, he set to work cataloging his plants.

It was actually a couple of hours after lunch before Kata and Lyell headed outside; but for Kata, as always, the joy of being out under the open sky made any and all preliminaries worthwhile. She enjoyed the lab, of course—the intellectual excitement of coaxing the secrets out of some new organism—but it was for the field work that she'd gone into biology in the first place. To tramp alien soil; to see, smell, and touch alien plants and animals in their own unique environment and ecological structure ... it seemed so natural a joy that she still found it hard to understand people like Rom Endursson, who treated all living things with equal disregard as he hunted his long-dead artifacts.

With forested areas dominating the Palladian landscape, Lyell had insisted they set up shop in that particular ecosystem, a demand that had reportedly brought frowns to the faces of those in charge of the expedition's budget. Lyell had ultimately prevailed, but the extra money for clearing out trees and undergrowth had had to come from somewhere, and the relatively cramped central building was the result. Kata had occasionally missed their usual self-contained structure—especially when sloshing through the mud to one of the outside storage sheds—but all in all she considered the trade-off a reasonable one.

"Where do you want to set these up?" Lyell asked as they passed the circle of sheds and started across the ten-meter strip of empty ground separating the buildings from the edge of the forest. "Same places as the last time?" ·

"More or less," Kata nodded, wincing involuntarily as her feet crunched the dry soil underfoot. The dead ring—their "cordon sanitaire," as Adler called it—had been saturated with a potent herbicide to keep the forest from regaining its former territory. Perfectly safe; but her feet somehow refused to feel comfortable walking across poison. "I haven't seen any evidence the tarsapiens have changed their habits, so those sites should still be the high-traffic areas."

"Agreed."

The local section of forest was nearly devoid of such obvious features as streams, hills, and natural clearings, but radar and Lostproof transponder readings had long since mapped the ground's more subtle undulations. Combined with Kata's record of the original trap sites, the task reduced to little more than an afternoon's stroll in the woods. It

should have been an enjoyable time . . . but somehow Kata found herself unable to relax as the two
of them moved in a rough circle around their
clearing. Something in the air felt odd, though she
couldn't for the life of her pin down what it was.
Twice she almost mentioned it to Lyell; both times
decided against doing so.

They were setting the last net when a full-bodied
tarsapien screech split the air from a dozen meters
away. "About time," Lyell commented, glancing
that direction. "I was starting to think all the
tarsaps had gone on vacation."

"They *have* been unusually quiet," Kata agreed,
realizing suddenly that that was what had been
bothering her. "You suppose there's a heloderm
loose out here?"

"Could be," Lyell said slowly, drawing the half-
meter-long lightning rod sheathed at his side and
adjusting its power setting. "That screech had a
lot of piercing ultrasonic in it."

"Yeah," Kata said, drawing her own weapon.
The single communications point on which she
and Lyell agreed was that high ultrasonic content
signaled the presence of an enemy. "We going to
be smart and make a dignified run for it?"

"Let's take a short look around first," Lyell
suggested, easing a bush aside with his rod. "I'd
very much like to take a heloderm alive."

"Lyell, that's crazy. We don't *know* their poison
won't hurt us."

"Oh, sure we do—the tests on that dead one's
venom, remember?"

"The electric shock could have degraded the
chemical," Kata argued; but Lyell was already
moving cautiously forward. Gritting her teeth, she
nudged her lightning rod to full power and followed.

They'd covered perhaps five meters and Kata was probing carefully into a nearby pora-grass thicket when Lyell abruptly jerked backwards with a yelp of surprise and pain. "What?" Kata snapped, trying to get around in front of him.

"My arm—*ahr*!" he grunted again, lurching sideways into her and throwing them both off balance.

Which may have saved her life. Even as she took a step backwards to try and support his weight something whistled past her ear and thunked audibly into a tree trunk behind her.

They were being shot *at!*

The total impossibility of it threw her muscle coordination all to hell, sending both of them crashing down into the undergrowth. "Lyell!" she hissed. "Where were you hit?"

"Right arm and shoulder," he gritted. "Feels . . . strange."

Another shot snapped at the leaves above them. "We've got to get out of here," she said, looking around as best she could without lifting her head. Her lightning rod was still gripped in her hand; Lyell's was nowhere to be seen. Not that glorified cattle-prods would be a lot of use, anyway. "Can you crawl?"

"But who—how—?"

"Never mind that," she snapped, tugging at his arm. *Don't go foggy on me, Lyell,* she pleaded silently. "Let's just get *out* of here."

Two more shots whistling overhead underlined her words and seemed to snap Lyell out of his torpor. Moving awkwardly on knees and elbows, he began to crawl back the way they'd come. Kata followed, tensing for the shot that would rip into her own body. . . .

Surprisingly, the shot never came. Another tarsapien screech sounded, farther away this time, reminding Kata of the heloderm that might still be skulking about. It hardly seemed important anymore, though, and she waited until she and Lyell had traveled a good fifteen meters before wriggling her jacket off and raising it on the end of her lightning rod. There was no response, and a minute later she cautiously sat up. "Looks clear," she whispered, helping Lyell up. "Can you make it back to the camp?"

"Sure." He had a funny sort of look on his face and he was gripping his right arm with a white-knuckled hand, but he seemed steady enough on his feet.

"Okay." Kata glanced at her Lostproof for the direction and got a good grip under Lyell's left arm. "Let's go. *Quietly.*"

And as they set off she sheathed her lightning rod and pulled out her communicator. The others had to be alerted.

Lyell's knees were starting to buckle by the time they reached the edge of the herbicide ring, but Mitch was watching for them and came out to help the last few meters. "Are *you* okay?" he asked Kata as he took some of Lyell's weight.

"Yeah," she puffed. "Adler make it back all right?"

"He's in the common room getting the medkit laid out." Mitch was very obviously bursting with questions, but restrained himself well. "Lyell, how do you feel?"

"Not much pain, but my arm feels funny," the other said. "I can feel something solid in there, too."

"All right, just take it easy till we get inside."

Mitch opened the door and together the three of them eased through it.

Adler had finished preparations in the common room when they arrived and was pacing nervously by the window, one of the expedition's only two laser pistols belted at his side. He came over as they got Lyell seated. "Lyell, what's going on here?" he demanded. "Mitch fed me some nonsense about a *sniper*? What kind of crazy story is *that*?"

"Wasn't any of *my* doing, Adler, believe me," Lyell grunted as Kata eased his arm out of its sleeve. "Doesn't seem to be any blood, does there?"

"Not much." There was a little, though, she saw, as if he'd been poked with a needle. "Mitch, hand me the fluoroscan, will you? Thanks. Now . . . ah. Wumph." She ran the hand unit over his shoulder next, feeling her jaw tighten. "They're there, all right. Two little needles, a few millimeters long. In pretty deep, too."

"*I* could have told you that," Lyell said dryly, wincing as Kata probed with her fingers. "You feel up to going in and getting them out?"

"Me? I don't have a medical certificate."

"Well, I can't very well operate on myself," he countered. "Just pretend I'm a frog or rhesus."

"But—"

"Don't argue!" Lyell snapped. "My arm doesn't feel this way solely because of shock. Those needles are putting something into me, and I want them *out*."

Gritting her teeth, Kata nodded and reached for the local anesthetic.

It wasn't as bad as she'd thought it would be. Focusing on a few square centimeters of skin as she manipulated the probe, she was indeed able to almost forget it was a human being she was working on. Still, it seemed like forever before she dropped the second needle into the gauze pad Mitch held for her. "There," she said, expelling her breath in a sigh of relief.

"Good job," Lyell grunted, touching the skin gingerly. "I think we should go to the biology lab right away and plug me into the blood analyzer."

"Right." Kata glanced around, noticed for the first time that they'd lost one of their number. "Where's Adler?"

"Checking to make sure all the windows are latched and watching for your sniper to stick his nose inside the cordon," Mitch told her. He'd rubbed some of the blood off the needles and was holding the gauze pad up to the light. "If that's really what's out there."

"What do you mean, 'if'?" Kata snapped. "What do you think those things are, tarsapien toenails?"

"Could be the seeds of some plant," he shrugged. "Pine needle shaped, thrown from a branch by the wind or the passage of some animal. Sort of a combination samara and cocklebur."

"Ridiculous—the *speed* they must have been traveling—"

"There's an easy way to settle this," Lyell interrupted mildly, standing up. "Run the needles under a microscope and look for Palladian-type cellular construction. If there isn't any—well, maybe Adler can run a composition test on them."

"Lyell, aren't you playing the dispassionate scientist part just a little too far?" Kata asked, glancing once toward the windows. "There's someone out there *shooting* at us. Shouldn't we be doing something to defend ourselves?"

"Adler's wearing our entire arsenal until the Endurssons come back," he pointed out. "As for defenses, what would you suggest we do? Sandbag the entrance? Rig a defensive force field out of our meson microscope and centrifuges?"

Her despair must have showed on her face, because Lyell smiled slightly and laid a hand on her shoulder. "It's not as bad as it looks, though—really it isn't. I'm sure you agree our assailant could have cut us both down long before we got back here if he'd either wanted to or been able to. The fact that he didn't implies we've got some breathing space." He glanced at the bandage on his shoulder. "And in that case our top priority is to figure out just what we're up against here."

It took a few minutes for Kata to get Lyell connected to the blood/tissue analyzer, about the same time it took Mitch to clean one of the needles and get it under the microscope. "Here goes," he announced, flipping on the projector.

Palladian cellular structure differed in any number of ways from that of terrestrial flora and fauna, but even so it was instantly obvious that the needle had never been part of an organic structure. Smooth and metallic, it was equipped with tiny fins that had the look of mathematical precision about them, and despite all it had been through the tip was still perfectly sharp. Long, thin pores, symmetrically placed, seemed to lead through the skin to a darker shaft beneath.

Mitch was the first to break the silence. "I think," he said quietly, "that we're in serious trouble."

"The understatement of the day," Lyell said. He stared at the needle's image a moment, then shook his head. "This just doesn't make sense. We *know* the tarsaps haven't got anywhere near enough brains or technology to make something like that, and there simply aren't any traces of anything more advanced down here."

"What about those ruins Rom and Shannon are working?" Mitch asked.

"I mean *recent* traces," Lyell amended. "Rom dates those structures as at least three hundred years old. *That*—" he gestured at the screen—"is practically new."

"Is it?" Mitch pulled out his communicator. "Maybe Adler will be able to tell us."

The geologist, when consulted, looked skeptical. "That's a pretty small sample to get both composition and age from."

"Just pretend it's a sliver of unknown ore," Lyell said, his eyes on the blood analysis data that was starting to come in.

Adler sighed. "I'll try. Mitch, you'd better take over sentry duty. Here's the laser; keep your comm ready."

The two men left, and Kata stepped to Lyell's side. "How's it look?"

"Strange, but so far doesn't seem all *that* dangerous." He pointed. "The stuff's getting into my red cells, but I don't see any effect on oxygen transport. Wait—here comes a preliminary molecular structure."

Kata watched with growing fascination as the foreign molecule began to appear. It was nothing she immediately recognized; and yet—"An azido group," she said suddenly, tapping that end of the schematic. "That settles it—this *is* a poison."

"Maybe," Lyell agreed, tight-lipped. "Still . . . seems pretty slow-acting."

Kata was already keying the analyzer's scrubbing capability. "Try to relax," she said, double-checking her coding. "It'll take an hour or so to flush the stuff out of your system. How do you feel?"

"Actually, a little better. I don't really think this drug was meant specifically for use against humans."

"Let's hope not." Kata hesitated, then removed Lyell's communicator from his belt and placed it on the table beside his hand. "If you feel any change, hit the emergency switch and I'll come running. I need to go see how Adler and Mitch are doing."

"I'll be fine," he assured her. "Let me know what Adler finds out."

She nodded wordlessly and left.

Adler's geology lab was just a short walk around the building's central hub, but Kata passed it by. Mitch would be circling the outer areas on guard duty, and it was Mitch whom she wanted to see.

She found him by the exit door, staring out the small window with his hand resting on the laser's grip. "Anything out there?" she asked.

"Apparently there is; but it's not showing itself." He turned to look at her, and she was startled by the tightness around his eyes. "How's Lyell?"

"The darts were poisoned, but the drug doesn't seem very virulent. It's being scrubbed out of his blood now."

Mitch nodded. "You're taking this pretty calmly," he said.

She opened her mouth to deny it, but no words came out. He was right, she realized suddenly; so far her physical and emotional responses had been totally on a scientific level. "I suppose the emotional impact just hasn't hit me yet," she said at last. "I had to get Lyell back and then take care of him. . . ." She shook her head. "You've had more time to think. What do *you* make of all this?"

"Oh, hell, *I* don't know." Mitch turned back to the window. "Lyell's right—nothing that's native here could have made those darts. We've got to be dealing with an outsider, maybe a survivor of a space ship wreck or something."

"Injured, perhaps, and not mobile?" That could explain how they'd escaped so easily. But—"Surely the seismographs or weather satellites would have picked up traces of any crash or forced landing."

Mitch shrugged. "The only other options I've come up with are an old survivor from one of Rom's ruined towns—a *very* old survivor—or else someone sent deliberately to drive us off. Take your pick."

Kata grimaced. "So what do we do?—hole up here and hope he'll go away?"

"For three more months?" Mitch shook his head. "I don't relish the idea of running through a hail of darts every time we need something from one of the sheds. And that assumes he doesn't have anything more powerful."

Kata felt a shiver run down her back. "Mitch . . . I think I'm starting to get scared."

"You're in good company." Taking one final look outside, Mitch took Kata's arm and started back toward the biology lab. "Come on; let's go talk to Lyell. Guarding the door like this is probably a waste of time, anyway."

Adler had also returned to the lab by the time they arrived, his bristly eyebrows knitted together in concentration. "If I could have the other needle as well," he was saying, "I might be able to get more information."

Lyell shook his head. "I want that one to do a better analysis on the drug it's carrying." He looked up at Mitch and Kata. "Anything?"

Mitch shook his head. "Nothing past our perimeter except forest," he said. "Lyell, it occurs to me that this place is about as defensible as the far end of a target range. Why don't we get Rom and the *Sunray* back and get out of here?"

"And go where?" Adler snorted. "We don't even know what it is you want us to run from."

"Peace." Lyell raised his hand, cutting off Mitch's own retort. "I indeed plan to call Rom and Shannon back, but not for purposes of escape. I believe what we have here is a castaway, a victim perhaps of a space accident, and I have no intention of simply flying off and leaving him."

Almost exactly what Mitch had suggested, Kata thought, glancing at him. But somehow it sounded a lot less threatening when Lyell said it.

Though apparently not to all of them. "So what're you going to do—invite him in for tea and fruit sticks?" Adler asked. "He *shot* at you, remember?"

"Perhaps he mistook the sound for local fauna," Lyell shrugged. "Or else he spotted our drawn lightning rods and thought we were coming to attack him. Either way, we can't afford to leave matters as they stand." He paused, and his face took on a thoughtful look. "I presume you all realize that we may be on the brink here of finding out why we've never before run into any intelligent species in this part of space."

"What, the old 'shy alien' hypothesis again?" Adler grunted. But even he had the beginnings of a gleam in his eye. "I suppose it's not impossible."

Lyell shifted his gaze to Kata. "You're being pretty quiet, Kata. What are your thoughts on all this?"

She shook her head. "I don't know," she admitted. "The Robinson Crusoe theory works as well as any other, I suppose, but there are still holes in it you could fly the *Sunray* through. If that dart gun of our theoretical alien is supposed to be a survival weapon, why doesn't it carry a more lethal poison? —cyanide, for trivial example; that'll kill most oxygen-breathers we know of. Furthermore, if he crashed this close to us why haven't our surveys picked up evidence of it? And if he hit far away, how in starnation did he find us?"

There was a moment of silence. Then Mitch cleared his throat. "This poison—it *is* a real poison, isn't it?"

"I'm sure it's supposed to be, but against us it hardly qualifies as one," Lyell told him. "It affects the nervous system locally to the extent of causing minor and temporary numbness, but that appears to be all it does. That's one reason I'm not especially worried about being gunned down en masse."

"I see." Mitch had a frown on his face. "Have you done any tests to see how the darts work on, say, tarsap physiology?"

Kata exchanged glances with Lyell. "Unh," Lyell grunted. "I see what you're getting at."

"I don't," Adler spoke up.

"On a biochemical level Palladian life is very similar to ours," Lyell explained, stroking his chin thoughtfully. "If the darts don't bother us much, they aren't likely to kill native animals either, at least not quickly enough to be useful for hunting or defense."

"Bang goes the survival weapon theory," Mitch murmured. "Lyell, this isn't getting us anywhere. If the drug isn't dangerous, maybe Adler and I should go out and see if we can find our trigger-happy guest. Before he figures it out and switches to a stronger weapon."

"You don't mind if I do my own volunteering, do you?" Adler snapped.

"First things first," Lyell shook his head. "No one's going back outside until we have the *Sunray* back to monitor things from the air. Kata, you and Mitch are to try and extract the main poison reservoir from the second dart and double-check the blood analyzer's chemical formula. Adler, I guess you can just go about your work. As soon as the scrubber here's finished with me, I'll give the Endurssons a call."

"If it's all the same to you," Adler said, "I think I'll continue watching the windows. Even high-impact plastic can be broken if you hit it hard enough. Mitch?"

Silently, Mitch handed over the laser. The geologist strapped it on and left the room, and Mitch stepped over to the table where the second dart lay on its gauze pad. "Come on, Kata," he said, picking it up. "Rom will have his standard snit if Lyell doesn't have some hard data to give him when he calls."

Mitch didn't hear the radio conversation Lyell had with Rom: but when the Endurssons finally arrived an hour after sunset Rom wasted no time in making his annoyance public. "All right—let's see these so-called poisoned needles," were his first words as Mitch met them at the door.

"Sure," Mitch said, swallowing the greeting he'd started to give. "The others are in the bio lab."

Rom snorted and strode past him. Shannon gave Mitch a smile that was half greeting, half apology, and hurried after her husband. Suppressing a grimace, Mitch followed, glad that the conversa-

tional burden would be shifting from his shoulders
to Lyell's.

Lyell and Kata were indeed waiting in the lab
when they arrived, Adler with a good sense of
timing having chosen that moment to be elsewhere.
"Lyell," Rom nodded briskly. "What's all this fuss
that you absolutely *had* to drag us away from our
work over?"

Lyell flipped on the microscope projector and
gestured to the screen. "I was shot with two of
those darts," he told the other without preamble.
"I was hoping you might have run into this kind of
weapon before in your studies."

Rom stepped up to the screen, and Mitch felt a
smile of admiration twitch at his lip. Only Lyell
would think of drawing the archeologist into this
by appealing to his professional judgment. "Composition?" Rom asked, adjusting the light a fraction.

"An alloy of nickel, iron, molybdenum, and
manganese," Lyell told him. "There may be a very
thin layer of a lacquer coating on it, too; Adler
wasn't sure. Its main claim to fame is that it's an
extremely ferromagnetic material."

"In other words, the gun that fired it uses magnetic rings instead of compressed gas or chemical
explosives," Rom said, his tone implying the others should have figured that out long ago.

They had, actually, but Lyell didn't bother to
say so. "Seems reasonable—neither Kata nor I
heard any sound except the whistle of the darts
themselves."

"Means a reasonably high technology," Rom continued as if Lyell hadn't spoken. "Could have come
from the ruins, I suppose. Have you done an alloy-
bond dating yet?"

"Adler couldn't get both age and composition

from the other dart, and I wouldn't let him have this one too."

Rom snorted. "Adler thinks you need a kilo of sample to do anything useful. I can probably get a good approximation from whatever he's got left."

"Wait a second," Kata spoke up. "Are you saying the sniper could be a survivor from a dead civilization?"

"More likely an outcast or someone accidentally left behind," Shannon said, the quiet patience in her voice forming its usual contrast with the lack of that quality in Rom's. "Or a descendant of such a group. The people who built those ruins seem to have arrived rather abruptly on Pallas and then have left equally abruptly. There is no 'dead civilization' here, just temporary visitors."

"Visitors?" Lyell frowned. "I got the impression from your reports that these ruins were more elaborate than a simple exploration team bivouac."

"They are," Rom said. "All of them so far have shown evidence of extensive permanent buildings— one of them even has a nested series of perimeter walls, which indicates periodic growth of the settlement."

"Sounds more like a fort setup," Mitch murmured.

"Doubtful," Rom shook his head. "The walls weren't thick enough to defend against any real attack. Probably they were just decorative." He peered at the magnified needle for another minute. "I gather you want me to take the *Sunray* up tomorrow and look for whatever's out there shooting these things. Suppose he doesn't want to be found?"

"We'll just have to flush him out, won't we?" Mitch said, and immediately regretted it as Rom sent him a look of disgust that could have sterilized culture plates at twenty paces.

"I don't suppose it occurred to you that he may not *want* our company," the archeologist said icily. "If he's used to being alone or part of a small group we'd probably scare the hell out of him charging in on him like that. In fact, maybe that's what started him shooting in the first place."

"We've been tromping all around this part of Pallas for well over six months, apparently without bothering him," Lyell pointed out. "Why should he start shooting now if he doesn't want any attention? If, on the other hand, he just got here, it may be he *is* in need of help or company."

"He's got a funny way of showing it," Rom grunted. "But my original question was how you intended to locate him in the first place. If you were counting on the *Sunray's* sensors to pick up the needles or magnets, you can forget it. A properly designed mag-ring gun doesn't leak very much field, even when it's being fired."

"Then we'll walk around and listen for the tarsapien enemy call," Kata put in.

"The what?"

"Lyell and I heard a tarsapien danger cry just before the needles started flying," she amplified. "At the time we thought it meant a heloderm was scuttling around, but now I'm not so sure."

"And why would the tarsaps identify this visitor as an enemy?" Rom snorted. "They don't treat *us* that way."

"I only meant—"

"It's as good a working assumption as any," Lyell interjected mildly. "The whole tarsap community was unusually quiet this morning, and I've never known even a family of heloderms to cause a reaction that widespread. Do you have any idea yet what the people who built those ruins looked like?''

Rom shrugged. "Bipedal, certainly; probably at least vaguely humanoid, as well. We haven't yet located any photos or sculptures that would tell us for sure, but all the more subtle indications are there." He favored Lyell with a sardonic smile. "Don't worry, I'm sure he'll be distinguishable from any tarsaps in the area. He'll be holding a gun, for one thing. When do you plan on organizing this hunt?''

Lyell winced slightly at the word *hunt* but didn't comment on it. "I thought early tomorrow morning you could take the *Sunray* up and just see if you can pick up any traces of our visitor from above. If not, Mitch, Adler, and I will go to the spot where I was shot and work outward from there. Unless you have another suggestion?''

"No, I suppose that's as good a plan as any," Rom said. "You won't object if I leave any details to the rest of you?—I've got some samples I want to get catalogued. I thought not. Good night, all." Without waiting for a reply, he turned and disappeared down the hall.

Always a pleasure, Mitch thought sourly, but he refrained from saying it aloud. Shannon was still in the room, and whatever he thought of Rom he *did* genuinely like her. So he merely gave her a friendly smile and strolled over to where Kata was tapping her fingers idly on her terminal. "Feeling any less scared than you were this afternoon?" he asked, pulling up a chair beside hers.

She didn't turn to face him, and her fingers halted their drumming only for a moment. "Yes or no," she answered over her shoulder. "I'm not as afraid of the needles as I was ... but the rest of it just keeps getting worse."

"You mean Rom's odd-man-out theory? I agree it's shot full of holes—"

"Doesn't that *bother* you?" she interrupted, turning to give him a strange look. "This isn't some nice, safe theoretical discussion about the ecological function of Frensky moss. There is a real someone out there, shooting real needles for real reasons—and it seems to me that charging into this without knowing what we're doing could be dangerous as well as plain stupid."

The intensity of her outburst startled Mitch, and he glanced over to see if Lyell had heard. But the other was deep in quiet conversation with Shannon. "If you feel that way," he asked Kata, "why didn't you bring it up a few minutes ago?"

She shook her head and turned away again. "Lyell had his mind made up—you saw that."

"But you're—" *his lover* "a long-time colleague. Someone he trusts. You could change his mind."

She snorted. "*No* one changes Lyell Moffit's mind once he's decided on a course of action."

Her face was still turned away, and Mitch abruptly realized what she was staring at. Crouching motionlessly in one corner of his cage, Swizzle had a preternatural alertness about him. Occasional ripples of muscle sent waves through his fur, and his flared nostrils were larger even than his unblinking eyes. "How long has he been like that?" Mitch asked quietly.

"I noticed it when we were working on the needle drug analysis earlier. I don't think he's moved half a meter since then."

Mitch shivered. Generalizing from one species to another was always an iffy proposition, but he'd rarely seen a more textbook example of herbivore danger reaction. "Could he have heard the tarsap enemy cry earlier?"

"I don't know. Actually, I'm not quite sure how to read this; he *acts* nervous, certainly, but he accepted his dinner from me without any hesitation I could detect."

"In other words, it's not *us* he's afraid of?"

"I wouldn't even swear to that. I just don't *know*." Kata's fingertips slapped the console one final time and came to a halt. "Well . . . maybe it'll all prove academic, after all. If you catch the sniper tomorrow we should be able to put all the pieces together easily enough."

"Maybe." Mitch glanced once more at Swizzle and then turned away. "Might be interesting to see if his wake-up call tomorrow has any of the 'danger' overtones in it, though."

"I've already got the recorder set up."

Mitch had planned to be listening when the tarsapien cry came the next morning; but though he was up well in advance of the event he wound up missing it entirely as he walked innocently into the common room and straight into a full-fledged war of words.

Lyell, it seemed, had finally run afoul of his own abundant self-confidence. Apparently simply assuming Adler's cooperation in the morning's activities, he hadn't bothered to clear his plans with the geologist . . . and Adler was not amused at having been volunteered for such clearly hazardous duty.

"I don't care," he was saying when Mitch arrived. "I'm not going out there to be shot at on a half-hour's notice. Not without better protection than these coveralls—certainly not without a better idea of what we're up against."

Even Lyell's temper was showing signs of strain. "I've told you what the darts contain—"

"And you've assured me it's not dangerous," Adler interrupted him. "And I'm sure you're not deliberately lying to me. But what about long-term effects of the residue you can't flush out? What about cumulative effects? Face it, Lyell; you haven't got nearly enough answers yet."

"I presume we're open to suggestions," Mitch said, sitting down next to Shannon. Rom, seated alone on the far side of the table with a look of sour amusement on his face, seemed to be staying out of the discussion.

"My idea's already been trampled on, thank you," Adler said, his voice frosty.

Lyell shook his head wearily. "Adler thinks we should just expand our herbicide ring—excuse me, our *cordon sanitaire*—by a factor of ten or so. Keep the sniper at a distance. Be reasonable, Adler; even if we had the herbicide to maintain it, we couldn't begin to clear that much space quickly and safely enough."

"If you say so. But I'm still not going out there."

The impasse lasted several minutes longer, with Lyell running through an amazing repertoire of persuasions and inducements before giving up. "All right, then," he said, standing up. "I guess Mitch and I will have to do it alone. You ready, Rom?"

"Whenever you are," Rom said. "If it would help, though, I suppose I *could* let Adler take the *Sunray* and go with you two myself."

You might have suggested that ten minutes ago, Mitch thought—and was opening his mouth to say so when Lyell beat him to the draw with a far more diplomatic comment.

"That's very generous of you, Rom; thank you. Well, Adler?"

Adler shot an irritated glance in Rom's direction; but having basically painted himself into a corner he had little choice but to accept the offer. Lyell pretended to take it all at face value, but even he couldn't quite carry it off, and it was a quiet group that headed out into the forest.

The forest, too, was quiet—quieter than Mitch had ever known it. He felt the eeriness of it all as he, Lyell, and Rom fanned out toward the spot where the mysterious sniper had first struck. Overhead, the *Sunray* was a humming blue-and-gray shadow drifting above the ginkgaps and manzanis; behind them, unseen but ever present, Kata and Shannon monitored the Lostproof and ground-to-air equipment and directed the search. It was, Mitch thought more than once, almost as if he were back in college playing the elaborate Search and Strike games that had been all the rage then. Those had been fun . . . but in those he'd been facing only chalk-dye pellets, not high-velocity needles.

"Still nothing," Adler's voice murmured from the communicator strapped to Mitch's shoulder.

"Computer enhancement's not getting anything from the data, either," Kata put in. "Lyell, I think Rom was right; that gun's not going to show on the *Sunray's* sensors."

"Well, we'll leave him up there—" Lyell broke off abruptly as a tarsapien screech split the air off to Mitch's left. "Report," Lyell said quietly.

"About thirty degrees left," Mitch whispered toward his shoulder, squeezing the "mark" button on his Lostproof to feed its position and orientation back to Shannon's monitor.

"Directly to my right," Lyell said. "Rom?"

"Straight ahead," the archeologist said calmly. "I guess I win."

"Stay there," Lyell ordered. "Mitch and I'll move in to flank him. Shannon. . . ?"

"Got a probable location—feeding to you."

Mitch glanced at the small white cross that had appeared on his Lostproof display and headed in that direction. There was no guarantee the loud tarsapien was sitting directly on top of the sniper, and he didn't want to blunder carelessly into a couple of those needles.

He was no more than twenty meters from the spot Shannon had marked when there was a rustle of movement in the trees ahead. "Lyell?" he whispered. "Something moving up there."

"I can see it," Rom put in. "Just a tarsap."

"Okay," Mitch nodded. He took a careful step forward, eyes scanning the undergrowth—

The needle jabbed in from almost directly above him, tracing a line of fire down his right shoulderblade. With a yelp he threw himself to the side, reflexively raising his lightning rod as if to ward off the attack. A second needle whistled down to nick his thigh as he scrambled toward the nearest tree trunk. Dimly, he heard Lyell calling his name. "In the trees!" he shouted as his brain unlocked for a second . . . and as a third needle slapped into the tree beside his cheek the forest seemed to explode with noise.

The crash of breaking branches overhead was the worst, giving Mitch the momentary feeling of being caught in a wood pulverizer. A swish of a body through the foliage and a glimpse of blue metal an instant later told him what had happened: Adler had rammed the *Sunray* through the upper tree branches in an attempt to dislodge the sniper. Simultaneously, a flash of laser light filtered through the undergrowth ahead. The scramble of something among low branches—Rom's bellow—three more laser flashes—

And with an unearthly scream something large crashed to the ground.

For a moment there was silence. "Mitch?" Lyell called, his voice echoed by the communicator jammed into his neck.

"Here," Mitch answered, struggling to his feet. There was a rustle of branches and Lyell appeared, an oddly tight look on his face. "You get him?" Mitch asked as the other gave him a hand up.

"Yeah. You okay?"

"Couple of needles—those damn things *hurt* going in. What's he look like?"

Lyell's expression tightened a bit more. "Come and see."

The body was lying on the crushed remains of a sarcacia bush, its fur marked with the red-in-black swaths of laser burns. Still gripped in its hand was a sleek, jet-black pistol—gripped so tightly, in fact, that Rom was having trouble prying it loose. For the moment, though, Mitch had little attention to spare for the weapon; his full and unbelieving gaze was on the creature holding it.

A tarsapien.

"Got to hand it to you biologists," Rom grunted as he straightened up, the pistol held loosely in his hand. "When you goof, you do it right. Canine-level intelligence, wasn't it? This one must have been a particularly fast learner."

"Lyell, what's going on?" Kata's voice said at Mitch's shoulder.

"We got the sniper," Lyell answered, the words seeming to stick in his throat. "It's—well, it seems to be a tarsap."

"*What?*"

"Yeah." Lyell shook his head in a gesture of bewilderment. "He must have found the gun somewhere; in one of the ruins, probably. Then figured out how to use it . . . somehow. . . ."

"Or else won it from a tourist in a card game," Rom put in sarcastically. Hefting the pistol, he sighted down the barrel, a slight frown creasing his forehead. "Don't worry—I'm sure you'll be able to salvage your theories somehow."

"We'll certainly take a crack at it," Lyell agreed, sounding more on balance. "Mitch, can you travel under your own power?"

"Uh . . . well, my leg feels sort of tingly—"

"Never mind." Lyell stepped to his side and offered a supporting arm. "Rom, if you can carry the tarsap I can take that weapon."

"Okay." Rom raised the gun, but halfway through the gesture hesitated and slipped it into his belt instead. "No, thanks; I can handle both." Reaching down, he manhandled the dead tarsapien onto one shoulder and checked his Lostproof. "Let's go," he said, heading toward home. Traveling only a bit slower, Lyell and Mitch followed.

They were halfway across the herbicide ring when the impossible happened; and because it *was* impossible none of them reacted during the precious handful of seconds that might have made the difference. From the treetops behind them wafted down a high-pitched tarsapien cry . . . and even as Lyell paused to look around the needles began to fly.

"Run!" Rom yelled, sprinting for the safety of the building. Mitch tried to follow, but Lyell had been caught flatfooted and it cost the two of them another second to get their feet moving in synch. Mitch bit down hard as a familiar sting scratched across his arm. Lyell seemed to falter, nearly pitching them headlong onto the ground; shifting his grip, Mitch managed more by luck than anything else to take Lyell's weight and keep them moving. The last four steps seemed to take forever . . . and then they were through the open door, slamming into Rom as the archeologist was starting back out. They fell together in a heap, another couple of needles ricocheting from the floor and walls before Mitch managed to get a foot free and kick the door closed.

It wasn't until he and Rom got to their feet that they discovered why Lyell was being so quiet.

The work on Lyell was slow, nerve-wracking, and frustrating, and by the time Kata remembered Mitch's injuries she already felt as if she'd been run backwards through a faulty garbage recycler. But despite the fact he'd been left lying on the dining table for over an hour there was no anger or impatience in his face or posture when she finally looked in on him. "How are you feeling?" she asked, hoping the deadness within her didn't come across as disinterest.

"I'm all right," he said quietly. "You can leave the needles in until later if you're still busy."

She shook her head. "I can't do anything more for Lyell now except let him sleep. Where were you hit?"

"Right scapula somewhere and left thigh rectus muscle, if I'm remembering my anatomy classes properly." He paused. "How is he?"

Something in his voice made her take another look at his face, and it finally penetrated her own cloud of fear and anxiety how hard he was taking this. "He's not doing too badly," she told him. "Still unconscious, but I'd have sedated him anyway. I think he'll pull through okay."

"Shannon told me there's a needle lodged in the heart muscle."

"Near, but not actually in it," Kata corrected, silently thanking heaven for small favors. "Unless it migrates it should be all right to leave it there."

He twisted his head up to look at her. "You're not going to take it out?"

Kata shook her head tiredly. "No, and I've already gone six rounds with Adler over the decision, so please don't you start. The needle went in between two ribs, just missing the spine, and there's simply no way I can get at it with the non-specialized equipment we've got here." She bit her lip as she applied a fresh layer of anesthetic to Mitch's shoulder wound. "Not to mention my own lack of skill, of course."

"Yeah."

She worked in silence for a moment, the part of her mind not actually involved with the operation trying to come up with words that would sound convincing. But Lyell was the one with the silver tongue, and eventually she gave up the effort. "It's not your fault, you know," she told Mitch.

"Isn't it? Rom made it in without a scratch . . . but he wasn't being slowed down by someone with only one and a half legs. Lyell could have let go of me and saved himself."

"In that case, it was his decision and again wasn't your fault." Kata shrugged. "Anyway, who's to say what would have happened if he'd let go? *You're the one who got* him *inside*, remember. Without you the tarsapien might have had time to put a dozen more shots into him."

"Maybe." Mitch sighed. "Kata . . . what the hell is going *on* here? Tarsaps with guns, shooting at us—it's like something out of a plot for *City of Night.* You know—the old Natives Rising To Throw Off The Human Conquerors gimmick. *Could* the tarsaps somehow have hidden a technological civilization from us?"

"No." There was a lot about this that Kata didn't understand, but of that one thing she was certain. "Remember the Bateson neural dexterity index? The tarsapiens are biologically incapable of inventing something as advanced as a needle gun."

"But that conclusion assumes Swizzle is a typical example. Is there any chance he's the tarsap equivalent of an imbecile, deliberately planted on us to skew our data?"

"You forget I've got disks full of data on tarsapiens in the wild as well. Anyway, if they were so intelligent that they could fool us that thoroughly, why tip their hand now?"

"I don't know." Mitch hissed between his teeth as Kata began easing the needle back along its original path. "But the option is to believe that they just happened to find at least two working needle guns in some multi-hundred-year-old ruin *and* that the tarsaps that found them both traveled several hundred kilometers to this same spot *and* that they only shoot humans and not each other with them." He ran out of breath and fell silent.

Kata withdrew the needle and laid it in a culture plate. *For future analysis,* a detached part of her mind said. "It doesn't make much sense either way, does it?" she admitted, moving down to work on Mitch's leg. "Well ... Rom and Adler are looking at the gun now. Maybe they'll come up with a better theory. I just wish we had better deep-probe equipment for them to use."

"*I* wish we had a way to call out-system for help," Mitch retorted.

Grimacing, Kata nodded. *If wishes were horses. . . .*

It took another half hour to remove the second needle and clean the wounds, and afterwards she helped Mitch to the bio lab for a session with the blood scrubber. She had finished the connections and was thinking about lying down for a while herself when Lyell woke up.

"I gather I took a fall," he said as Kata came over to the cot they'd set up for him.

"Of a sort," she said, checking the sensor readings and trying to keep her voice reasonably cheerful. "Tried running away from a needle that was running faster."

"So that part wasn't a dream," he murmured. "I was almost sure. . . ." He closed his eyes briefly and seemed to come a bit more awake. "Did the tarsap we killed get lost?"

"No, we've got both it and the gun," Kata said.

"We need to do an autopsy on it," Lyell said. "Find out why it was different. Why it shot at us."

"It's probably not—" Kata clamped her teeth firmly across the sentence. Already Lyell's eyelids were drooping; now was not the time to attempt a rational discussion with him. "You just sleep and get yourself well," she said instead. "We can handle things until you're back on your feet again."

"All right," Lyell's eyes were closed now, but with an obvious effort he forced them open a crack.

"Kata? Until I'm better . . . you're in charge of the expedition."

"Me? But—"

"Please. You're the only one who can do it."

She gritted her teeth; but the important thing was that Lyell should get to sleep without any added burdens on mind or body. "All right, Lyell, I'll do my best to keep everything running smoothly."

"Thank you." Lyell's eyes closed, and with a sigh he settled back to sleep.

For a moment she watched the sensors, wishing she knew what normal readings ought to be in this kind of situation. *We shouldn't have let him go out there*, she thought miserably. *We should have made him stay here, or at least up in the* Sunray. *No matter* how *safe the needles seemed we should have made sure our only doctor was as protected as possible.*

But with all the advances of modern technology no one had yet come up with a way to make second-hindsight profitable. Putting the chain of what-ifs from her mind, Kata went to Lyell's lab table and the dead tarsapien lying there. Her nap would just have to wait until after the autopsy.

It was a somber group that assembled in the bio lab that afternoon—an atmosphere undoubtedly not helped by the presence of Lyell lying unconscious on his cot against the wall. Kata didn't care much for the constant reminder of their danger either, but she was becoming increasingly reluctant to leave him alone.

"To start," she said, looking around the circle of people clustered around her lab table, "I'd like to get the tarsapien himself out of the way. The preliminary autopsy shows nothing especially out of the ordinary about him: no extra brain mass, no anomalies in coloration or organ size—in short, no indication whatsoever that he's a member of a theoretically superior sub-species of tarsapien. The computer's doing a detailed biochemical analysis now, but I believe it's safe to say he did *not* make the gun himself."

Rom snorted. "I told you that hours ago." Besides him, Shannon shifted slightly in her chair, but said nothing.

"It's nice to have proof, though," Mitch murmured. There was still a haunted look about his eyes, Kata noted uneasily: mute testimony to the fact that he still felt some responsibility for Lyell's injury. "How far did *you* two get with the pistol?" he added.

"Depends on what you want," Rom said. He glanced at Adler, as if expecting the other to say something. But the geologist was staring in the direction of Lyell's cot, his mind obviously light-years away, and with a quiet snort Rom pulled the black weapon from his belt and held it up. "Length, about fifteen centimeters, main body about four by three, grip about six long and an oval cross-section about twelve centimeters in circumference. The front half of the main body contains a series of seventy rings that, judging by their reaction to applied magnetic fields, are room-temp superconductors."

Abruptly, Kata noticed that the pistol, which had started out being held by the fingertips of Rom's right hand, had slipped imperceptibly into a cozy position in the archeologist's palm. There was nothing overtly hostile about that—certainly Rom wasn't pointing the thing at anyone—but something about the action nevertheless sent a quiet shiver through her body. "Rom, can we put it under the fluoroscan here?" she cut into his monologue. "See what it looks like inside?"

He glanced down at the gun in his hand, almost as if seeing it for the first time. "No need," he told Kata, lowering the gun to his lap but maintaining his grip on it. "It's all on the computer—Datapack ALP."

Feeling vaguely disturbed, Kata reached to her terminal and accessed the proper disk. A moment later, she had an x-ray view of the pistol on the screen.

Mitch whistled softly. "Crowded in there, isn't it? What *is* all that stuff?"

"Looks like some sort of relatively simple sensor at the tip of the barrel, probably part of the firing mechanism," Rom said. "The stuff behind the rings is more electronics and what seems to be a small powerpack. That narrow thing around the inside edge of the grip is a reservoir of some liquid, probably a lubricant. The rectangular block taking up the rest of the grip—" he hesitated—"appears to be the ammunition."

"The whole thing?" Kata asked, her eyes and brain trying to reconcile the sizes of the tiny needles she'd become far too familiar with and the solid-looking mass on the computer screen. "There must be—oh, *thousands* of needles in there."

"Something under nine thousand, actually," Rom said. "The reservoir also appears to be about half empty."

Mitch was the first to break the silence. "An eighteen *thousand* shot clip? What were they fighting, anyway, the Hundred Years' War?"

"How should *I* know?" Rom retorted. "Maybe it was just their version of the disposable flashlight—a sealed unit that you throw away when it's empty."

"Sealed?" Kata frowned. "You mean you can't figure out how to open it?"

"If I'd meant that I would have *said* that," Rom said, his voice heavy with scorn. "I mean there *is* no way to open it. Not unless you want to ruin part of the mechanism getting in."

Clamping her mouth firmly shut over her irritation, Kata looked back at the image on the computer screen. "I think we're going to have to risk it," she said. "There's only so much we can learn from indirect study—"

"Well, forget it," Rom interrupted. "I know you biologists are used to cutting up everything in sight, but you're not taking your scalpels to my gun."

"*Your* gun?" Kata asked. "Since when?"

"Since when do *you* give orders around here?" Rom countered.

"Since Lyell put her in charge this morning," Mitch spoke up.

"He did *that*?" Shannon asked, frowning. "Why?"

"Well, obviously he's not in any shape to run things himself," Mitch shrugged. "He woke up long enough to order an autopsy on the tarsap and then told Kata to run things until he was better."

"Ridiculous," Rom snorted. "Lyell must've been delirious."

"Now *you're* being ridiculous—"

"Enough," Kata interrupted. Mitch had a lower threshold of irritation than even Adler, and the last thing they needed was a knock-down argument about who got the dubious honor of Lyell's hot seat. "In case you've all forgotten, there's a tarsapien out there with a gun—one of *those* guns, Rom. Wherever he got it, we need to know everything we can about the thing if we're going to come up with a defense."

Rom's face was settling in along well-defined frown lines; but before he could reply Shannon spoke up. "Surely there are other tests and studies we can do before we have to risk damaging the gun," she said. "After all, the immediate problem seems to me to be learning how to locate or defend against the weapon, not necessarily learning all the details of how it works."

Kata hesitated ... but it wouldn't cost them more than a little time, and if they could postpone this fight until Lyell was back in charge the final decision would probably be reached with less emotional bloodshed. "All right," she said with a sigh. "Rom, why don't you take the gun back to your lab and—oh—set it up in the NMR chamber. We could have dinner while the thing's getting a good composition profile."

"I know what to do," Rom snorted, getting to his feet and starting for the door. There he paused, staring for a moment at the alien weapon still gripped in his hand. "Don't hold dinner for me—I may just wait until the analysis is finished."

He left, and Kata felt a prickling of the hairs of her neck. It was the sort of parting shot they all expected from a loner like Rom ... but there'd been something about the way he'd looked at that pistol that bothered her. *You're getting hypersensitive*, she told herself firmly. *Hypersensitive and maybe a little paranoid*.

Beside her, Mitch cleared his throat. "Shannon, is he okay?" he asked quietly. "I mean . . . he seems a little. . . ."

"Preoccupied?" Shannon suggested. Her eyes were on the empty doorway and there was a slight furrow between her eyebrows. "Yes. He does, doesn't he."

So I'm not imagining things, Kata thought. "Why did he refer to the gun as *his*?" she asked Shannon.

"Because it's like the other artifacts you're always digging up?"

"Archeologists don't become attached to the things they find," Shannon shook her head. "We nearly always wind up giving them to someone else. And Rom's always been even less possessive than most of the others I know."

"He's sure making up for it now," Adler spoke up.

Kata turned to him in some surprise—she'd almost forgotten he was there—and found him still gazing at the unconscious Lyell. "What do you mean?"

"I mean he wouldn't so much as let me *touch* that damn gun while we were working on it," the geologist said. "*He* held it under the fluoroscan, *he* took all the caliper measurements, *he* moved it between machines when necessary. All he'd let me do is punch in the data."

"Um." That *did* seem excessive, Kata thought. Still, Rom had never been at his best in group situations. "Well . . . Rom doesn't ask much of the rest of us. I suppose we can indulge him this once."

"He still shouldn't carry that gun around like a personal sidearm," Shannon said, standing up. "I'll try to get that through to him, at least. Oh, and please don't wait for me, either—I'll make a private supper for Rom and me after you've eaten." With her usual half-apologetic smile she left.

"Going to be a small group for dinner," Kata remarked, trying for a light tone. "I don't know about you two, but I'm famished."

"Yeah." Mitch got up from his seat, his eyes flicking once to Lyell and then—Kata thought—guiltily away. "My turn to cook, I suppose. I've certainly had the easiest day of everyone."

"Adler?" Kata asked, turning to the geologist. "You coming?"

"In a while," the other answered. "I'm not really hungry yet."

Kata followed his line of sight. "There's nothing you can do for him right now," she said. "I've programmed the sensors to alert me in case of any change."

"I know. I just want to sit here a while." He hesitated. "I'm not afraid of dying, Kata—I'm not, really. I just don't want to die *now*, with my career and professional reputation as low as they are. I—well, I'm sure you didn't know it, but the main reason I came to Pallas was that so many of Lyell's companions have returned from these trips to publish outstanding papers. I rather hoped some of that luck would rub off on me."

"I see," Kata said. The revelation wasn't exactly news to her—Lyell had read Adler's motives correctly right from the start—but there wasn't any point in telling him that. "Okay. Call me if he wakes up; otherwise, I'll be back in an hour."

The dinner Mitch fixed for them was quick, simple, and under other circumstances would probably have tasted quite good. But with all the strains and uncertainties of the situation buzzing around her like a swarm of sweat gnats the food went down like so much untextured protein supplement. Midway through the meal Shannon unexpectedly appeared, and though she acted civil enough the single meal she heated and sat down to eat spoke volumes about how her talk with Rom had gone. *First Adler goes all quivery*, Kata thought glumly, *and now Rom and Shannon are having some kind of polemic. Please get well quick, Lyell—I can't hang onto this tiger much longer.*

But that hope proved cruelly short-lived. Four hours later the medsensor alarms signalled Lyell's lapse into a coma, and despite Kata's best efforts his condition steadily worsened.

Two hours later, he was dead.

The morning sun was filtering through the trees by the time Kata called them together again. "The best guess I can make is that the drug in the needle interfered with Lyell's autonomic nervous system enough to cause a slowdown of his heart," she told them quietly. "I don't know whether the drug also caused the subsequent metabolism drop or whether that was a reaction to the slower heartbeat—" She caught her breath as her voice began to tremble, and Mitch winced in sympathetic pain. To have had to perform even a biochemical autopsy on a man she'd loved; wondering probably the whole time whether different treatment could have saved his life. . . . "Whichever," she continued, once again under control, "he seems to have just drifted off . . . and died."

"So your 'harmless' poison turns out not so harmless after all," Adler said heavily.

"We never said it was harmless; only that—" Kata waved a weary hand. "Oh, never mind. Rom? What more have you found out about the weapon?"

Kata had been up most of the night, handling what was undoubtedly the most emotionally draining situation of her life, and she looked it. And yet, as Mitch studied Rom, he decided the archeologist looked even worse. His face was drawn and pale, as if he'd spent a month with a debilitating illness, and even in the cool of the morning there was a sheen of perspiration on his forehead. He hadn't bothered to shave, and his eyes seemed unable to shift from their steady gaze at the floor. But his voice was clear enough, and the hand that gripped the alien pistol in his lap showed no signs of infirmity. "Nothing very useful," he said, staring at a spot near Kata's feet. "I've got the feed mechanism figured out—an unorthodox but straightforward scheme that seems totally jam-proof. I also took a sliver of metal from the underside of the barrel, and it looks like the gun's twenty to fifty years *older* than any of the ruins we've studied."

"It is?" Shannon frowned, and Mitch felt his eyebrows lift at her surprise. Freezing Adler out of the work had been par for the course with Rom; but Shannon's reaction meant he'd kept her out as well, and that was well-nigh unheard of. Mitch glanced at Kata, saw the same thought flicker briefly across her face.

"Yes," Rom said, "and it sort of blows the theory that that's where the tarsaps found them."

"Unless the settlers brought twenty-year-old guns with them," Kata suggested.

Rom snorted. "I thought we'd established these things were useless for hunting local animals. I suppose they brought a bunch of semi-infinite repeaters to use on each other?"

Kata flushed. "Maybe the different settlements weren't put up by the same people. You ever think of *that*?"

For a second Rom's eyes locked with Kata's and Mitch braced for an explosion. But apparently Rom wasn't in the mood. "Yeah, I've thought of that," he said, his gaze slipping to the floor again. "But the building styles are virtually identical. Besides, the weapons don't seem very practical for warfare."

"They kill well enough," Adler murmured.

Kata seemed to wince, and Mitch hastened to

step in. "What happened to Lyell was a fluke," he pointed out. "Anyway, there are other reasons Rom's probably right. Those needles have practically no stopping power, and they'd be useless against any kind of body armor. The gun's designed more like a child's toy than like a weapon for a trained soldier."

"Or like a test for civilization, perhaps," Shannon said.

All eyes turned to her. "What do you mean?" Mitch asked.

"I've been thinking over the same questions lately," she said, her gaze flickering around and coming to rest on the gun in her husband's hand. "Suppose you came upon a planet like Pallas and wanted to see how stable or adaptable the tarsap social structure was. One way you might do that would be to give a group of them superior tools or weapons and observe what happens."

"Shades of Satan in the garden," Mitch said. "What a rotten trick to play on a species."

"Is it?" Rom retorted. "Is it any different really than netting Swizzle and hauling him here to perform in a maze? You should know by now that biologists are always playing God with the things they find."

Mitch clamped his teeth together and counted to ten; but before he reached it Kata returned his earlier favor and took back the conversational ball. "You're suggesting, then," she said to Shannon, "that when it came time to collect the guns and leave they missed a couple?"

"Or else didn't bother to collect them at all," Shannon shrugged. "Mitch told me earlier that you'd never found a tarsap with needles in him, so maybe they never learned to shoot each other."

"Which again leaves us the question of why they shoot at *us*," Mitch reminded her.

"Maybe they just don't like people," Rom murmured. "I can sure understand that." He looked up abruptly, and for a long second the gun in his hand wavered like a snake unsure of its target. Mitch caught his breath, heard Kata do the same . . . and Rom stood up, jamming the gun back into his belt. "I need some air," he said and strode out of the room. Even before he was out of sight, he was fumbling the pistol back into his hand.

Carefully, Mitch let out the breath he'd been holding. "Is it my imagination, or was he really thinking about opening up with that thing?"

"He *was*." Adler's face was a dirty white, his preoccupation with Lyell's death momentarily pushed into the background. "And if he did he would have started with *me*. He doesn't like me— you all know that."

"Rom wouldn't do a thing like that," Shannon said. But her voice lacked conviction, and her face was almost as pale as Adler's. "He's not—I mean, he's not very sociable, but . . . did any of you see his face right then?"

The others shook their heads. "I was watching the gun," Mitch said. "Why?"

"He looked . . . confused, sort of. Or like he was in pain." Shannon looked at Kata. "I think he's coming down with something, Kata. I know you and Lyell said that shouldn't happen, but with the way he's acting and the way he looks—" She waved a hand helplessly. "I just think he's ill."

Kata nodded grimly. "He sure looks like someone with untreated intestinal flu," she agreed. "And it's not completely impossible for one of us to catch something here; the different surface protein cues keep the local bacteria and viruses from entrenching themselves into our systems, but the DNA and RNA structures are similar enough for a rogue plasmid or something to conceivably make trouble." She looked at the doorway. "I'd better try and talk him into an examination."

But Rom didn't like Kata much; and with the shorter fuse this illness seemed to have given him. . . . "I'll go," Mitch said, getting quickly to his feet.

"You sure?" Kata asked, her voice a mixture of relief and guilty concern.

"Sure. Rom doesn't seem as angry at botanists this semester as he is at biologists. Anyway, I can always remind him I supported one of his arguments a few minutes ago. You want a full medcheck?"

"If you can get it," Kata said. "But don't push too hard."

"No kidding." Wondering briefly about the stupid things done in the name of chivalry, Mitch went in search of Rom.

He found the other, predictably enough, in the archeology lab, staring out the window and ignoring the bits and pieces of ancient rubble laid out around the room. "Mind if I come in?" he asked from the doorway.

Rom half turned, then resumed his outward gaze. "Don't touch anything," he said shortly.

Swallowing, Mitch stepped inside and closed the door. "How are you feeling?" he asked casually, moving carefully toward the other.

"Why?"

"To be honest, you look like you're coming down with something and we're worried about you."

Rom snorted. "Afraid I'll pass it on to you?"

"Not especially," Mitch said, determined not to let the other get to him. "We're more afraid of what it might do to *you*."

"Oh, come on—none of you cares what happens to me."

"Not even Shannon? She's the one who suggested—"

"Shannon can go swim an ocean with the rest of you," Rom snapped.

Surprise tangled Mitch's tongue, cutting off the rest of his sentence. As uncaring as Rom was about everyone else's sensitivities, Shannon had always before been exempted from the verbal abuse. To hear that immunity crumbling was in a way more disquieting even than the other's fixation with the alien weapon.

And Rom knew it. "Bothers you, does it?" he said as Mitch was still trying to find something to say. "Shows you've never tried marriage yourself. Half the time you'd be better off rooming with your worst enemy. At least then you'd know exactly where you stand."

If things are that bad . . . ? Mitch wondered. *No. They've just had a fight, that's all. That and/or this illness.* "Deep down you know better than that," he said, hoping it didn't sound as trite to Rom as it did to him. "We care about you—all of us—and Shannon most of all."

"Deep down," Rom countered softly, "you're all my enemies. Tell me, do you believe in ghosts?"

The verbal blockbusters were coming too fast. "I . . . don't know," he managed. "Do you?"

"Not really. But I think there are ghosts on Pallas. I can . . . I can feel them, almost. Hear them, too."

Oh, terrific. "What do they say?" he asked, choosing the safest response he could think of.

"They tell me I'm in danger." Rom's voice was calm, almost as if he were reciting from a stone tablet he'd dug up. "There are enemies here, enemies I have to try and fight. To drive away. We did that once, a long time ago."

"We?" The word slipped out before Mitch could stop it.

"I mean *they*," Rom replied. "They. The abandoned ruins are proof of that, I think. Someone tried to settle here and the ones with the guns drove them off."

Mitch's mouth was beginning to feel dry. "That's not what you were saying about the ruins before."

"I didn't know about the guns before, did I?" Rom retorted with a touch of his old acerbity. "Anyway, it's obvious now."

"Not to me." This whole line of conversation was becoming more than a little creepy, but somehow Mitch had the feeling he'd better stick with it as long as he could. "You said the people who built the settlements were gone, but then you also said they were still here."

"No. I said there were *enemies* here. Not the same ones that were here before . . . well, sort of the same . . . no. . . ." Rom trailed off, and for a long minute stared out the window in silence. "I know who they are," he murmured at last, almost inaudibly. "If necessary. . . ."

He shook suddenly, like a dog throwing off bathwater. "So what did you want, anyway?" he asked.

"Uh. . . ." It took Mitch a second to remember. "I think it'd be a good idea to run a quick medcheck on you. In case you *have* picked up some bug."

"Shannon's idea, right?"

"Sort of a group consensus, actually," Mitch told

him, wondering if he should be lying about such things. Rom's personality was shifting too rapidly for Mitch's meager knowledge of psychology to keep up with. "We all care about you—"

"Yeah, sure. All right; if it'll get you all off my back—" Hauling himself out of his chair, Rom swung to face Mitch . . . and froze.

For that first, awful instant Mitch thought the most horrible creatures from all the *City of Night* shows he'd ever seen had silently lined up behind him. But Rom's eyes were locked squarely on Mitch's face; and the other's look of horror, hatred, and fear was directed squarely toward him. Peripherally, he saw the gun in Rom's hand snap up into firing position, but for once even that couldn't distract his attention. Eyes fixed on Rom's, unable to move and knowing it would be useless anyway, he waited with tensed stomach muscles for the needles to cut into him.

They never did. Slowly, almost unwillingly, Rom turned his head; and as his gaze broke from Mitch's face his body seemed to sag. "No," he growled as Mitch shook off his own paralysis and took a step forward. "I'm all right—don't *touch* me. Go ahead; I'll follow you to the bio lab."

With that pistol trained at my back. . . . But Rom had already had ample opportunity to gun him down. Swallowing painfully, Mitch turned and headed toward the door.

His original hope—*was that really only five minutes ago?*—had been that Kata and the others would clear out of the lab before he and Rom arrived. Now, after all that had happened, he hoped fervently that Kata, at least, would still be there. The blood/tissue analyzer, poor cousin to the Diagnizer machines in common use these days, was easy enough to set up for a medcheck . . . but adjusting it to administer medication took more knowledge than Mitch possessed.

But Kata hadn't been around to see Rom's latest reaction . . . and the bio lab was thus indeed deserted when they arrived.

The analyzer took ten minutes to collect its data, and it was among the longest ten-minute blocks Mitch had ever lived through. Rom was cooperative enough—almost docile, in fact—as Mitch got him into the chair and hooked up the twin armbands. But the other's carefully averted eyes and restless fingering of the alien pistol were continual reminders of the emotions bubbling a millimeter beneath the surface. Twice during that time Mitch reached silently for the keyboard, prepared to gamble that he could locate a strong enough sedative among the machine's pharmaceuticals and flood Rom's system with it before the other could figure out what was happening and riddle him with needles. But both times he withdrew his hand, letting it curl into an impotent fist at his side. Fast sedatives were generally dangerous ones as well, and there was no guarantee whatsoever that Kata would be able to neutralize that kind of overdose before it proved fatal.

And so he watched silently as the machine finished its job, then helped Rom off with the armbands. And then, because he couldn't think of any way to stop him, he let the other leave.

It was early evening when Kata finally pushed her chair back from her lab table and rubbed her eyes. "That's it," she told Mitch. "I'm out of ideas on what to try next."

Mitch nodded; he'd spent most of the day looking over her shoulder as she ran her tests, and he likewise saw the study at a dead end. The nucleic acid anomalies in Rom's system had shown up quickly enough, but tracking down any likely carrier—or even pinpointing the foreign molecules themselves—had proved impossible. "You're sure we're not dealing with a hitherto quiescent Terrestrial virus or something?"

"Positive—the analyzer would have picked that up right away. No, there's something new in there . . . and the crazy thing is it acts like it just dropped out of the sky into his bloodstream. No broken virus fragments, no plasmids or plasmid hosts— nothing."

"Could he have inhaled something?" Mitch asked, though he was pretty sure he knew the answer.

"There's no way a naked nucleic acid could survive long enough in an unprotected environment," she said, confirming his guess.

"How about dug into a crevice or something in the gun?"

"It'd still have to get through his skin." She frowned. "Maybe we should check his hands for cuts or scrapes."

"I'd recommend waiting until he's asleep tonight," Mitch said, grimacing at the memory of their last encounter that morning. "You still haven't told me what you're going to do with him, by the way."

"You mean sedate him or not?" Kata shook her head wearily. "Mitch, I know you're not given to flights of fancy and all, but you have to understand that I can't do something like that on the basis of a single subjective feeling that Rom's somehow becoming dangerous. If I can get something— *anything*—objective from this machine then maybe we can risk it. But otherwise—" She waved her hands helplessly.

Mitch nodded, tight-lipped, and stared for a moment out the lab's window. The sun had set within the past few minutes, and the forest beyond their herbicide ring was darkening rapidly against the blue sky above. "Whatever's wrong with Rom," he said, "we still aren't any closer to solving our original problem. You given any thought to that?"

"The armed tarsapiens?" She sighed. "Yes, but you couldn't tell from the results. Every idea I've come up with so far has had one or more flaws in it. We haven't got anything that would make realistic body armor, we don't know enough about tarsapien physiology to come up with a safe repellent, and we've already proved we can't locate the guns themselves from any distance. I guess we're just going to have to hole up here until the ship comes back, dashing out to the sheds for food as we need it and letting everything else slide."

"And hope the tarsaps with the guns aren't fast enough on the uptake to pick us off each time we run outside." He shook his head. "I don't know, though. Three months cooped up here—we'll be at each other's throats within a week."

"Especially without Lyell here to smooth the ruffled feathers," Kata murmured.

He looked at her closely; but she wasn't, as he'd expected, on the verge of tears. *Holding up well*, he thought. *Unless this is going to hit her as a delayed reaction.*

Behind him the door opened, and he turned as Shannon stepped into the lab. "Have you seen Rom anywhere?" she asked, her voice tight.

"Not since the medcheck this morning," Mitch said. "What's the matter?"

"I can't find him," she said, her eyes darting around as if he might have somehow sneaked in without their knowledge. "I've been through the entire building and I simply can't find him."

"That's ridiculous," Mitch said . . . but even as he spoke that unearthly look of Rom's floated back up from his memory. "Have you tried calling him?" he asked, trying to keep his sudden chill from showing up in his voice.

"He left his comm on our bed," Shannon said. "And his Lostproof, too."

"He's gone outside." It wasn't what Mitch had planned to say, but suddenly all of it clicked together in some recess of his mind and the words simply forced their way out. "He's taken the gun to go fight the 'enemies.' Come on, Kata—we've got to get him back inside."

"Wait a minute," Shannon said, grabbing at Mitch's arm as he and Kata headed for the door. "What enemies? What's going on?"

"I'll explain later," Kata told her. "Right now we've got to act fast. The lasers are locked up in the—wait a second." She raised her communicator, punched a button. "Adler, this is Kata. Are you still carrying one of the lasers? . . . Good. Meet us at the outside door right away."

Mitch half expected to see Rom lying face-down halfway across the herbicide ring, but that fear at least wasn't realized. *Unless he's on the far side of one of the sheds*, he grimaced, studying as much of the forest as he could see through the small window. *And there's only one way to find out.* "Adler!" he shouted over his shoulder. "Hurry it up!"

"What do you see?" Kata demanded, trying to squeeze in for a look.

"Nothing—but that doesn't mean much," he told

her shortly. "I'm going to go out and see if I can find him. Adler!—there you are," he added as the geologist puffed into sight behind Shannon. "I'm going out. Stand here in the doorway, and if I yell start shooting into the trees. *High* into the trees—don't forget I'll be out there, too."

"What? Wait a minute—"

"Just do it." Wondering whether he was being heroic or just stupid, Mitch eased the door open and slipped outside—

And was barely two paces away from the building when the needles began whining all around him.

The smart move, he quickly realized, would have been to beat a hasty retreat; but momentum and surprise kept him moving forward, and seconds later he was flat up against the closest shed, gulping air and waiting with itchy skin for the needles to find their mark.

But, surprisingly, they didn't. For a few more seconds the hail of impacts against his shelter continued, then ceased. Behind him, he could hear a sort of muffled confusion at the doorway, but no laser flashes lit up the dusk. "Rom?" Mitch called. "Rom, can you hear me? You're in danger out here—you've got to come back in." He paused, listening, but his bellow had silenced even the animals in the area. *Already too far away to hear?* he wondered tensely. *Or did the tarsaps already get him?* "Rom!" he shouted, louder this time. *Would he have headed for one of the ruins? And if so, which? We'll have to take the* Sunray *up, try to spot him—*

"You'll never get me, Drzewicki!"

The reply would have made Mitch jump if he hadn't been pressed so hard against the shed. Rom's

voice was firm and clear, with nothing of an injured man about it . . . and it came from no more
than fifteen meters away. "Go away or I'll kill you.
I mean it!"

Mitch licked his lips without obvious effect.
"Rom, I want to help you," he called. Out of the
corner of his eye he saw the muzzle of Adler's laser
poke cautiously around the doorway. *Not now, you
idiot*, he thought furiously; but there was nothing
he could do but try and hold Rom's attention.
"We'll help you hunt down the enemies," he improvised rapidly. "You're right, they're still out
there—"

A clatter of needles on metal cut him off, and
when he glanced around the laser had vanished
back inside. "You must really think I'm a fool,"
Rom snarled. "You don't think I can recognize
enemies when I see them? I'm wise to you now,
Drzewicki—you won't fool me again."

This was starting to get sticky. "Rom, no one
here's trying to fool you, but if you want me to go
back inside I'll do so. Just hold your fire, okay?"
He paused. "Okay?"

"Why?—so you can plot against me?" Rom
answered, punctuating his words with a few more
shots. The ricochets seemed to be changing direction, Mitch noticed uneasily. Was Rom working
his way around the circle to a point where he
could get a clear shot?

The unexpected beep of his communicator made
him start. Moving as little as possible, he snared
the instrument. "What?" he whispered.

"Get ready to move," Kata's voice said tensely.
"I'm going to throw a flare out, try and dazzle
him. When I do, make for the door. Got it?"

"Yeah. Hurry it up—he's getting ready to nail me to the shed."

His answer was a faint creak of hinges; and with the sputter of burning magnesium the clearing was abruptly bathed in blue-white light. Shoving off the shed wall, Mitch threw himself into a desperate sprint toward the gaping door. A wild spray of needles spattered all around him, but none of them connected, and with one final surge he hurled himself through the shadowy rectangle and into Kata's waiting arms. Someone slammed the door behind him; and for the moment, at least, he was safe.

"Mitch, what's happening out there?" Shannon asked as he and Kata regained their balance. "Did you remind him there are tarsaps with guns on the loose?"

"The tarsaps are welcome to him," Mitch panted. "I'm sorry; I didn't mean that—but it was *Rom*, not any tarsap, who was shooting at me. He's gone crazy—thinks we're his enemies." He looked at Kata. "Could you hear what he was saying?"

"I got most of it," she nodded grimly. "I'm sorry Mitch; I should have listened when you first told me about him."

"There wasn't much we could have done even then—" Mitch broke off and took a long step backwards, intercepting Shannon as she started for the door. "Hold it; you're not going out there."

"Get out of my way," Shannon said. Her voice, no louder than a whisper, had a touch of hysteria building at its edge. "He's my husband—I've got to help him."

"You can't do anything for him now," Kata told her firmly, stepping to Mitch's side. "We have to figure out what's happened before we can help him."

"What do you mean, *what's happened*? He's ill, that's what, and we have to cure him." Abruptly, Shannon pushed, sending Mitch staggering back. "Let me go to him—I'll get him back inside."

"No!" For Mitch it was a tossup whether Shannon going out or Rom coming in would be a greater disaster; but for now, at least, both would be averted. Even as Shannon tried to push past Kata, Adler reached from behind to pinion the archeologist's arms. For a moment she thrashed in his grip; but as Kata and Mitch moved in to assist she abruptly gave up and stood quietly, tears welling up in her eyes.

"Don't you understand?" she half demanded, half pleaded. "He *needs* me."

"Come on, Shannon," Kata said, taking her arm and walking her down the hall toward the bio lab. "Let me get you something to calm you down. You're not helping Rom like this."

They disappeared around the curve, and Adler turned haunted eyes on Mitch. "What the hell's *happening* here, anyway?"

"You know about as much as I do," Mitch answered shortly, stooping to study the door's latch mechanism. It should be possible, he decided, to jam the thing well enough to keep Rom from sneaking in in the middle of the night. "I'm going to need some wire and a flat chunk of metal the size of a—"

"First Lyell gets killed, and now Rom goes totally rock-happy," Adler went on as if Mitch hadn't spoken, "and all on a supposedly safe world. How are we going to look to the rest of the scientific community?"

"We're going to look dead if we don't get this door sealed," Mitch snapped. "Now go get me—"

"Better dead than having to live through the end of a career," Adler murmured. Mitch opened his mouth, but before he could speak Adler's eyes seemed to refocus on him. "What did you say you wanted?"

"Some strong wire and a chunk of metal the size of a microscope slide," Mitch repeated. "Try Rom's tool kit—and leave the laser here."

Adler nodded and headed off. Clutching the laser like a good-luck talisman, Mitch waited tensely by the door, belatedly wishing he'd sent Kata for the equipment instead. But Adler was back within five minutes with a double handful of wire, metal chips, and tools, and in ten minutes more the door was as secure as Mitch could make it. "At least he won't break in without making a lot of noise," he concluded, testing the latch one final time. "Come on—let's go find Kata and Shannon and try to figure out what we're going to do."

"If you don't mind, I think I'll check first to make sure Rom didn't unlatch one of the windows for himself," Adler said, that distant look drifting onto his face again. "I'm . . . not likely to be much help just now."

With an effort Mitch controlled his tongue. "All right. But don't take too long. We're going to need your help."

A bitter smile tugged briefly at Adler's lips. "Sure. I'll do what I can . . . whatever little that is."

Hiding his grimace, Mitch nodded and left. He could vaguely understand the demons Adler was wrestling with, but the geologist would just have to handle the battle by himself.

Kata was alone in the bio lab when Mitch arrived,

staring grimly at her computer display. "Shannon?" he asked, pulling a chair up beside her.

"I gave her a strong sedative and put her to bed. What's the situation out there?"

"Not good," Mitch admitted, eyeing the screen. "We've got the door sealed against casual entry; but with Rom in a position to keep us away from our supplies, locking him out seems sort of futile. I've been trying to figure out a way to sneak out in the dead of night to collect some food, but if Rom anticipates us properly whoever goes out there won't have a chance."

"Well . . . we've got a few days' worth of food already inside—more, if we ration it. Rom's got to sleep *some*time."

"Does he? We don't have any idea yet what's happened to him. If he could be turned into a homicidal maniac, why not into a sleepwalker with the same qualities, too?" Mitch nodded at the screen. "Rom's psych profile?"

"Yes," Kata nodded. "I was hoping to find some basis for his actions—some latent paranoia that had cancered out of control, maybe. But aside from his well-known loner tendencies nothing seems particularly abnormal."

"I doubt if Lyell would have brought him along if there'd been anything obvious." He hesitated. "Stop me if this sounds weird . . . but we know those guns were made by some alien race, and I told you Rom thought he was hearing ghosts. Could . . . well, *something* have entered him and taken control?"

Kata shook her head. "I don't believe in ghosts, alien or otherwise."

"Maybe they weren't a corporeal race to begin with," he suggested, a bit warmly. It wasn't *that* ridiculous an idea. "It's possible they were pure spirit or pure energy or—"

"They fought with needle guns."

"Oh. Right."

Reaching forward, Kata blanked Rom's medical record from the screen and typed up a new file. "That gun's the key, Mitch—it's *got* to be the gun." On cue, an x-ray view of the pistol appeared on the screen. "He's the only one who ever touched it, and all this started at the same time." Abruptly, she called up a file index and leaned forward to study it. "On a hunch ... Rom must have taken some ultra-high-resolution pictures. Let's see...." A new picture appeared and she centered the screen on one edge of the grip. "Let's try about a thousand magnification...." She pressed some keys, the picture changed—and Mitch inhaled sharply.

The smooth edge had become a gently curving hill forested with squat but exquisitely sharp needles. A glance at the scale confirmed his first guess: Rom would probably never have felt them poking into his skin. "I think," he said, "we've found the delivery system for those nucleic acids in Rom's blood."

"I think you're right," Kata agreed. "That angle must mean we're focused on one of the indented finger grips. Let's just confirm...." She tapped controls and the image rotated a few degrees. "Yeah, the needles are hollow, all right. Probably take from that reservoir around the magazine. Damn! Well, I guess that answers the *how*. All we need now are the *what* and *why*." She drummed her fingers against the table. "And for at least the *what* we're going to have to figure out what that reservoir contains. I don't suppose you have any idea of how to write an interior-analysis program for x-ray diffraction data?"

Mitch snorted. "Not hardly. But maybe we can get a sample directly."

"From where?"

"From the gun's previous owner." Mitch waved back toward the lab's refrigerator.

"The tarsapien! Of course—I'd forgotten all about him. As a matter of fact. . . ."

She busied herself with the keyboard again. Mitch, too, hadn't thought about tarsapiens lately, but now he looked over at the corner where Swizzle was squatting in a precarious-looking position on top of his jungle gym. "Swizzle seems to have loosened up from a couple of nights ago," he commented.

"Yes," Kata agreed. "Whatever was in that danger call he reacted to, he's apparently decided since then that we're okay." Her fingers paused, and Mitch looked back in time to see her blink something from her eyes. "More evidence of intelligent modification of instinctual patterns . . . but I'll never get the chance to convince Lyell now. Never mind. Here's the biochemical comparison of the dead tarsapien with Swizzle . . . yes! Look—nucleic acid differences. Now, if only the molecules didn't degrade too much before the data was taken. . . ."

In that, though, they were only half lucky. The odd nucleic acids had indeed begun to unravel, and their concentrations were far too low for a composite/extrapolation to be made. "Well?" Mitch asked as a diagram of an incomplete molecule slowly rotated on the screen. "Can you make any guesses as to what it's supposed to do?"

"I think so," she said slowly. "That tail looks like a tag to get the molecule through the tarsapien brain-blood barrier, which implies we're on the right track. I've got a reasonable data base on their brain chemistry; and if worst comes to worst I suppose we could try and synthesize some and give it to Swizzle."

"And then we come up with a way to block whatever it does?"

"Starnation." Kata shook her head. "I can't even think that far ahead right now. Let me do what I can with this and we'll go on from there." Abruptly, she looked around. "Where's Adler?"

Mitch frowned, glancing back at the door. "I told him to join us here. He's probably still wandering around pretending he's on guard while he tries to figure out how he's going to explain all of this to his colleagues."

"What's to explain? None of this is his fault."

"*I* know that. But *you* try telling him his life is more important than his reputation."

Kata said a word Mitch had never heard her use before. "Great. Just great. Between him and Shannon we're really rising to the challenge. Well, Mitch, until the rest of our team get their brains back on-line I guess it's up to us."

"Looks that way," he agreed. *So here we are,* he thought, *thrown together in battle against something that'll probably kill us if we can't figure it out damn fast. How the* hell *do fiction writers make this sort of thing sound so romantic?*

But he had too many serious questions on his mind to bother with trivial ones as well. "Okay," he sighed. "What can I do to help?"

Kata had known on an intellectual level since her senior year at college—and on a far more personal level since her first grueling year of grad school—that even the safest of sleep-substitute drugs extracted their price in both subtle and not-so-subtle ways. Once she'd finally accepted this truth she had made it part of her personal rule book to avoid such drugs like Sirian leopard snakes. But rules were servants, not master, and it was almost without notice—let alone qualm—that she spent the next day and a half drugged to the eyeballs as she worked to reconstruct and understand the enigmatic molecule that seemed to be at the bottom of Rom's psychotic behavior. On one level, the results were worth the price, as her studies began to bear fruit . . . but on another, it meant that when Adler's fuse ran down that afternoon she was in the worst possible shape to handle it.

The explosion occurred an hour after lunch—a meal which Kata had taken care not to dawdle over. Adler's growing touchiness and barely controlled nervous energy were hard enough to take by themselves, but when contrasted against Shannon's almost ghostly quietude the effect was to leave Kata feeling positively twitchy. Mitch, who usually managed to be an island of relative stability at such gatherings, was back in his room catching a couple of hours' sleep, and Kata had therefore stayed in the common room only as long as basic civility and hunger required before escaping back to the lab.

She was at her table, sweating over a particularly tricky simulation, when Adler stalked in. "I need some ten percent hydrochloric acid," he growled, walking over to the chemical cabinet. "Where do you keep it?"

"Number six locker; out the door and turn left," she replied without looking up. "Help yourself."

A second later she literally jumped out of her

chair as the crash of the cabinet door against the wall echoed through the room. "Adler!" she yelped.

He was fumbling with the back row of bottles, his hand trembling. "The hydrochloric, damn it!" he demanded.

"I told you I don't have any," she snapped, dimly aware that she was losing her temper but not really caring. "What are you trying to do, earn yourself a vacation in a psycho-ward snuggy?"

His face darkened. "You'd like that, wouldn't you? You'd like to be able to spread the blame around to the rest of us. You imply in your report that I went rock-happy and maybe they won't notice how badly *you* botched things."

"*I* botched things? What are you talking about?"

"Not so eager to be in charge now, um? Now that Lyell's dead and Rom might as well be and you've got us cooped up in here like your pet tarsap while the whole project turns to organic fertilizer?"

"I am trying," she said icily, "to keep all of us alive. If this double-damned project and your triple-damned reputation are that important to you, then why don't you go out there and bring Rom back in?"

"I might just do that," he snarled. "You'd at least have to list me as a hero if I did." Turning, he stomped back out.

Slowly, the blind fury died within Kata, and as it did so she started to shake with reaction and guilt. *Some terrific leader I am,* she berated herself. *Lyell wouldn't have blown up like that—he'd have let Adler drain off some of his tension and that would have been the end of it. Obvious thing to do.* But instead she'd fought back, and in the process simply added to both parties' resentment. *I can't believe I did something that stupid. Stupid* and—

Did I really suggest he go out after Rom? Oh, my God—

She didn't even stop to put her half-finished program on standby as she took off toward the exit as fast as the curving corridor permitted. If Adler was feeling as irrational as he'd sounded. . . .

But the exit door was still sealed when she arrived. For a moment she leaned against it, catching her breath and feeling a little silly. Of *course* Adler wasn't crazy enough to—

"Out of my way, Kata," a voice behind her growled, spinning her around and kicking her heart back into high gear.

Adler had put on gloves, hat, and the heaviest coat he had, and had a hip pack belted to his left side. With the laser riding his other hip he looked like a child's version of a Starlane Patroller, and under other conditions the effect might have been laughable.

But there wasn't anything amusing about the expression on his face.

"Adler, this isn't going to do any good," Kata said carefully, staying where she was. "You don't know anything about hunting animals, let alone people; and even if you did Rom's got a flashless weapon and his pick of places to ambush you from. All you can possibly do is get yourself shot."

"You agreed yourself that what happened to Lyell was an unlikely accident," Adler pointed out. There was a deadly calm to his voice that suggested reasoning with him was a waste of time. "A few needles, if he gets that lucky, won't slow me down much—and my weapon *is* ultimately superior to his."

"Lyell's death was an accident because tarsapiens don't have the eye-hand coordination to be marksmen," Kata retorted. "Rom does. Furthermore, he also knows where the vital organs are, and he's had plenty of time to practice his shooting. Chances are good he'll kill you before you even get a shot off."

Adler's lip twitched. "And if he does? My career will never have time to recover from this trip, Kata. I might as well die here as live out my last few years in some tenured dead-end position somewhere."

"Adler, that's—" She broke off before the work *crazy* could slip out and tried again. "Look, this isn't going to be nearly the drag on your reputation that you seem to think. The alien gun actually qualifies as pretty exciting stuff—"

"For you, Mitch, and Shanon, perhaps," Adler interrupted her. "But for me? No. I'll just suffer under the sensationalistic hammer without so much as a new geological formation to balance it with." Again, his lip twitched in an almost-smile. "I've seen it happen before; been the target of it, in fact, more than once. Colleagues—people you thought were your friends—concentrating on everything but the paper you're presenting or the results you're reporting on. 'But what *really* happened on Draconis Minor, Dr. Zimmerman?' 'Do these two really fight as much in private as they do in the journals?' " 'How were *you* involved in that incident with the site break-in?' I can already hear what they'll ask me about Pallas: 'So things were falling apart, eh? What did *you* do to help out? Oh, you stayed in your room and sorted rocks? How *help*ful of you.' "

"Adler—"

"No, Kata. When they ask those questions I intend to have answers for them." Carefully, he drew his laser and settled it firmly into his gloved fist. "Please; just go away. I really don't want to have to hurt you."

Wordlessly, Kata moved aside. Adler knelt by the door and within half a minute had undone the makeshift lock. "Seal it up behind me," he instructed her, getting back to his feet. "If I get Rom I'll call you." Taking a deep breath, he abruptly swung open the door and slipped outside.

Only then did Kata's drug-fogged mind think to call for help.

Mitch was obviously still half asleep when he answered her call; but he wasn't that way for long. "Stay there," he told her when she'd given him a two-sentence summary of the situation. "If anyone heads for the door, holler. I'll get the other laser and meet you there in a couple of minutes."

He was there in less time than that, the weapon in his hand forming an odd contrast to his robe and disheveled appearance. "I've got Shannon warming up the Lostproof monitor," he said, glancing out the window. "Did he get to the trees?"

"I don't know—he broke to the left just past the sheds. Mitch, I'm sorry—"

"Never mind the brow-beating," he cut her off. "Get back there and help Shannon. And leave your comm open."

It was a slow and painful wait. Despite his apparent recklessness Adler wasn't simply beating the bushes and waiting for Rom to attack. His blip on the Lostproof screen showed he was in fact making his way slowly and—presumably—quietly through the forest, halting occasionally in the shadow of a tree before continuing his rough spiral around the clearing. Each time he stopped Kata's stomach tightened, relaxing again only when he started moving again.

He was almost halfway around when his blip abruptly threw itself sideways. "Mitch!" Kata barked. "I think he's been hit."

"Where?" her communicator snapped.

"Thirty-five meters by forty-two degrees," she read off the coordinates.

"Okay. Come here and take the laser—I'm going to take the *Sunray* up."

"But *Rom*—"

"If he's with Adler I've got a clear path," Mitch cut in impatiently. "Hurry up; I don't want to just leave the laser here on the floor."

She hurried, and two minutes later the *Sunray* hummed its way overhead in the direction of Adler's motionless Lostproof blip. A minute after that Mitch called in the bad news.

"There's just no way at all for me to get in on top of him," he reported tensely. "I'm going to have to put down and go out to get him."

"No," Kata snapped, the pain of the decision twisting like a knife in her gut. "It's too risky— you'd be a walking target out there."

"Kata, I can't just *leave* him—"

"You have to. Maybe Adler's not dead; if so, you may have distracted Rom's attention enough to let him escape. But if you wait too long Rom'll have time to get back before you—and he'll then be in perfect position to shoot you when you try to come back inside."

For a second she thought he was going to refuse . . . and that she would be forced to add another death to her conscience. "All right," he sighed. "I'm coming in."

*   *   *

She sat in the common room for a long time after Mitch made it in, staring into a cup of coffee and trying hard not to break down into borderline-hysterical sobbing. *Those damn drugs*, she told herself over and over; but she and the others knew better than that. Kata simply didn't have what it took to play chess with people's lives.

Oh, Lyell—why did you have to will this burden to me?

"That coffee's going to curdle if you don't drink it," Shannon murmured from across the table.

The attempted humor deserved an attempted smile, which was about all Kata could manage. *At least I've got Shannon acting human again*, she thought, sipping her cooling drink. *Maybe if I'd fallen apart sooner none of this would have happened. Is that an irrational thought?*

"Nothing seems to be moving out there," Mitch said as he came into the room and sat down next to Kata. He'd dressed and run a comb through his hair, but such trappings of normalcy merely emphasized the tension lines about his eyes. "I can't tell for sure, but it looks like Adler's Lostproof blip may have moved slightly. That could mean he's still alive and conscious."

"You can't go out after him," Kata said dully.

"I wasn't going to ask." He paused, and she could feel his eyes on her. "You made the right decision, you know. Make that *decisions*, plural. There wasn't a thing in the world you could have done for Rom, Adler was stir-crazy beyond rational argument, and I probably *would* have gotten myself perforated if I'd tried to get him into the *Sunray*."

"You pointed out to me two days ago that we'd have trouble if I kept everyone indoors," Kata said, perversely refusing to be comforted. "I should have listened, tried to do something about it."

"There wasn't anything you could have done," Shannon put in quietly. "In fact, I rather think driving us stir-crazy was the basic idea behind all this."

"All what?" Mitch frowned. "You think someone's out there trying to drive us off Pallas?"

Shannon shook her head. "Not us personally; and I don't think anyone's actually watching us. What I meant was that whoever left the guns here did so specifically to keep people like us off the planet."

Kata's first reaction was incredulity . . . but even as she opened her mouth to voice her doubts the pieces started clicking into place. Multiple-shot, maintenance-free weapons in the hands of native animals; combined with the lab results of the past few hours—

Mitch might have read her mind. "Kata, have you got anything on that odd nucleic acid yet?"

"Yes." She took a deep breath. "The results aren't complete by any means, but it appears the drug is designed to teach any tarsapien who finds the gun how to use it. And, if Shannon's right, exactly who to shoot it at."

"It *what*?" Shannon whispered. "How? I mean, memory alteration methods are supposed to require huge temporal-lobe induction machines."

"Ours do," Kata acknowledged. "The—what do I call them? How about the 'Gunners'? The Gunners seem to have come up with a method using nothing but a sequence of enzymes to stimulate and guide the false memory development. How they provide the motivation I don't yet know, but it would have to couple a recognition pattern with either a glandular or mental fear reaction and then induce the proper physical motions. Probably need a reinforcement mechanism, as well—" She cut off abruptly.

"Sounds awfully dicey," Mitch shook his head. "To coordinate that many different activities within such a short time of each other?"

Kata shrugged. "I argue from the results that they managed it."

"Even worse, how could they possibly set up a recognition pattern that way? You'd need sensory input of *some* kind—" He paused. "Oh. Sure. All of that winds up as chemical signals anyway. Why not just skip the middleman?"

"That seems to be the case," Kata nodded. "Part of the molecule appears designed to break away along with one of the several tags. The tags on my sample have degraded pretty far, but the one that's most intact looks suspiciously like it should attach itself to a group of receptor sites found mainly in the brain's visual cortex."

"Human or tarsap?" Shannon asked.

"Either, as it turns out." Kata hesitated, then continued. "I'm afraid that's what's happened to Rom. We must look enough like the Gunners' enemies to have triggered the chemical sequence."

Mitch bit at his lip. "If that's true, though, why'd they wait six months before they started shooting?"

"Probably took that long for the ones with the guns to get here once they learned about us," Kata shrugged. "Remember Swizzle's morning news service? I guess the tarsapien information network is even more efficient than I thought."

"Um. That would explain why Rom and Shannon didn't get shot at out at the various ruins, too, wouldn't it? They didn't spend enough time anywhere for the gun carriers to catch up with them."

Shannon's eyes held a faraway look. "That morning—the last one he was here—Rom looked like he hadn't slept all night, and I suggested a shower and shave might make him feel better. He took a shower, but didn't comb his hair and absolutely refused to shave. I thought he was just being grouchy ... but now it makes sense. He didn't want to look in a mirror."

"Because he knew he'd see an enemy." Mitch looked at Kata. "So you're saying what we had here was a sort of wind-up proxy war. The Gunners didn't want to risk their own lives pushing their enemies off Pallas, so they armed the local animals and turned *them* loose to do it." He shivered visibly. "What a cold-blooded scheme."

"It gets worse," Kata sighed. "Remember Rom's report?—the guns arrived here long *before* the settlements were put up. The Gunners weren't throwing anyone off; they were making sure no one showed up in the first place."

"Disputed planet? But then why didn't the Gunners move in to colonize?"

"Maybe they lost the war. Or maybe they never wanted Pallas in the first place."

"Meaning?"

"Well, one of the first things *we* did here was make sure the forest didn't get too close to our buildings," Kata said, waving out the window at the herbicide ring. "Maybe we're sitting on part of the Gunners' own cordon sanitaire."

There was a long silence. "Incredible," Mitch

said at last, shaking his head. "Seal off a whole planet—maybe a whole *group* of planets—to keep your opponents off your doorstep. You know, I never thought about it before ... but have you noticed that the gun's finger notches angle upwards, and that the angle is steeper for the lower notches? Means a creature with a small hand and thin fingers will get about as comfortable a grip as one with large hands and thicker fingers."

"Which implies they can parachute the things wholesale onto practically any world with DNA-based life and *some* species there will likely be able to use them," Kata said. "In fact, I'd bet even a tentacle or prehensile tail could get an adequate grip. Add an attractive scent or coloring to the guns to get the whole thing started, and the system probably perpetuates itself—you can just go away and forget it. Makes sense. Makes a *lot* of sense."

"So what are we going to do about Rom?" Shannon asked.

The grand vision of interstellar rivalry collapsed like a popped balloon back into the life-and-death problem at hand. "I don't know yet," Kata admitted. "Bear in mind that we're not really fighting Rom, or even the tarsapiens—we're fighting the damn aliens who built these guns in the first place."

"But it's Rom who's actually shooting at us," Shannon sighed, adding the part Kata had intended to leave unsaid. "I understand. What can I do?"

Back to being in charge, Kata thought, the reminder an almost tangible constriction around her chest. "Stay by the Lostproof and watch both Adler and the transponder in his laser; holler if either of them moves. Mitch and I'll get back to work, see what we can come up with."

Mitch was silent all the way back to the lab, but once inside he let out a hissing breath. "The laser," he muttered. "Somehow, I never even thought of that. What are we going to do if Rom starts shooting at us with *that*?"

"I don't think he will," Kata sighed, slumping into her chair. The drug-enhanced depression was fading, to be replaced by fatigue. "Aside from the fact that carrying it lets us trace him . . . well, I didn't want to mention this in front of Shannon, but the Gunners did indeed add a cute reinforcement kicker to their training method. I've located a set of low-power electrodes on the grip and firing button that seem to send signals along the sensory nerves to the brain, where they induce their versatile little molecule to briefly jump enkephalin production."

"Like a poke in the pleasure center," Mitch grimaced. "No wonder he wouldn't let anyone take it away from him. That sort of stimulation is supposed to be pretty addictive, too, isn't it?"

"It sure is." Kata shook her head. "Mitch, we're in way over our heads here. How can we possibly fight aliens who we've never even met? We don't have anything but the vaguest idea what they were trying to accomplish with their guns."

"Well. . . ." Mitch bit at his lip as he gazed out the window. "It's pretty clear that, whatever the details, the scheme *did* work—remember Shannon telling us the ruins were abruptly abandoned? Now, similar biochemistry or not, I refuse to believe we fit the target profile *exactly*. If we can reproduce the Gunners' thinking well enough, we may be able to find a loophole somewhere."

Kata snorted. "May I repeat, we don't even know what they *looked*—"

"For instance," Mitch overrode her, "they weren't trying to prevent military bases from being built here. Soldiers with body armor wouldn't be bothered by the needles. Underground or fully enclosed bases could've been built, too, but they weren't. So question: why did the—let's call them the *Rivals*—why did the Rivals need to wander around outside without armor?"

Kata frowned thoughtfully, impressed in spite of herself. In a handful of sentences Mitch had converted a seemingly infinite problem to one with almost manageable dimensions. *I should have been able to come up with that*, she groused to herself. *Come on, brain: back to work.* "Maybe it wasn't the Rivals themselves that were the target," she suggested. "Maybe their food supply included a grazing animal that had to be kept outdoors."

Mitch nodded slowly. "Or else the targets were unarmored civilians. Either way, we're talking about a permanent colony rather than a military base."

"So point one: the scheme was directed against permanent settlements." Kata yawned widely enough to make her jaw hurt. "Pretty odd cordon sanitaire that doesn't care if the enemy brings troops through, though. Or am I just too tired to think straight?"

"It *does* seem odd; but you very definitely are too tired for a think-tank session," Mitch told her. "Let's postpone this until you've had some sleep."

"You sound just like Lyell," she sighed. "His Standing Order Number Six was always 'go take a nap.'"

A shadow seemed to pass over Mitch's face. "I'm

sorry; I didn't mean to—well, remind you of—what happened."

"It's likely to be hard to forget for a while," she replied dryly.

"Yeah." He hesitated. "You cared a lot for him, didn't you?"

"Lyell? Of course. We worked for seven years and three planets together."

"I meant—never mind."

It was just one more indication of her fatigue that it took several seconds to pick up on what he was trying not to say. "If you meant on a more personal level, the answer is no," she said. "Lyell offered the best opportunities to do biology—*real* biology, not the robot-line busywork multiversity expeditions parcel out. He was a good boss and colleague, but I wouldn't have even considered any other kind of relationship with him."

That seemed to surprise him. "Why not?"

"Oh, come on Mitch—you saw how Shannon reacted when Rom first ran out on us. She was all set to go out and get herself killed. Even now she's not all that functional. That's what deep relationships do to you—foul up your mind as well as your glands."

"Well, at least she's worried about someone besides herself," he replied with unexpected heat. "What about Adler, who couldn't think of anything except his precious reputation? Is that more rational thinking?"

"No, but who said I had to be like either one? Anyway, don't we have better things to worry about right now?"

"You're right." Mitch rubbed at his eyes. "Sorry. Look, why don't you tell me what I should do here and then go get some sleep. The chance that Rom's

getting addicted gives us a tighter deadline than
we used to have."

"Right." *Now what,* she wondered, *was* that *all
about*? But she was too tired to puzzle over Mitch's
reaction. It was probably just the tension, anyway.

Mitch got the machine going on the simulation
Kata had requested, and then sat back and glow-
ered at the flickering indicator lights. *So much for
riding into the sunset with her after all this was over,*
he thought, embarrassment flooding his face with
warmth. To have missed that badly on such an
assumption . . . and the truth, naturally, left him
in just as hopeless a position as before. Kata cher-
ishing Lyell or his memory was bad enough; but if
she hadn't fallen for *him,* then Mitch was completely out of the running. *I wonder if she noticed
how close I came to making a blithering idiot of
myself? Maybe Rom was right—maybe I ought to
trade in the rest of my teen-age romanticism for
some healthy cynicism.* It wasn't an especially original idea; he made similar resolution every time
one of his castles in the sky fell on top of him.
*Though if it took Rom ten years of marriage to get
that way—*

His communicator beeped, cutting through the
flood of self-reproach. *Kata*? he wondered, rather
hoping it wasn't. "Yes—?"

"Mitch, Adler's blip is beginning to move,"
Shannon's voice cut him off.

The conversation with Kata was abruptly forgotten. "Which way?" he snapped.

"Parallel to the herbicide ring—the Lostproof
shows a shallow furrow right there. And his laser's
moving with him."

Adler trying to find cover? Or Rom dragging the

body out of the way? There might be a way to find out. "Keep watching," he told her. "I'm going to the door to try and get Rom's attention."

"Be careful."

"You bet."

No one was visible through the exit door window when he arrived, but he nevertheless had his laser in hand as he unsealed the door and eased it open. "Rom?" he called tentatively. "Rom, I want to parley." He held his breath, eyes and attention focused toward the place where Adler's blip was moving.

"We've got nothing to talk about," Rom's voice wafted in from the forest.

From the forest—but nearly forty-five degrees around the circle from where it should have been.

Mitch let his breath out, feeling better than he had in hours. *Score one for our side—Adler's still alive. Now, what do I say to Rom?* "We're willing to leave here, Rom," he improvised, hoping their guess about the Gunners' intentions was at least close. "Would you give us safe-conduct to the *Sunray?*"

"So you can either hunt me down or just set up somewhere else? Forget it."

Mitch grimaced; but unfortunately it made sense. Whatever the Gunners' actual goal, they wouldn't have bothered programming the details into their pawns. "We don't want to hunt you down—we want to help you," he called. "The gun you've got is giving you a false set of memories and motivations, making you think we're your enemies. But we're not—"

"You think I don't know who my enemies are?" Rom cut in harshly.

"Rom, listen to me! The enemies the ghosts are telling you about?—they left Pallas hundreds of years ago. They're *gone*; *all* of them—the abandoned ruins, remember? What you're trying to do is hammer us into the mold the ghosts are giving you. But we *don't fit*; try and see that. We aren't the ones you need to be afraid of—"

"No! You're just trying to confuse me!"

"Rom—"

Mitch dropped back, losing both his sentence and train of thought as a needle ricocheted off the door jamb and whistled past his ear. Slamming the door, he hurriedly sealed it and returned to the common room.

Shannon looked ten years younger. "I talked to Adler," she announced before Mitch could speak. "He heard you and Rom shouting and decided to risk calling me."

"And?"

"He's very weak and tired, but said he'll be okay for a while unless he gets shot again. He thinks it was a tarsap that got him, not Rom, and he only took four or five needles before it ran away."

Mitch nodded; Rom would certainly have known enough to stay and finish the job. *Using herbivorous animals to fight for you* does *have some disadvantages*, he reminded himself. "Any of the needles hit vital organs?"

"He didn't think so, but he twisted his ankle when he fell, which is why he can't get back." She hesitated. "He also said Rom almost found him when you buzzed the area in the *Sunray*, but that he left when you did."

Mitch felt his stomach tighten. So not only had his quixotic rescue mission failed, it had nearly gotten Adler killed in the bargain. *I'd better quit trying to be a hero before I lose every friend I've got*, he thought bitterly. "Four or five needles, you said?"

"Yes. I told him he'd be able to survive that much of the drug." Her eyes were very steady on him. "Was I telling the truth?"

"I hope so." *Though on my record to date.* . . .
"Did you hear any of my talk with Rom?"

She shook her head.

"I tried to get him to see that the motivations the Gunners' drug is giving him don't make sense. But he wouldn't listen."

Shannon was silent a long moment. "I know next to nothing about biochemistry," she said at last, "but I wonder if it's possible you and Kata are overcomplicating things with this recognition pattern to fear reaction to specified physical response sequence. It seems to me that, since most animals already have their own inborn enemy-recognition apparatus, the Gunners could save one or more steps by linking the most obvious physical characteristic of their enemies directly into this existing pattern. That also solves the timing problem, because the memory matrix for shooting the gun can be learned essentially independently and stored away until needed."

Mitch frowned. "An interesting idea. I don't know how the chemistry would work out, but it sure *sounds* simpler than Kata's description. Though it seems to me Rom would need more than his normal dislike of us to explain the drugs's effect on him. He'd almost have to see us as enemies, wouldn't he?"

Shannon sighed. "Mitch, Rom sees the entire human race as his enemies. Not in the way you think," she added as his face apparently mirrored his reaction. "He's not paranoid in the sense that he thinks people are deliberately out to get him. It's more like he's a kitten stuck in a room with a hundred clumsy elephants. He's convinced that, whether we mean it or not, we're all likely to end up hurting him."

"That seems a pretty extreme reaction," Mitch frowned. "Sure, we all bump egos occasionally—" his last exchange with Kata rose up to mock him— "but that's no reason to bury yourself in—well—"

"In archeological digs on deserted planets?" Shannon's smile was brief and painful. "Not for us, no. But Rom's always been hypersensitive to peer opinion and he takes such ego bumps very hard. The roots of this go back to early childhood, to times and places he won't even talk much about with me."

"Um. And that hardhead image he projects—the defense of a strong offense?"

"Yes. Actually, he was a lot worse when I first married him. He's relaxed quite a bit lately, with more habit than real intent behind his cynicism. I'm . . . worried about what this is going to do to him."

Not to mention to us, Mitch thought, but kept that depressing reminder to himself. "I'll discuss this with Kata when she wakes up, but I don't know offhand how it'll help. At the moment we're sort of trying a different tack." He started to get up, abruptly sat down again. "Frensky moss—what am I using for brains? Listen—you're the resident expert on reconstructing human and alien cultures out of minuscule pieces, right? Let me tell you what we're trying."

Quickly, he sketched out the logic he and Kata had tried to apply to the Gunner-Rival conflict and the deductions it had led them to. Shannon listened, gazing off into space, and when he'd finished she nodded. "It makes sense," she told him. "We found one ruin with an expanding series of outer walls, useless for serious defense but perfectly adequate for stopping those needles. Either your civilian courtyard or grazing area models would fit with that."

"But I keep hitting the question of why they didn't simply wear body armor outside; they *or* their animals. After all, people in cold climates regularly bundle their children into snowsuits when they leave the house. This wouldn't be all that different."

"Perhaps, but you're missing an important psychological point. Colonizing a world—*really* colonizing it—is possible only when you can live out under the open sky without anything that can be termed life-support gear. It's like that for humans, it's like that for virtually all the intelligent races we've come into contact with. You may have to import your water or flood your crops with compound nitrates, but if you can stand outside with the wind and sun in your hair you can believe down deep that the world is *yours*. If you *can't*—" She shrugged. "You wind up with a base instead of a colony. Luna was the first example; there've been dozens since then."

Mitch digested that. "So you're saying that, for some reason, the Rivals wouldn't settle for bases. Why not?"

"I don't know, and we may never find out. Perhaps they were too socially oriented to exist in small groups; alternatively, perhaps one gender or the other couldn't or wouldn't adapt to staying indoors all the time. It certainly looks like they *tried* to hold out; they were clearly here for years before giving up. There's also the possibility that the Gunners had more powerful weapons that they had qualms about using against civilians. In that case, the Rivals would know that setting up a purely military base on Pallas would be a waste of time." She thought for a moment. "Is there anything you could get on the Rival biochemistry if you assume the needle drug was more lethal to them than it was to us?"

"Mm. I don't know how we'd get anything conclusive from it. There must be hundreds of ways the drug could kill, depending on what specific part of the system it attacks. Kata might be able to narrow it down some, but I'm not sure how it would help us in any case. We already *know* what it does to us, after all, and that's the really critical thing at the moment."

"True," Shannon murmured. "I was just looking at the puzzle pieces we have, trying to see what we can do with them. Are you assuming the Gunners never intended to colonize Pallas themselves?"

"Or else that the Rivals somehow prevented them from doing so. Is it important?"

"Well . . . when an army mines a section of land, they usually leave themselves the option of locating and clearing those mines away at some future date—"

"We've already shown our sensors aren't good enough to find the guns."

"—or of deactivating them."

Mitch opened his mouth, closed it again. "Deactivating. Now *that's* an interesting thought. Any ideas how you might do that?"

"It can't be an easy method to stumble across," Shannon said, gazing into space again. "Ideally, it should be something the Rivals couldn't do even if they knew roughly how."

"A coded radio signal, perhaps? Something involving the power pack or sequencing in the magnetic rings?"

"Or maybe something involving that sensor Rom mentioned—the one in the muzzle of the gun."

"Point it at a Gunner and it shuts down?" Mitch suggested, feeling a cautious excitement growing within him. If they could figure out the mechanism and trip it themselves. . . . "No, that would be too easy. A cardboard cutout, or a Rival in a Gunner costume—" He stood up. "Let's go back to the bio lab. Some more data should be ready on the instinct-drug molecule by now, and we can see what Rom found out about that muzzle sensor. Give me a hand with the Lostproof gear; we'll take it with us."

They spent the rest of the afternoon going over the gun analysis with a fine mesh, but the results were disappointing. The muzzle sensor itself showed insufficient detail on any of the x-ray photos for them to get more than the vaguest idea of what it actually did. There was an optical component to it, certainly; but there was also a magnetic detector coil and something else that Mitch couldn't even hazard a guess about. The connections between all of it and the rest of the gun were equally cryptic, and they spent a frustrating half-hour tracing one optical fiber on the high-resolution x-rays only to have it disappear into another enigmatic component.

And as the initial excitement faded into the disappointments and blind alleys, Shannon seemed to withdraw into herself, offering comments less and less frequently until she merely sat in her chair and watched Mitch work. By the time Kata reemerged from her room the archeologist had drifted even farther from both the lab table and the investigation and was standing by the window gazing outside. Kata's own initial enthusiasm slipped somewhat as Mitch described the lack of progress, but it was clear she intended to be as outwardly optimistic as possible.

"I think you've hit the nail dead-center, Shannon," she nodded. "You really wouldn't want to scatter such long-lived weapons indiscriminately around and not be able to either locate or shut them down. Why don't we start with that sensor again; maybe I'll see something you overlooked."

"Maybe." Shannon took a deep breath and turned to face them, and with a shock Mitch saw that the laser he'd left on the table beside the Lostproof monitor was now dangling loosely from her hand. "But you'd better work fast ... because in one hour I'm going to try bringing Rom in."

She's finally snapped, was Mitch's first frantic thought; and *what the hell do we do now*? his second. Beside him Kata straightened up and he waited tensely for her reaction.

But it was far milder than he'd feared. "Be reasonable, Shannon," she said calmly. "Rom will shoot you on sight; you know that."

"Maybe not." Shannon's voice was also calm, but with an undertone of black tension beneath it. *How long since* she's *had any sleep*? Mitch wondered abruptly. Just because she hadn't been able to help with any of the work the past couple of days didn't mean she'd been relaxing. In fact, her forced idleness might have made things even harder for her. "If this whole enemy-recognition thing is right," she continued, "then I'm the only one among us who has any chance at all of getting to him. The only one who might register as a friend even through the drug's influence."

"And what if you're wrong?" Kata countered. "You'll be throwing your life away for nothing. At least give Mitch and me a few more days to follow this lead down."

Shannon shook her head. "We can't wait that long. Every minute we spend here means more of that drug going into Rom's blood and brain. At the moment he seems to be fighting it, at least to the extent of being willing to talk to us. But that can't last—you know that better than I. I've got to try this before he loses the battle completely . . . before the drug becomes a permanent part of him."

Mitch glanced up at Kata, saw her jaw tighten. *So much for keeping the possibility of addiction secret*, he thought. "You're still risking your life unnecessarily," he put in.

"Am I? What about Adler?"

Mitch's argument died in his throat. "Yeah. Adler."

"He's going to need medical attention soon, not to mention food, if he's going to survive," Shannon pointed out unnecessarily. "And the longer he's out there the greater the chances that Rom or another armed tarsap will come across him."

"And what if a tarsapien comes across *you*?" Kata asked.

"I'll just have to risk that, won't I?" Shannon smiled, and Mitch saw that her lower lip was trembling. "Please, Kata; I know you don't understand why I have to do this, but you're just making it harder for me to be brave. Don't make me fight you and Mitch—I can't handle that along with all the rest of it."

For a long moment the two women stared at each other across the room . . . and finally Kata sighed. "I'll compromise with you," she said. "You offered us an hour; but by then the sun will be almost down and the forest already getting dark.

The last thing you want is for Rom to mistake you for me in the gloom. Give us until morning and we'll let you try it, whether we've got any results or not. Okay?"

Shannon's lips compressed into a thin line. "What about Adler?"

"My guess is that he can survive the night if he makes it to sundown. Certainly it won't get too cold for him, and the tarsapiens will be quiescent until almost dawn, as well. If he was able to move and talk soon after he was shot, I don't think the needles he's carrying are going to kill him."

"But you don't *know* for sure."

Kata shrugged. "It's at least as good an assumption as the one you're going on."

Shannon smiled briefly. "All right. Dawn tomorrow, then. Your word?"

"Yes." Kata extended her hand, palm up.

Stepping forward, Shannon laid the laser across it. "I'm going to my room," she said. "Let me know if there's anything I can help with."

"Sure," Kata said softly. "We'll be up to see you out."

Shannon nodded and left the lab. "You going to let her go?" Mitch asked Kata, not sure which answer he wanted to hear.

Kata sat down. "I promised her she could," she sighed. "Besides, she's right. On all counts."

"Except maybe the point about her being off Rom's enemies list." Mitch hesitated. "When I was doing that last medcheck on Rom he said something about Shannon being an enemy along with the rest of us. I think they must have had a fight or something."

"Oh, terrific." Kata closed her eyes briefly. "Well, that just makes it all the more crucial that we find a way to shut down those guns." For a moment she gazed out the window, fingers tapping on the lab table. "Along with all we *don't* know about the Gunners, we *do* know that they were whizzes with complex organic chemistry—the instinct drug shows that. Maybe we should be looking for a chemical cutoff switch instead of an electromagnetic one or whatever."

"You mean something you set off like a gas bomb upwind of the guns?" Mitch asked doubtfully.

"Sure. You've already admitted there's a component of the muzzle sensor you don't understand."

"Agreed; but we're back then to the question of why the Rivals wouldn't be able to do that themselves. Not to mention the mechanics of how a whiff of gas would set up that kind of signal."

"Let's forget the mechanism for now." Kata pursed her lips. "Could they never have gotten ahold of a working model. . . ? No. Even if the Rivals could be trapped by the gun like Rom was, they surely must have figured things out quickly enough to have safely studied at least a couple of the weapons. And it's practically guaranteed their equipment was more elaborate than ours—they were a settlement, after all."

"So they *must* have figured out everything about the guns," Mitch concluded. "And they gave up and left anyway. Not a good sign."

"Let's not give up ourselves just yet," Kata said tartly. "What about multiple designs? A hundred different varieties of cutoff switches, say."

"Should've just taken them longer to clear the planet. Remember, they *wanted* Pallas—they had settlements already built—and they would hardly have quit without a fight."

"Which puts us right back at square one," Kata

murmured. ". . . Unless it was a cutoff the Rivals *couldn't* use."

" 'Couldn't'?"

"Say the cutoff was a poison to them—a heavy, viscous chemical that'll coat the ground and foliage. That would've eliminated the guns but left them just as bad off."

"Interesting idea," Mitch said slowly. "Especially since what's poisonous to them might not be so to us. Unfortunately, that also means we don't have the foggiest idea what sort of chemical to try."

Kata sent him a tight smile and scooted her chair up to the computer terminal. "Sure we do; because the Gunners almost certainly loaded their needles with the nastiest stuff they could think of." A molecular diagram appeared on the display in response to Kata's commands, and for a long moment she gazed at it. "I suppose we could try to synthesize some of the stuff and shoot it into the forest, but I hate to do that without knowing exactly what it'll do. If we had better data on the muzzle sensor we could try a simulation. But barring that . . . wait a second."

Again her fingers skipped across the keyboard. "This is a weird idea, but since the actual mechanism is a complete unknown anyway, let's see what happens when the needle drug meets the instinct drug . . . oh, my *God*."

"What?" Mitch snapped.

Kata's face had turned an ashy white. "Wait a minute—I want to try it again with a larger target population."

The display images shifted twice. "Well?" Mitch demanded.

Kata seemed to shrink in her seat. "Catalytic reaction," she said with a shiver. "You get anything upwards of a dozen needle-drug molecules into the grip resevoir and it'll break the entire mass of instinct drug into five separate types of cyanide . . . the whole thing under pressure."

"Pressure? As in to drive it through the delivery system all the more quickly?" Mitch hazarded, a funny feeling in the pit of his stomach.

"Yeah. So if you're not a Rival, all you need to do is spray the forest with Rival-killer . . . and all the tarsapiens holding the guns fall over dead."

Mitch broke the silence that followed. "Well. So much for *that* approach. Unless you think this is possibly just a coincidence?"

Kata shook her head. "The chemistry's been too carefully set up to be anything but deliberate. This is the Gunners' cutoff switch, all right. And they've got us as neatly stymied as they did the Rivals."

Unless and until, Mitch added silently, *we decide Rom can't be saved*. The whole idea made his stomach churn . . . but down deep he knew they might eventually have to make such a decision. "They must have been really great to have on your side in a war," he growled.

Kata reached over and blanked the screen. "It shouldn't be all *that* surprising a revelation, actually—if they'd cared a tuft of Frensky moss about the tarsapiens they wouldn't have turned them into cannon fodder like this in the first place. What would they care if a few more got killed?"

Another silence descended on the lab, and Mitch found himself gazing out the window. *Now what?* he wondered bleakly. *Our best chance, and the Gunners have already closed the door on it. We can't let Shannon go out there now—promises or no. If Rom doesn't get her the tarsaps will, and there's not a thing—*

The train of thought vanished, buried abruptly beneath a realization that was so obvious he was astonished it hadn't occurred to him earlier. "Kata," he said carefully. "What's keeping Rom alive?"

She turned puzzled eyes on him. "You want to specify?"

"He's been out there two days now," Mitch said, "out with one or more tarsaps who—"

"Hell and breakfast," Kata breathed. "You're right, Mitch. For some reason they *aren't shooting at him*."

"If we can figure out why—"

"Yeah, yeah," Kata shushed him. "Let me think." She bit at her lip. "Shannon must have been right—it's the tarsapiens' enemy-recognition mechanism that's being used ... and it's *not* a visual one. Rom surely doesn't look any different; but with a new set of enzymes in his system he must *smell* different. Enough different, anyway—and that gives us our own defensive approach."

Mitch looked over at Swizzle in his cage, for the first time really seeing the huge nostrils. "We must be right on the edge of the Rivals' scent pattern for that small a change to protect him, though," he pointed out. "The problem will be to make sure we don't use a perfume that pushes us the wrong direction."

"Oh, we can do better than that," Kata smiled—her first real smile, Mitch thought, since this whole thing had started. "We know at least one other odor the tarsapiens don't shoot at—*and* have the perfect template for making some up." She gestured.

"Reasonable enough, I suppose," he said. "But won't they be able to detect our scent beneath it?"

"Trust me," she replied grimly. "We'll spread it

on so thick Swizzle himself won't recognize us. Even tarsapien noses can be overwhelmed."

"If you say so." He hesitated. "That's still only half of the problem, you know. Human recognition centers on sight, not smell. Unless Shannon can pull her miracle off we're still going to have Rom to deal with."

"Yes, well, I've got a couple of ideas on that," Kata nodded. "It occurs to me that there's one other human recognition system we might be able to use once we don't have to worry about the tarsapiens ... and we've certainly got someone here who Rom would consider his enemy. Come on; we can discuss it while we work on our olfactory camouflage."

When dawn came, they were ready.

"Rom?" Shannon called tentatively through the open door. "Rom, this is Shannon. Your wife. Can you hear me?"

Behind her, Mitch shifted his feet silently, heart thudding in his ears. Artificial tarsapien odor hung thickly around them, creating the nagging illusion of being in an especially pungent peat bog. To tarsapien senses it would probably be overpowering ... but that had yet to be tested.

"What do you want?" Rom's voice cut through the silence.

"About ten degrees right of the door," Shannon breathed.

"Got it," Mitch said tersely. "Keep him talking."

Shannon raised her voice again, but Mitch didn't wait to hear any more. If Rom stayed put, the window in the geology lab should offer an exit the other couldn't see; and if the armed tarsapiens reacted to Kata's concoction like they were supposed to that end of the forest should be safe.

Should be.

The window made only the faintest of protesting squeaks as he unlatched and swung it open, and seconds later he was striding quickly across the herbicide ring. Behind him he could hear snatches of the Endurssons' shouted conversation on the far side of the building . . . and with a feeling akin to having just walked across the Amazon he reached the edge of the forest without being shot at.

He took a moment to let his heartbeat settle down as he checked his bearings on the Lostproof. Kata and Lyell had set ten tarsapien nets on their last trapping run, and he could only hope the one or two closest ones hadn't yet been triggered. Easing the cap off the intravenous drip bottle strapped to his right boot, he made sure it was dribbling its contents properly onto the ground and started off around the circle toward Rom's voice.

In some ways, he discovered quickly, it was more unnerving than the short trek across open ground had been. Visually, he was certainly better hidden, but the advantage was almost swallowed up by the stretches of dry leaves and the occasional brittle branch underfoot. Besides watching out for such noisemakers, he also had to trace out a reasonable route and stay alert in case Rom tired of talking with his wife and moved in his direction. Approximately once per step he reminded himself of how crazy this whole plan was.

But Rom's attention remained with Shannon, and Mitch penetrated to within perhaps ten meters before thankfully beginning a silent retreat in a direction that would take him deeper into the forest and, ultimately, to the net listed on his Lostproof.

And a few minutes later he found luck was indeed with them. The three-meter-square mesh was still stretched across a gap between two trees, waiting like a giant spiderweb for a victim to blunder into it.

It took less than a minute for Mitch to complete his job and find a hiding place behind a large sarcacia bush. Raising his communicator, he punched for Kata. "Ready," he hissed. "You?"

"I hope so," she answered, her voice betraying her own tension. "Mitch . . . if this doesn't work—"

"It'll work," he told her. "Come on now; before Shannon loses him. The trail starts between two big ginkgap trees just opposite the geology lab window."

"Right. Cross your fingers."

For a minute nothing happened. All around him were the normal chirps and clicks of the forest; in the distance he could just make out Rom's voice. *A few more minutes, Shannon,* he willed silently. *Just let Kata get in position—*

"All right," Kata's voice came suddenly from somewhere between Mitch and Rom. "You keep saying you want to kill us?—well, here's your chance. Come and get me."

Mitch had half expected Rom to let loose a bellow like a charging bull, but nothing like that accompanied the abrupt sound of bodies crashing toward him through the undergrowth. His hands tightened around his drawn lightning rod as he tried to guess from the noise whether or not Rom was gaining. Surely he was already shooting blindly; if any of the needles connected—or if he got close enough to see—

"Promise the others they can leave safely and I'll stop," Kata's voice came, much closer this time. Rom made no answer, but as Kata also fell silent Mitch found he could now hear the *snick-snick-snick* of needles cutting through leaves. They were almost within sight—he could see movement of low branches—

And with a final crash of leaves Swizzle burst into sight, the communicator strapped to his back bouncing wildly as he ran for all he was worth. Mitch caught just a glimpse of dilated nostrils bare centimeters off the ground as the animal followed the trail of jasmine he had carefully laid down; and then the tarsapien veered around the net and disappeared back into the forest—

Rom, bare seconds behind, had no way of detecting the safe path even if he'd known it was there. He hit the net at full speed, the alien weapon knocked from his hand by the impact as the mesh wrapped itself solidly about its prey.

Rom didn't bellow this time, either. The sound he made was much more like an anguished scream.

"Well?"

Kata sank down into the seat next to Mitch, gratefully sipping the coffee he'd poured for her. "Uncertain, but hopeful. Adler should have no problems unless the dart drug carries something potent in the way of aftereffects—his body was actually doing a reasonable job of eliminating the stuff on its own, though I'm going to leave him on the scrubber another hour to be on the safe side. Rom—" She shrugged tiredly. "No way of telling. We can keep him sedated or under restraint and try the scrubber when it's free, but we'll just have to wait and see how firmly the drug is entrenched in his system. I'd hate to keep him tied up until the ship comes, but we could do so if absolutely necessary."

"Or we could put him in Swizzle's cage," Mitch offered. "I've got a feeling we won't be needing it again."

Kata smiled. "Swizzle still eluding you, eh?"

"Well, we might be able to trap him using the *Sunray* but even that's doubtful. On foot, forget it."

"Probably not worth the effort. Besides, we owe him a lot, and maybe letting him go free's the best way to clear the ledger. I don't think I would have liked leading Rom into that net in person."

Mitch cocked an eyebrow. "Rom's comment about biologists playing God really got to you, didn't it?"

"A little," she admitted. "But then, you already know how much I try to keep my relationships on an intellectual level. I suppose that applies to my relationships with test subjects, too."

He shrugged, looking a bit uncomfortable. "That's how scientists are supposed to be."

"Maybe. But maybe I've just been using that as an excuse."

"An excuse for what?"

Kata took a deep breath, steeling herself. This wasn't going to be easy to say, but it'd been rehearsing itself in the back of her mind for the past hour and she was determined to let it come out. "I get the feeling that you were rather upset by what I said yesterday about relationships fouling up your mind."

He waved a hand in dismissal. "Forget it. I've always had a tendency to go overly starry-eyed.

Too much *City of Night* influence on my early life, I suppose."

"Yeah, I noticed. Rushing out there to rescue Rom and then Adler. . . ." She smiled ruefully at the memory. "I don't think I'd like to go quite *that* far overboard."

"You don't want most of the rest of it, either," Mitch said. "Overly romantic isn't any better for getting close to people than overly intellectual. I'm forever winding up having my bubble popped."

She shrugged fractionally. *So he does it, too,* she thought. "Yours is a more subtle approach, I'd say, but it seems just as good as my method . . . or Rom's or Adler's, for that matter."

"Come again?"

"Our methods for keeping other people at a safe arm's reach," she amplified. "Don't you see? Rom's belligerent cynicism, Adler's all-consuming attention to his career—they're just different versions of what you and I are doing. We all have our own—"

"Our own personal cordons sanitaires?" Mitch offered with a wry half-smile.

"My words exactly."

"It was an obvious metaphor. Sort of makes sense, I suppose—human gregariousness *does* have certain boundaries." He looked at her curiously. "May I ask what got you started on this line of thought?"

She shrugged again. "Oh, I don't know. Probably because Shannon held up so much better than I expected her to. You know; the old problem of theory versus reality."

"Besides which, you really *didn't* understand why she was willing to risk her life for Rom?"

Kata felt herself flush. "I suppose that's part of it," she admitted. "Knowledge and understanding *are* supposed to be my stock in trade, after all. Being told I can't do something has always bugged me."

"Um." He eyed her, a touch of wariness in his face. "So now what? We break down the barriers and joyfully embrace in the clear light of the rising sun?"

She chuckled, fully aware that he was only half-joking. "I'm not ready to scrap my entire cordon sanitaire quite *that* fast, thanks. I just thought . . . well, that maybe we both ought to start re-thinking how we deal with people. Remember how hard Shannon said it was for Rom to break his antisocial image? I wouldn't want that kind of rigid attitude getting a grip on *me*." She hesitated. "Or on you, either," she added with only a little difficulty.

A twitch at the corner of his mouth showed he'd caught the small concession, but he had the grace not to push it. "Especially one like Rom's," he nodded. "That brand of active defense can be pretty hard on friend *or* foe. Or innocent bystander."

Kata looked out the window, suppressing a shiver. "We'll go looking for them, you know, once all this gets out. You think we'll find them?"

"I hope not," Mitch said fervently. "If they could do this on Pallas, who knows *what* they've done to booby-trap their own system?"

"I don't even want to think about it."